THE NEW PROPHECY

WARRIORS

MOONRISE

WARRIORS

WARRIORS:
THE NEW PROPHECY

THE NEW PROPHECY
WARRIORS
MOONRISE

ERIN HUNTER

HarperCollins *Children's Books*

First published in the USA by HarperCollins Children's Books in 2005
First published in Great Britain by HarperCollins Children's Books in 2011
HarperCollins Children's Books is a division of HarperCollinsPublishers Ltd,
77-85 Fulham Palace Road, Hammersmith, London W6 8JB
www.harpercollins.co.uk
www.warriorcats.com

10

MOONRISE
Copyright © Working Partners Limited 2005
Series created by Working Partners Limited.

ISBN 978-0-00-741923-4

Printed and bound in England by
Clays Ltd, St Ives plc

Special thanks to Cherith Baldry

ALLEGIANGES

THUNDERCLAN

LEADER   **FIRESTAR**—ginger tom with a flame-coloured pelt

DEPUTY   **GREYSTRIPE**—long-haired grey tom

MEDICINE CAT   **CINDERPELT**—dark grey she-cat
APPRENTICE, LEAFPAW

WARRIORS   (toms, and she-cats without kits)

MOUSEFUR—small dusky brown she-cat
APPRENTICE, SPIDERPAW

DUSTPELT—dark brown tabby tom
APPRENTICE, SQUIRRELPAW

SANDSTORM—pale ginger she-cat
APPRENTICE, SORRELPAW

CLOUDTAIL—long-haired white tom

BRACKENFUR—golden brown tabby tom
APPRENTICE, WHITEPAW

THORNCLAW—golden brown tabby tom
APPRENTICE, SHREWPAW

BRIGHTHEART—white she-cat with ginger patches

BRAMBLECLAW—dark brown tabby tom with amber eyes

ASHFUR—pale grey (with darker flecks) tom, dark blue eyes

RAINWHISKER—dark grey tom with blue eyes

SOOTFUR—lighter grey tom with amber eyes

APPRENTICES (more than six moons old, in training to become warriors)

SORRELPAW—tortoiseshell and white she-cat with amber eyes

SQUIRRELPAW—dark ginger she-cat with green eyes

LEAFPAW—light brown tabby she-cat with amber eyes and white paws

SPIDERPAW—long-limbed black tom with brown underbelly and amber eyes

SHREWPAW—small dark brown tom with amber eyes

WHITEPAW—white she-cat with green eyes

QUEENS (she-cats expecting or nursing kits)

GOLDENFLOWER—pale ginger coat, the oldest nursery queen

FERNCLOUD—pale grey (with darker flecks) she-cat, green eyes

ELDERS (former warriors and queens, now retired)

FROSTFUR—beautiful white she-cat with blue eyes

DAPPLETAIL—once-pretty tortoiseshell she-cat, the oldest cat in thunderclan

SPECKLETAIL—pale tabby she-cat

LONGTAIL—pale tabby tom with dark black stripes, retired early due to failing sight

SHADOWCLAN

LEADER   **BLACKSTAR**—large white tom with huge jet-black paws

DEPUTY   **RUSSETFUR**—dark ginger she-cat

MEDICINE CAT   **LITTLECLOUD**—very small tabby tom

WARRIORS   **OAKFUR**—small brown tom
APPRENTICE, SMOKEPAW

TAWNYPELT—tortoiseshell she-cat with green eyes

CEDARHEART—dark grey tom

ROWANCLAW—ginger she-cat
APPRENTICE, TALONPAW

TALLPOPPY—long-legged light brown tabby she-cat

ELDERS   **RUNNINGNOSE**—small grey and white tom, formerly the medicine cat

WINDCLAN

LEADER   **TALLSTAR**—elderly black and white tom with a very long tail

DEPUTY   **MUDCLAW**—mottled dark brown tom
APPRENTICE, CROWPAW—dark smoky grey, almost black tom with blue eyes

MEDICINE CAT   **BARKFACE**—short-tailed brown tom

WARRIORS

ONEWHISKER—brown tabby tom

WEBFOOT—dark grey tabby tom

TORNEAR—tabby tom

WHITETAIL—small white she-cat

ELDERS

MORNINGFLOWER—tortoiseshell she-cat

RIVERCLAN

LEADER

LEOPARDSTAR—unusually spotted golden tabby she-cat

DEPUTY

MISTYFOOT—grey she-cat with blue eyes

MEDICINE CAT

MUDFUR—long-haired light brown tom
APPRENTICE, MOTHWING—beautiful golden tabby she-cat with amber eyes

WARRIORS

BLACKCLAW—smoky black tom

HEAVYSTEP—thickset tabby tom

STORMFUR—dark grey tom with amber eyes

FEATHERTAIL—light grey she-cat with blue eyes

HAWKFROST—broad-shouldered dark brown tom

MOSSPELT—tortoiseshell she-cat

QUEENS

DAWNFLOWER—pale grey she-cat

ELDERS

SHADEPELT—very dark grey she-cat

LOUDBELLY—dark brown tom

CATS OUTSIDE CLANS

BARLEY—black and white tom that lives on a farm close to the forest

RAVENPAW—sleek black cat that lives on the farm with Barley

PURDY—elderly tabby tom that lives in woods near the sea

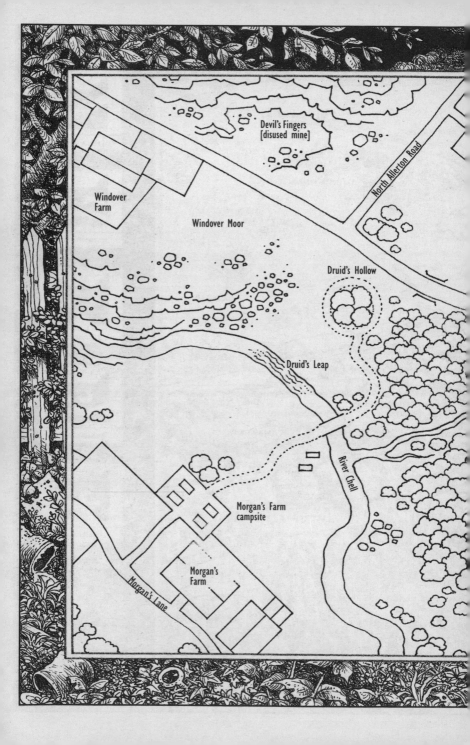

Devil's Fingers
[disused mine]

Windover
Farm

Windover Moor

Druid's Hollow

Druid's Leap

North Allerton Road

River Chell

Morgan's Farm
campsite

Morgan's
Farm

Morgan's Lane

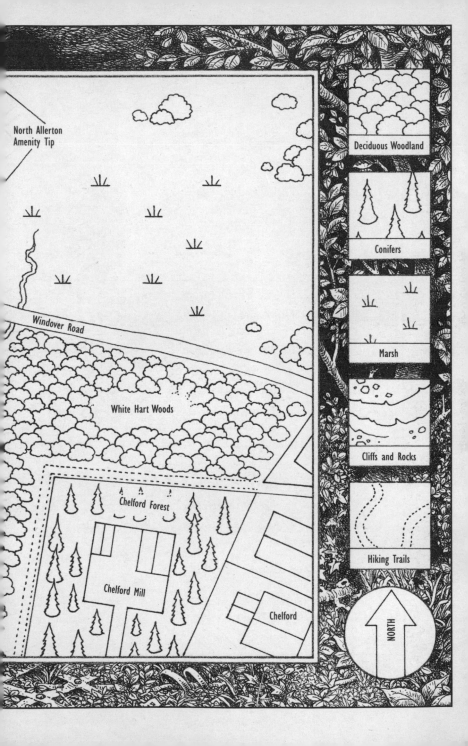

North Allerton
Amenity Tip

Windover Road

White Hart Woods

Chelford Forest

Chelford Mill

Chelford

Deciduous Woodland

Conifers

Marsh

Cliffs and Rocks

Hiking Trails

NORTH

PROLOGUE
❧

One by one, the cats crept into the cave. Their fur was streaked with mud and their eyes stretched wide with fear, reflecting the cold moonlight that filtered through a crack in the roof. They crouched low with their bellies close to the ground, their gazes flickering from side to side as if they expected to see danger lurking in the shadows.

The glimmer of moonlight was caught in pools of water on the cave floor. It lit up a forest of pointed stones, some rising from the ground and others hanging from the cave roof. Some of the stones joined in the middle to form slender trees of gleaming white rock. Wind gusted through them, ruffling the cats' fur. The air smelled damp and clean, and was filled with the distant roar of falling water.

A cat stepped out from behind one of the pointed stones. He was long-bodied, with lean, muscular limbs, and his pelt was completely covered in mud that had dried into spikes, so that he looked like a cat carved in stone.

"Welcome," he meowed in a rasping voice. "Moonlight lies on the water. It is time for a Telling, according to the laws of the Tribe of Endless Hunting."

One of the cats crept forward, dipping his head to the mud-covered cat. "Stoneteller, have you had a sign? Has the Tribe of Endless Hunting spoken to you?"

Another cat spoke from behind him. "Is there hope at last?"

Stoneteller bowed his head. "I have seen the words of the Tribe of Endless Hunting in the pattern of moonlight on rock, in the shadows cast by the stones, in the sound of raindrops as they fall from the roof." He paused, letting his gaze sweep over the cats around him. "Yes," he went on. "They have told me there is hope."

A faint murmur, like the rustle of leaves in the wind, passed through the group of cats. Their eyes seemed to grow brighter, and their ears pricked. The one who had come forwards first mewed hesitantly, "Then you know what will rid us of this dreadful danger?"

"Yes, Crag," Stoneteller replied. "The Tribe of Endless Hunting has promised me that a cat will come, a silver cat not from this Tribe, who will rid us of Sharptooth once and for all."

There was a pause, then: "Are there other cats, not in the Tribe of Rushing Water?" a voice asked from the back of the group.

"There must be," another cat replied.

"I have heard tell of strangers," meowed Crag, "though we've seen none here in our lifetimes. But when will the silver cat come?" he added desperately, and other mews rose from all around him.

"Yes, when?"

"Is it really true?"

Stoneteller signalled for silence with a twitch of his tail. "Yes, it is true," he meowed. "The Tribe of Endless Hunting has never lied to us. I have seen the sheen of his silver fur myself, in a moonlit pool."

"But *when?*" Crag persisted.

"The Tribe of Endless Hunting has not shown that to me," Stoneteller replied. "I do not know when the silver cat will come, or from where, but we will know it when he arrives."

He raised his head towards the cave roof, and his eyes shone like two tiny moons. "Until then, cats of my Tribe, we can only wait."

CHAPTER 1

Stormfur opened his eyes, blinking away sleep, and struggled to remember where he was. Instead of his nest of reeds in the RiverClan camp, he was lying curled in dry, crunchy bracken. Above his head was the earth roof of a cave, crisscrossed with tangled roots. He could hear a rhythmic roaring sound faintly in the distance. At first it puzzled him; then he remembered how close they were to the sun-drown water, washing endlessly onto the edge of the land. He flinched as a vision burst into his mind, of how he and Brambleclaw had struggled in the water for their lives; he spat, still tasting the salty tang at the back of his throat. At home in RiverClan he was used to water—his was the only Clan that could swim comfortably in the river that ran through the forest—but not this surging, salty, pushing-and-pulling water, too strong even for a RiverClan cat to swim in safely.

Other memories came rushing back. StarClan had sent cats from each of the four Clans on a long, dangerous journey, to hear what Midnight had to tell them. They had fought their way across unknown country, through Twoleg nests, facing attacks from dogs and rats, to make the last incredible discovery: that Midnight was a badger.

Stormfur felt ice creeping along his limbs as he recalled Midnight's dreadful message. Twolegs were destroying the forest to make a new Thunderpath. All the Clans would have to leave, and it was the task of StarClan's chosen cats to warn them and lead them to a new home.

Stormfur sat up and looked around the cave. Faint light filtered down the tunnel that led out onto the clifftop, along with a gentle current of fresh air that carried the scent of salt water. Midnight the badger was nowhere to be seen. Close beside Stormfur, his sister, Feathertail, was sleeping, her tail curled over her nose. Just beyond her was Tawnypelt, the fierce ShadowClan warrior; Stormfur was relieved to see that she was resting quietly, as if the rat bite she had suffered in the Twolegplace was troubling her less. Midnight's store of herbs had yielded something to soothe the infection and help her sleep. On the opposite side of the cave, a little way apart, was the WindClan apprentice Crowpaw, his dark grey pelt barely visible among the fronds of bracken. Nearest the cave entrance, Tawnypelt's brother, Brambleclaw, was stretched out beside Squirrelpaw, who slept in a tight ball. Stormfur felt a stab of jealousy at the sight of the two ThunderClan cats close together, and tried to push it away. He had no right to admire Squirrelpaw, and her courage and bright optimism, as much as he did, when they came from different Clans. Brambleclaw would make her a much better mate.

Stormfur knew that he ought to rouse his companions so that they could begin their long journey back to the forest. Yet he was strangely reluctant. *Let them sleep a little longer*, he thought. *We'll need all our strength for what lies ahead.*

Shaking scraps of bracken from his pelt, he picked his way across the sandy floor of the cave and out through the tunnel. A stiff breeze ruffled his fur as he emerged onto the springy grass. He was dry at last, after his near-drowning the night before, and sleep had refreshed him. He stood gazing around him; just ahead was the edge of the cliff and beyond it lay an endless stretch of shimmering water, reflecting the pale light of dawn.

Stormfur opened his jaws to drink in the air and catch the scent of prey. Instead his senses were flooded by a strong reek of badger. He caught sight of Midnight sitting on the highest point of the cliff, her small, bright eyes fixed on the fading stars. In the sky behind her, on the far side of the moorland, a strip of creamy light showed where the sun would rise. Stormfur padded over, dipping his head respectfully before sitting beside her.

"Good morning, grey warrior," Midnight's voice rumbled in welcome. "Sleep you have enough?"

"Yes. Thanks, Midnight." Stormfur still found it strange to be exchanging friendly greetings with her, when badgers had always been deadly enemies of the warrior Clans.

Yet Midnight was no ordinary badger. She seemed closer to StarClan than any warrior, except perhaps the medicine cats; she had travelled far and somehow had found the wisdom to foretell the future.

Stormfur gave her a sidelong glance, to see her eyes still

fixed on the remaining stars in the dawn sky. "Can you really read signs there from StarClan?" he asked curiously, half hoping that her terrible predictions from the night before would vanish in the light of morning.

"Much is to be read everywhere," the badger replied. "In stars, in running water, in flash of light on waves. Whole world speaks, if ears are open to listen."

"I must be deaf, then," Stormfur meowed. "The future seems dark to me."

"Not so, grey warrior," rasped Midnight. "See." She pointed with her snout across the sun-drown water to where a single warrior of StarClan still shone brightly just above the horizon. "StarClan has seen our meeting. Pleased they are, and help they will give in dark days coming."

Stormfur gazed up at the brilliant point of light and let out a faint sigh. He was no medicine cat, accustomed to sharing tongues with their warrior ancestors. His task was to offer his strength and skill in the service of his Clan—and now, it seemed, of all the forest cats. Midnight had made it clear that each and every Clan would be destroyed if they could not ignore the ancient boundaries and work together for once.

"Midnight, when we go home—"

His question was never finished. A yowl interrupted him, and he turned to see Squirrelpaw burst out of the tunnel that led down into the badger's sett. She stood in the entrance, her dark ginger fur fluffed up and her ears pricked.

"I'm starving!" she announced. "Where's the prey around here?"

7

"Budge up, and let the rest of us out." Crowpaw's irritable voice sounded behind her. "Then we might be able to tell you."

Squirrelpaw bounced forwards a few paces, and the WindClan apprentice emerged, followed closely by Feathertail. She stretched with pleasure in the sunlight. Stormfur got up and bounded over the tough moorland grass so he could touch noses with his sister. He had not been one of StarClan's original chosen cats, but he had insisted on coming on the journey to protect Feathertail. With their mother dead and their father living in a different Clan, the two cats were much closer than ordinary siblings.

Midnight lumbered after him and nodded a greeting to the cats.

"Tawnypelt's much better this morning," Feathertail reported. "She says her shoulder hardly hurts at all." To Midnight she added, "That burdock root you gave her really helped."

"Root is good," the badger rumbled. "Now injured warrior travel well."

As she spoke, Tawnypelt herself appeared from the tunnel; Stormfur was relieved to see that she looked stronger after her long sleep and was scarcely limping at all.

Following Tawnypelt, her brother, Brambleclaw, pushed his way out of the tunnel and stood blinking in the growing light. "The sun's nearly up," he meowed. "It's time we were on our way."

"But we have to eat first!" Squirrelpaw wailed. "My belly is growling louder than a monster on the Thunderpath! I could eat a fox, fur and all."

Stormfur had to agree with her. Hunger clawed at his own belly, and he knew that without food they would not be able to face the long and exhausting journey back to the forest. Yet he shared Brambleclaw's urgency; how would they feel if they delayed too long, and then discovered cats had died because of it?

A look of exasperation flitted over Brambleclaw's face. His voice was firm as he replied, "We'll pick up some prey as we go. And once we get back to the woods where we made camp, we'll have a proper hunt."

"Bossy furball," Squirrelpaw muttered.

"Brambleclaw's right," Tawnypelt meowed. "Who knows what's happening at home? There's no time to waste."

A murmur of agreement rose from the other cats. Even Crowpaw, who usually challenged Brambleclaw's decisions even more than Squirrelpaw, had nothing to say. With a slight shock, Stormfur realised that their long journey, and the threat to all their Clans, had changed them from a group of squabbling rivals into a unified force with a single purpose, to save their Clanmates and the warrior code that had protected them for so long. A warm feeling of belonging swept over Stormfur. His loyalty towards RiverClan was complicated— knowing how their half-Clan heritage made other warriors suspicious of him and Feathertail—but here he knew he had found friends who judged him without thinking about Clan differences all the time.

Brambleclaw paced forwards until he stood in front of Midnight. "The thanks of all the Clans go with you," he mewed.

Midnight grunted. "Time is not yet for farewell. I come with you as far as woods, make sure you know right path."

Without waiting for the cats to agree or thank her, she lumbered off across the moor. Ahead of her, the sky had become too bright to look at as the sun began to edge its way above the horizon. Stormfur blinked gratefully at the yellow light. The setting sun had guided them on their journey to find the sun-drown place; now the rising sun would guide them home.

The four chosen cats—along with Stormfur and Squirrelpaw, who had come with Brambleclaw after an argument with her father, Firestar—had set out from the forest blindly following a half-understood prophecy from StarClan. Now that they had discovered what the prophecy meant, it was easier to decide what to do next, but at the same time it was terrifying to know just how much danger their Clans were in.

"Well, what are we waiting for?" Squirrelpaw asked, dashing off to overtake Midnight.

Her Clanmate Brambleclaw followed more slowly, looking deep in thought, as if he were imagining all the difficulties they would have to face on their way back to the forest. At his side, Tawnypelt seemed refreshed from her night's rest, and even though she was still limping, her eyes showed nothing but determination to make the long journey home. Feathertail trotted with her tail up, clearly enjoying the bright morning, while Crowpaw loped along beside her, keeping his ears pricked and his muscles tense, as if he were already anticipating trouble.

Stormfur, bringing up the rear, breathed a swift prayer to StarClan. *Guide our paws, and bring us all safely home.*

As the sun climbed higher, the sky became a deep, clear blue, dotted with fluffy scraps of cloud. The weather was warm and kind for so late in leaf-fall. A breeze swept over the grass, and Stormfur's mouth watered as he caught the scent of rabbit. Out of the corner of his eye, he spotted a white tail bobbing as the rabbit vanished over the crest of a gentle slope.

Instantly Crowpaw darted after it.

"Wait! Where are you going?" Brambleclaw called after him, but the WindClan apprentice was gone. The tabby warrior's tail lashed irritably. "Does he ever listen?"

"He won't be long," Feathertail soothed him. "You could hardly expect him to ignore a rabbit when it pops up right under our noses."

Brambleclaw's only reply was another swish of his tail.

"I'll fetch him back," Stormfur meowed, bunching his muscles to spring in pursuit.

Before he could move, the dark grey apprentice reappeared at the top of the rise. He was dragging the rabbit with him; it was almost as big as he was.

"Here," he meowed ungraciously as he dumped it on the ground. "That didn't take long, did it? I suppose we're allowed to stop and eat it?"

"Of course," Brambleclaw replied. "Sorry, Crowpaw. I'd

forgotten how fast WindClan cats can be. This . . . this moorland must feel like home to you."

Crowpaw acknowledged the apology with a curt nod as all six cats crowded around the fresh-kill. Stormfur stopped short when he noticed a glow of admiration in Feathertail's eyes. Surely his sister couldn't be interested in Crowpaw? All he ever did was argue and push himself forwards as if he were already a warrior. A cat from another Clan—and an apprentice at that!—had no right to start padding after Feathertail. And whatever did Feathertail see in him? Didn't she know the problems this sort of thing could cause—hadn't she learned that from their own parents?

Then Stormfur's gaze slid across to Squirrelpaw. Had he any right to criticise Feathertail, when he liked Squirrelpaw so much? But then, he told himself, any cat would like the brave, intelligent ThunderClan apprentice. And he knew better than to start something with a cat from another Clan, when they couldn't possibly have a future together.

Stormfur sighed and began gulping his share of the rabbit. He hoped he was imagining things; after all, any cat might admire Crowpaw's speed in catching them prey when they were all hungry. Surely that was all Feathertail was feeling.

While the cats ate, Midnight waited a few paces away. Stormfur saw her tearing at the moorland grass with her strong, blunt claws, snuffling up the grubs and beetles she disturbed. Her eyes were screwed up, as if she found it hard to search for food in the strong sunlight, but she said nothing, and as soon as the cats had eaten all they could of

Crowpaw's prey, she set off once more towards the rising sun.

Even with Midnight to lead them by the most direct route, it was sunhigh by the time they reached the crest of a gentle hill and saw the edge of the woods in front of them. The shade underneath the trees looked as inviting as running water to Stormfur after travelling through the heat of the unprotected moorland. For one brief moment, he let himself imagine an afternoon of hunting, then settling down full-fed for a sleep under the arching fronds of bracken, but he knew there was no chance of that.

As they drew closer to the woods, he spotted what looked like a heap of mottled brown fur in the long grass underneath a bush. His tail twitched in rueful recognition at the sight of the elderly tabby who had guided them—and nearly lost them forever—in the Twolegplace.

"Hey, Purdy!" Brambleclaw called. "We're back!"

A large round head emerged from the bundle of fur, whiskers twitching and eyes blinking in confusion that gradually turned to welcome. The old cat scrambled to his paws and took a couple of paces towards them, shaking bits of dead leaf from his untidy pelt.

"Great StarClan!" he exclaimed. "I never reckoned I'd see you again." Suddenly he broke off, his eyes fixed on something over Stormfur's shoulder. "Don't move a whisker!" he hissed. "There's a badger behind you. Just let me deal with it. I know a few fightin' moves that—"

"It's OK, Purdy," Stormfur interrupted, while Squirrelpaw's tail curled up with amusement. "This is Midnight. She's a friend."

The old tabby stared at Stormfur, his jaws gaping in astonishment. "A friend? You don't make friends with a badger, young fellow. You can't trust 'em a single mouselength."

Stormfur gave Midnight an anxious look, wondering if the badger was offended by Purdy's words. To his relief, she looked as amused as Squirrelpaw, her tiny black eyes gleaming.

"Come and meet Purdy," Stormfur mewed to her. "He guided us through Twolegplace."

Midnight plodded forwards until she stood in front of the old tabby tom. Unconvinced, Purdy crouched down with his neck fur bristling and his lips drawn back in a snarl to reveal snaggly teeth. Stormfur felt a twinge of admiration for his courage, even though the badger could have flattened him with one swat of her powerful front paws.

"Here is not fight," Midnight assured him. "Friend of my friends is my friend also. Much of you they have told me."

Purdy's ears twitched. "Can't say I'm pleased to meet you," he muttered. "But I suppose you must be all right if they say so." Backing away, he turned to Brambleclaw. "Why are we hangin' around here?" he demanded. "There are Upwalkers and dogs all over the place. Say goodbye and let's be on our way."

"Hang on!" Squirrelpaw protested loudly to Brambleclaw. "You said we could hunt."

"We can," he mewed.

He paused to taste the air; Stormfur did the same, and was relieved to find that although he could distinguish several different dog scents, they were all stale. He guessed that Purdy was using the danger of dogs as an excuse to get away from Midnight.

"OK," Brambleclaw went on, "let's split up and hunt quickly. We'll meet in that place where we camped last time. Tawnypelt, do you want to go straight there?"

The ShadowClan warrior's eyes flashed as she replied, "No, I can hunt as well as any of you."

Before any of the cats could respond, Midnight padded up to her and gave her a gentle nudge. "Foolish warrior," she rumbled. "Rest while able. Show me camping place. I will stay while sun is high, go home in dark."

Tawnypelt shrugged. "OK, Midnight." She headed further into the woods, following the stream to the hollow where the cats had rested on the outward journey.

The air was cooler in the dappled shade of the trees. Stormfur began to relax, feeling safer here than on the open moorland, though the chattering stream, too shallow for fish, was no substitute for the river he loved. A pang of loss stabbed through him at the thought that, even if he saw the river again, it would not be for long; Midnight had told them that the Clans would have to leave the forest as soon as the six cats returned.

A rustle in the undergrowth reminded him of how hungry he was. It would be good to go off for a while and hunt with

Feathertail, just as they did at home. But when he swung round to speak to his sister, he saw that Crowpaw was saying something in her ear.

"Do you want to hunt with me?" the apprentice muttered, sounding half grudging, half embarrassed. "We'd do better together."

"That would be great!" Feathertail's eyes shone; then she spotted Stormfur, and looked even more embarrassed than the WindClan cat. "Er—why don't we all hunt together?"

Crowpaw looked away, and Stormfur felt the hairs on his neck begin to prickle. What right did this apprentice have to invite Feathertail to be his hunting partner? "No, I'm fine on my own," Stormfur retorted, spinning round and plunging into the undergrowth, trying to pretend he hadn't seen the hurt in his sister's blue eyes.

But once he slipped beneath the lowest branches of the bushes his irritation faded. His ears pricked up and all his senses were alert in the hunt for prey.

Before long he spotted a mouse scrabbling among fallen leaves, and dispatched it with one swift blow. Satisfied, he scraped earth over the little brown body until he was ready to collect it, and looked around for more. Soon he added a squirrel and another mouse to his hoard—which was as much as he could carry—and set off for the meeting place.

On the way he began to wonder how Feathertail was getting along, asking himself if he should have stayed with her after all. He was not one of StarClan's chosen cats; he had come on this mission especially to look after his sister. He had been wrong to abandon her in this strange place, just because Crowpaw had annoyed him. What would he do if something happened to her?

When he reached the camping place he saw Tawnypelt stretched out in the shade of a hawthorn bush, her tortoiseshell fur hardly visible in the dappled sunlight. Midnight was beside her, dozing, and there was more chewed-up burdock root laid on Tawnypelt's injured shoulder. The badger must have found some growing by the stream. Brambleclaw was perched above Tawnypelt on a steeply arching tree root, obviously keeping watch, while Feathertail and Crowpaw shared a squirrel just below. As Stormfur dropped his catch on the small pile of fresh-kill in the center of the hollow, Squirrelpaw appeared at the top of the slope, dragging a rabbit, and Purdy followed with a couple of mice in his jaws.

"Good, we're all here," meowed Brambleclaw. "Let's eat and then get moving."

He leaped down into the hollow and chose a starling from the pile. Stormfur took one of his mice over to Feathertail, settling down next to her on the opposite side from Crowpaw.

"Good hunting?" he asked.

Feathertail blinked at him. "Brilliant, thanks. There's so much prey here! It's a pity we can't stay longer."

Stormfur was tempted to agree, but he knew that the danger to their home was too desperate for them to delay. He began to devour his mouse in famished gulps, his paws already itching for the next stage of their journey.

He had swallowed the last of the fresh-kill and was beginning to groom his thick grey pelt when he heard a low snarling behind him. He saw Brambleclaw raise his head, alarm flaring in his yellow eyes.

Stormfur whipped round to see what had spooked the ThunderClan warrior. A familiar smell hit his scent glands a heartbeat before two slender, tawny shapes emerged from the bracken beside the stream.

Foxes!

CHAPTER 2

Leafpaw wrinkled her nose at the foul scent and tried not to hiss in disgust. Shaking her head, she parted Sorreltail's tortoiseshell fur with one paw and dabbed the wad of bile-soaked moss on the tick clinging to her shoulder.

Sorreltail wriggled as she felt the bile soak through her fur. "That's better!" she meowed. "Has it gone yet?"

Leafpaw opened her mouth and dropped the twig that held the moss. "Give it time."

"There's only one good thing about ticks," Sorreltail mewed. "They hate mouse bile just as much as we do." Springing to her paws, she gave herself a vigorous shake and flicked the tick off her shoulder. "There! Thanks, Leafpaw."

A breeze rustled through the trees that surrounded the medicine cat's den. A few leaves drifted down; there was a chill in the morning air that warned Leafpaw of how few moons there were before leaf-bare. This time there would be more than the cold and shortage of prey to face. Leafpaw closed her eyes and shuddered as she remembered what she had seen the day before on patrol with her father, Firestar.

The biggest monster the cats had ever seen had been

forging a dreadful path through the forest, scoring deep ruts into the earth and tearing up trees by their roots. The huge, shiny monster had rolled inexorably through the bracken, roaring and belching smoke while the cats scattered helplessly before it. For the first time, Leafpaw began to understand the danger to the forest, which had been prophesied twice now, once in Brambleclaw's dream that had sent him on the journey with Squirrelpaw, and once in Cinderpelt's vision of fire and tiger. The doom that had been foretold was coming upon the forest, and Leafpaw did not know what any cat could do to stop it.

"Are you ok, Leafpaw?" meowed Sorreltail.

Leafpaw blinked. The vision of smoke, splintered trees, and shrieking cats faded away, to be replaced by soft green ferns and the smooth grey rock where Cinderpelt made her den. She was safe, ThunderClan was still here—but for how long? "Yes, I'm fine," she replied. Firestar had ordered the patrol to keep quiet about what they had seen until he had decided how to break the news to the Clan. "I've got to go and wash this mouse bile off my paws."

"I'll come with you," Sorreltail offered. "Then we could go along the ravine and pick up some fresh-kill."

Leafpaw led the way into the main clearing. Whitepaw and Shrewpaw were scuffling outside the apprentices' den in warm shafts of early morning sunlight, while Ferncloud's three kits watched them with huge admiring eyes. Their mother sat at the entrance to the nursery, washing herself while keeping one eye on her litter. The dawn patrol—Dustpelt, Mousefur, and

Spiderpaw—were just pushing their way into the clearing through the gorse tunnel, Dustpelt's eyes narrowing with pleasure as he caught sight of Ferncloud and his kits. Leafpaw gazed at the busy, peaceful camp, and could hardly keep back a wail of despair.

As soon as the apprentices spotted Leafpaw, they stopped their practice fight and stared at her, then started whispering urgently together. Even the cats in the returning patrol gave her an uneasy look as they padded over to the fresh-kill pile. Leafpaw knew that rumours about yesterday's patrol were starting to fly around the camp. At daybreak Firestar had called his deputy, Greystripe; Leafpaw's mother, Sandstorm; and Cinderpelt into a meeting in his den, and every cat had begun to suspect that something unusual had happened the day before.

Before she and Sorreltail could reach the gorse tunnel, Firestar appeared from his den at the foot of the Highrock. Greystripe and Sandstorm followed him out into the clearing with Cinderpelt limping after them. Firestar leaped to the top of the rock, leaving the other three cats to find comfortable places to sit at its base. In the slanting leaf-fall sun, his flame-coloured pelt blazed like the fire that gave him his name.

"Let all those cats old enough to catch their own prey join here beneath the Highrock for a Clan meeting," he called.

Leafpaw felt her belly lurch as Sorreltail nudged her gently towards the front of the gathering cats. "You know what he's going to say, don't you?" the tortoiseshell warrior murmured.

Leafpaw nodded bleakly.

"I knew something weird happened yesterday," Sorreltail went on. "You all came back looking as if the whole of ShadowClan were clawing at your tails."

"I wish it were just that," Leafpaw muttered.

"Cats of ThunderClan," Firestar began, then paused to take a deep breath. "I . . . I don't know if any Clan leader has ever had to take his Clan into the darkness that I see ahead." His voice faltered and his eyes met Sandstorm's, seeming to draw strength from the she-cat's steady gaze. "Some time ago, Ravenpaw warned me about more Twoleg activity on the Thunderpath. Back then, I didn't think it was important, and there was nothing we could do anyway because that is not our territory. But yesterday . . ."

A tense silence had fallen in the clearing. Firestar did not often sound so serious; Leafpaw could see how reluctant he was to go on, how he had to force himself to speak.

"My patrol was not far from Snakerocks when we saw a Twoleg monster leave the Thunderpath. It tore into the earth and pushed trees over. It—"

"But that's ridiculous!" Sootfur interrupted. "Monsters *never* leave the Thunderpath."

"This isn't another of his dreams, is it?" Dustpelt's question was too low for Firestar to hear, though Leafpaw caught the muttered words. "A tough bit of fresh-kill too late at night?"

"Shut up and listen." Cloudtail, Firestar's kin, glared at Dustpelt.

"I saw it too," Greystripe confirmed from his place at the foot of the rock.

Dead silence followed his words. Leafpaw watched the cats glance at one another with uncertainty and fear in their eyes. Sorreltail turned to Leafpaw. "Is that really what you saw?"

Leafpaw nodded. "You can't imagine what it was like."

"What does Cinderpelt have to say?" Speckletail called from where she sat among the elders. "Has StarClan shown you anything?"

The medicine cat rose to her paws and faced the Clan, her blue eyes steady. Of all the cats, even Firestar, she seemed the calmest.

Before she replied, she looked up to meet Firestar's gaze; Leafpaw could almost see flashing between them the memory of the prophecy of fire and tiger that Cinderpelt had seen in a clump of blazing bracken. She wondered how much they had decided to tell the Clan, in the meeting that had just ended. Then Firestar nodded as if he was giving Cinderpelt permission to speak; she acknowledged his signal with a brief dip of her head.

"The signs from StarClan are not clear," she admitted. "I see a time of great danger and change for the forest. A terrible doom hangs over us all."

"Then you have had warnings about this! Why haven't you told us before?" Mousefur challenged with a lash of her tail.

"Don't be mouse-brained!" Cloudtail growled. "What good would it have done? What could we do? Leave the forest—and go where? Wandering around in strange country with leaf-bare coming on? You might fancy that, Mousefur, but I don't."

"If you ask me, Brambleclaw and Squirrelpaw had the right idea," Sootfur muttered to his brother Rainwhisker. "Getting out when they did."

Leafpaw wanted to leap to the missing cats' defense, but she made herself sit still and keep quiet. She was the only cat in the Clan who knew that Squirrelpaw and Brambleclaw had left on a mission from StarClan to try to save the forest from this terrible danger. Stormfur and Feathertail, Greystripe's RiverClan children, had gone with them, and cats from WindClan and ShadowClan too. However much their Clanmates missed them, Leafpaw knew it was for the good of all the Clans that they had gone.

Yet the danger was here now, she thought, apprehension gripping her belly, and the missing cats had not returned. Did that mean they had failed? Did it mean StarClan had failed, in spite of the warnings they had sent?

Cinderpelt's calm gaze rested on the hushed and waiting Clan. "There will be great danger," she repeated. "But I do not believe that ThunderClan will be destroyed."

The Clan cats looked at one another, bewildered and afraid. The silence seemed to stretch out for a thousand heartbeats, until it was broken by a single eerie wail rising from the group of elders. As if that were a signal, more yowls and cries of terror broke out. Faced with the terror of approaching monsters, few of the Clan could believe Cinderpelt's reassurances.

Ferncloud swept her tail protectively around her three kits, drawing them into the shelter of her flecked grey fur. "What are we going to do?" she cried.

Dustpelt got up and pressed his nose comfortingly into her side. "We'll do something," he promised. "We'll show the Twolegs this is *our* place."

"And how do you propose doing that?" Mousefur asked, her voice harsh. "When have Twolegs ever cared about us? They do what they want."

"Their monsters will frighten all the prey," Ashfur added. "We already know the forest is emptier than it's ever been, and leaf-bare is coming. What are we going to eat?"

More terrified caterwauling broke out, and several heart-beats went by before Firestar could make himself heard again.

"We can't decide what to do until we know more," he meowed, when the noise had died to apprehensive muttering. "What happened yesterday was near Snakerocks, well away from here. It's possible that the Twolegs won't come any further."

"Then why would StarClan send any warnings at all?" Thornclaw asked. "We've got to face it, Firestar—we can't pretend this isn't happening."

"I'll arrange extra patrols," Firestar assured him, "and I'm going to try speaking to ShadowClan. This was near their border, and they may have had trouble too."

"You can't believe anything ShadowClan tells you," Cloudtail growled. "They wouldn't give you a mousetail if you were starving."

"Maybe not," Firestar replied. "But if the Twolegs have invaded their territory, they might be prepared to talk if it meant we could help one another."

"And hedgehogs might fly," Cloudtail grunted. He turned away from Firestar and muttered something into the ear of his mate, Brightheart, who pushed her nose into his fur as if she were reassuring him.

"Everyone must keep alert," Firestar continued. "If you see anything unusual, I want to know. We survived the flood and the fire. We survived Tigerstar's dog pack, and the threat from Scourge and BloodClan. We will survive this too."

He leaped down from the rock to show that the meeting was at an end.

Immediately the cats in the clearing broke into anxious little knots, discussing what they had just heard. Firestar and Cinderpelt spoke briefly together, and then Cinderpelt padded over to Leafpaw.

"Firestar is going to see ShadowClan right away," the medicine cat announced. "He wants you to come too."

Mingled excitement and apprehension clawed at Leafpaw. "Why me?"

"He wants both medicine cats with him. He thinks that if we're there Blackstar will realise that ThunderClan isn't looking for a fight." Cinderpelt's blue eyes flashed. "All the same, Leafpaw, I hope you've practiced your fighting moves recently."

Leafpaw swallowed. "Yes, Cinderpelt."

"Good." With a wave of her tail, she led the way to where

Firestar was waiting at the entrance to the gorse tunnel. Greystripe and Brackenfur were with him.

"Let's go," meowed Firestar. "And remember, I don't want any trouble. We're only going to talk."

Greystripe snorted. "Try telling that to ShadowClan. If a patrol catches us on their territory, they'll claw us as soon as they see us."

"Let's hope not," Firestar replied with feeling. "If the Twolegs are threatening both our Clans, we can't afford to waste our strength in fighting one another."

Greystripe still looked doubtful, but he said nothing more as Firestar led them up the ravine towards the ShadowClan border. Leafpaw kept her ears pricked for any unusual sounds, and every hair on her pelt stood on end. The forest that had been safe for as long as she could remember was suddenly a frightening place, invaded by the Twolegs and their monsters.

Firestar led his patrol directly towards Snakerocks, and soon Leafpaw realised that he was heading for the spot where the monster had left the Thunderpath. Before they came in sight of it she picked up the reek of the monster and the rich earthy smell of the torn ground. When she came to the top of the slope above the Thunderpath, she stopped and peered through a clump of bracken.

Just below her, a swath of churned-up grass stretched as far as the Thunderpath. Trees lay on the ground, their roots tangling in the air. Everything was silent; Leafpaw couldn't hear a single bird, or the scuffling of prey in the grass. But the monster had gone, and when she opened her jaws to drink in the air, the scent of Twolegs was stale. Even the reek of the monster was beginning to fade.

"They haven't been here today," Greystripe meowed. "Perhaps they've finished whatever they were doing."

"I wouldn't count on it," Firestar replied tersely.

"This is . . . terrible." Brackenfur sounded stunned. He had not been on the original patrol. "Why are they destroying the forest, Firestar?"

The tip of Firestar's tail twitched back and forth. "Why do Twolegs do anything? If we knew that, our lives would be a lot easier."

Skirting the edge of the damaged area, he led the way along the Thunderpath. Leafpaw's belly lurched as she saw that more trees had been felled in ShadowClan's territory, and more ground had been churned up.

Every one of the ThunderClan cats stopped to stare across the hard black surface. Brackenfur dropped into a crouch as if he were about to spring into attack, but there was no enemy to fight.

"Look at that!" Greystripe's voice shook with horror. "You were right, Firestar. ShadowClan is having exactly the same trouble."

"Then that should make it easier to talk to Blackstar." Firestar was trying to sound confident, but his ears were laid flat against his head.

Cinderpelt gave the scarred area a long look before turning away, shaking her head. Though she said nothing, her blue eyes were filled with dread and confusion.

A monster roared by on the Thunderpath, smaller than the tree-eating monsters but still deafeningly noisy. Leafpaw flinched, half expecting it to veer into the forest where they were standing. But it stayed on the Thunderpath and growled away until it vanished among the trees. Another monster followed it; then a third raced along in the opposite direction.

"I don't want to cross here," Greystripe muttered, blinking grit out of his eyes.

Firestar nodded. "We'll cross the stream by Fourtrees and go through the tunnel," he decided. "And just hope we don't meet any ShadowClan warriors on this side of the Thunderpath."

When they reached the stream, Firestar crossed in a couple of bounds by a stepping-stone in the middle. Leafpaw kept an eye on her mentor, making sure that Cinderpelt crossed safely in spite of the old injury to her leg from a Thunderpath accident seasons before. Then she followed her across as Firestar climbed the opposite bank.

A light breeze was blowing towards them, carrying the rank scent of ShadowClan. At the border, Firestar and Greystripe renewed the scent markings, before Firestar led the way towards the tunnel under the Thunderpath.

To Leafpaw's relief, there was no sign of ShadowClan cats in this section of their territory. The elders had told her many stories about that Clan's dark-hearted history, from the murderer Brokenstar, who had killed his own father, to treacherous Tigerstar, who had made himself ShadowClan leader when he was exiled from ThunderClan. The present leader, Blackstar, hadn't caused any trouble so far, but Leafpaw knew that Firestar didn't really trust him. As she followed him into the tunnel, she admired him even more for his courage in trying to make allies of his old enemies for the sake of the forest.

Leafpaw shivered as she plunged into the gloomy silence beneath the Thunderpath, broken only by the drip of water and the plashing of their paws in the mud that covered the bottom of the tunnel. On the ShadowClan side the harsh scent was stronger than ever. The ground under Leafpaw's paws was dank and marshy, covered with coarse scrubby grass. Here and there were pools fringed with reeds; there were few tall trees, unlike those that sheltered the ThunderClan camp. It felt like another world.

"The ShadowClan camp is this way," Firestar meowed, heading for a clump of bushes. "Leafpaw, Cinderpelt, keep close to me. Greystripe and Brackenfur, spread out and keep watch. And remember that we're not looking for trouble."

Leafpaw padded behind Firestar as they headed deeper into ShadowClan territory. She hated the way her paws sank into mud at every step. She kept wanting to stop to flick away the moisture. It was hard to imagine ShadowClan cats putting up with it every day of their lives. Surely they would have grown webbed paws by now? Her muscles began to ache from the strain of keeping alert; when Brackenfur called out she jumped nervously and then hoped that no cat had noticed.

"Firestar, come and look at this." Brackenfur pointed with his tail to a thin piece of wood, too smooth and regular to be the branch of a tree, standing upright in the ground about the height of a cat. Firestar padded over to and sniffed at it suspiciously. "It reeks of Twolegs," he reported.

"There's another over there," Leafpaw called, spotting a matching stick a few fox-lengths further away. "And another – all in a line! What are they –"

Her voice died away. As she bounded towards the next piece of wood, the bushes in front of her rustled and three cats stepped out into the open. She quickly recognised Russetfur, the dark ginger she-cat who was ShadowClan's deputy; the other warriors, a dark grey tom and a lean tabby with a torn ear, were strangers to her.

Leafpaw swallowed nervously.

Firestar was already bounding up to her. "Greetings, Russetfur," he meowed.

"You're trespassing on our territory," snarled the Shadow-Clan deputy.

With a flick of her tail she summoned her warriors forwards. Leafpaw barely had time to dodge, as the dark grey tom sprang at her; she felt claws rake down her side as she rolled away and scrambled to her paws, trying to remember her fighting moves. She caught a glimpse of Cinderpelt and Russetfur stalking around each other; a tail-length away, Greystripe had the tabby pinned down, while Brackenfur and the other tom writhed together in a screeching bundle of grey and ginger fur.

For a moment she could not see Firestar. Glancing around wildly, she saw that he had leaped on to one of the fallen tree trunks. His voice rose in a yowl above the hissing and spitting.

"Stop!"

CHAPTER 3

"You lot stay here," Purdy *ordered* in an undertone. "Let me deal with this."

Stormfur stared in dismay as the old tom shuffled forwards towards the foxes, his rumpled fur on end, his tail lashing back and forth. Frozen by shock, the others might have let Purdy attack and be torn to pieces if Stormfur had not stepped forwards at the last moment and pushed him aside.

"Wha'?" Purdy protested. "Let me get at 'em. I've chased off more foxes than you've had mice, young fellow."

"Then give the rest of us a chance," Stormfur retorted grimly.

The two foxes were creeping slowly up the bank, their eyes flicking from one cat to the next. Too late Stormfur realised that he and his friends had been wrong to assume the woods held no danger for them.

He saw that Crowpaw had stepped forwards to shield Feathertail, while Brambleclaw tried to do the same for Squirrelpaw. But the ThunderClan apprentice slipped out from the shelter of his flank and stood beside him with her ears flattened and one paw extended threateningly.

"What are you doing, treading on my tail?" she growled. "I can take care of myself!"

"You did say you could eat a fox," Tawnypelt pointed out wryly. "Now's your chance."

The foxes crept nearer. Stormfur braced himself, his gaze fixed on their narrow snouts and coldly glittering eyes, trying to guess where they would attack first. Back home, foxes weren't much of a threat to cats who kept alert. They could be avoided, but these were obviously young and spoiling for a fight, eager to defend their territory. Stormfur was sure that the six of them could drive the creatures off eventually, but not without serious injuries. And what would that mean for their journey? *StarClan help us!* he prayed desperately.

Crowpaw, who was nearest to the foxes, crouched to spring. There was barely a tail-length between him and the first of them when Stormfur heard a strange sound behind him, half growling and half barking. The leading fox abruptly lifted its head and stood very still.

Stormfur flicked a glance over his shoulder. Midnight had lumbered forwards, thrusting her way between Purdy and Feathertail until she stood in front of the foxes. She said something else in the same mixture of barks and growls. Although Stormfur could not understand what she was saying, there was no mistaking the threat in the way her shoulders hunched, or the hostility in her black eyes.

Then his ears pricked in shock as the first fox barked what was obviously a reply. "I'd forgotten Midnight told us she could speak fox," he muttered, glancing at Brambleclaw. The

ThunderClan warrior nodded without taking his eyes off the foxes.

"They say this is their place," Midnight reported. "To come here is to be their prey."

"Fox dung to that!" Crowpaw burst out. "Tell them if they try anything, we'll rip their fur off."

Midnight shook her head. "No, small warrior. Cat fur be ripped also. Wait."

Crowpaw backed off a pace or two, still looking furious, and Feathertail pressed her nose against his flank.

Midnight said something else to the foxes. "I tell them you only pass through," she explained to the cats when she had finished. "I tell them much prey is here in woods, easier prey that does not rip fur."

The leading fox was looking confused now, perhaps out of surprise at hearing a badger speak fox, perhaps because it was taking her arguments seriously. But the second—a lean dog fox with a scarred muzzle—was still glaring past Midnight at the group of cats, his teeth bared. He snarled out something that was a threat in any language.

Midnight barked a single word. Taking a step forwards, she raised a paw, her massive body poised to strike. Every hair on Stormfur's pelt prickled as he braced himself for a fight. Then the dog fox started to back away, growling a last curse at Midnight before turning and vanishing into the bracken. Midnight's gaze swivelled to his companion, but the other fox paused only to bark out something rapidly before following.

"And don't come back, if you know what's good for you!"

Crowpaw yowled after them.

Stormfur relaxed, feeling his fur lie flat again. Squirrelpaw flopped down on the ground with a noisy sigh. All the cats, even Purdy, were looking at the badger with new respect.

Brambleclaw padded over to her and dipped his head. "Thanks, Midnight," he meowed. "That could have been nasty."

"They might have killed us," Feathertail added.

"I suppose it's a bad time for a fight," Crowpaw admitted. Stormfur sighed at the aggressive note in the apprentice's voice as he went on, "All the same, I'd like to know why you didn't warn us about the foxes. You said you can read everything in the stars, so why didn't you tell us they'd be here?"

Even though he would never have asked the question, Stormfur waited tensely for Midnight's reply. She had told them so much already about the threat to the forest and how they must go home and lead the Clans to safety. If they did not trust her, they and all their Clanmates would be helpless in the face of destruction. Could she have warned them about the foxes?

For a moment the badger loomed over the WindClan apprentice, her black eyes furious. Crowpaw could not hide a flash of alarm in his eyes, though to his credit he did not back down. Then Midnight relaxed. "I not say everything. Everything indeed StarClan not want me to say. Much, yes, how Twolegs tear up forest, leave no place for cats to stay. But many answers lie within ourselves. This you have already learned, no?"

"I suppose," Crowpaw muttered.

Midnight turned away from him. "Foxes say you must go now," she told the cats. "If you still here at sunset, they attack. That dog fox, he says he tasted cat once, liked it fine."

"Well, he's not going to taste it again!" snapped Tawnypelt.

"We have to leave anyway," Brambleclaw pointed out. "And we're not looking for trouble from foxes. Let's go."

They paused for a few moments to gulp down the rest of the prey. Then Midnight took the lead, and brought them after a short time to the edge of the forest. The sun was dipping below the trees, and where they stood was already in shadow. In front of them, Stormfur saw yet more open moorland, with a range of mountains in the distance; over to one side were the hard reddish shapes of the Twolegplace they had travelled through on the outward journey.

"Which way now?" he asked.

Midnight raised one paw to point straight ahead. "That quickest way, path where sun rises."

"It's not the way we came," Brambleclaw mewed uneasily. "We came through Twolegplace."

"And I'm not going back there!" Crowpaw put in. "I'll climb as many mountains as you like before I face all those Twolegs again."

"I'm not sure," Feathertail meowed. "At least we know the way through Twolegplace, and we've got Purdy to help us."

Crowpaw replied only with a contemptuous snort. Stormfur half agreed with him; they had spent many frightening, hungry days wandering in Twolegplace, and Purdy had seemed as lost as any of them. But the mountains were unfamiliar too; even from here, Stormfur could see that their upper slopes were bare grey rock, with a streak of white here and there that must be the first snow of the approaching leaf-bare. They were far higher than Highstones, and he wondered how much shelter or prey they would find there.

"I agree with Feathertail," he meowed at last. "We made it through Twolegplace once, so we can do it again."

Brambleclaw glanced from one to another, undecided. "What do you think, Tawnypelt?"

His sister shrugged. "Whatever you like. There'll be problems whichever way we go; we all know that."

True enough, Stormfur thought grimly.

"Well, *I* think—" Squirrelpaw began, and broke off with a gasp. Her green eyes had widened with an expression of horror; they seemed to be fixed on something in the distance that no other cat could see.

"Squirrelpaw? What's the matter?" Brambleclaw meowed urgently.

"I . . . I don't know." Squirrelpaw gave herself a shake. "Just make your mind up, Brambleclaw, and let's be off. I want to go that way if it's the quickest route—" She flicked her tail towards the distant mountains. "We'll waste days and days going through Twolegplace again."

Stormfur's whiskers began to tingle. Squirrelpaw was right. They already knew that the route among the Twoleg nests was confusing and difficult. What dangers could there be in the mountains that could be worse than the rats and monsters they knew they would meet in Twolegplace? All that mattered was to get back to the forest without delay.

"I think she's got a point," he meowed. "I've changed my mind. I vote we should go through the mountains."

Squirrelpaw's dark ginger tail twitched to and fro, and she flexed her claws into the grass. "Well?" she spat at Brambleclaw. "Are you going to make up your mind or not?"

Brambleclaw took a deep breath. "OK, the mountains it is."

"Eh? Wha'?" Purdy had been scratching one ear with his hind paw. But when Brambleclaw made his decision he looked up in alarm, blinking his wide amber eyes. "You can't go that way. It's dangerous. What about the—"

"Danger is all around," Midnight broke in, silencing Purdy with a fierce glare. "Your friends great courage will need. The path has been laid out for them in the stars."

Stormfur shot a sharp look at the old tabby. What had Purdy been trying to say when Midnight interrupted him? Did he know of some particular danger in the mountains? And if so, why had Midnight stopped him from telling the rest of them? He thought that he could see wisdom in her face, and something like regret. Just what did she mean by "the path has been laid out"?

"Choice is hard, young warrior." The badger spoke in a low tone to Brambleclaw. Stormfur edged a pace closer so that he could hear. "Your path before you lies, and many challenges you will have to return safe home."

Brambleclaw gazed into the badger's eyes for a long

moment before padding forwards a few paces across the moorland. Whatever these challenges might be, he seemed ready to face them, and Stormfur couldn't help admiring his resolve, even though he came from a rival Clan. When Purdy scrambled to his feet to follow, Midnight put out a paw to hold him back.

The old tom bristled, his amber eyes glaring. "Get out o' my way," he rasped.

Midnight did not move. "With them you cannot go," she rumbled. "The way is theirs alone." Her black eyes gleamed in the dusk. "Young and rash they are, and tests will be many. Their own courage they need, my friend, not yours. Too much on you they would rely."

Purdy blinked. "Well, if you put it like that . . ."

Feathertail darted up to him and gave his ears a quick lick. "We'll never forget you, Purdy, or everything you've done for us."

Just behind her, Crowpaw opened his mouth with his eyes narrowed, as if he was about to say something cutting. Stormfur froze him with a glare. He doubted they would see the old cat again, and although Purdy had made mistakes, he had stood by them and brought them safely to Midnight in the end.

"Goodbye, Purdy. And thank you. We could never have found Midnight without you." Brambleclaw echoed Stormfur's thoughts. "And thank you, too, Midnight."

The badger inclined her head. "Farewell, my friends. May StarClan light your path."

The rest of the cats said their own goodbyes, and began to follow Brambleclaw out on to the moor. Stormfur brought up the rear. Glancing back, he saw Midnight and Purdy sitting side by side under the outlying trees, watching them go. It was impossible to read their expressions in the gathering dusk. Stormfur waved his tail in a last farewell, and turned his face toward the mountains.

CHAPTER 4

❧

At Firestar's yowl of command, Brackenfur and the grey ShadowClan warrior broke apart. Greystripe looked up from the tabby, but still kept a paw firmly on his neck.

"Let him go," Firestar ordered. "We're not here to fight."

"It's hard to do anything else when they jump us like that," Greystripe hissed. He stepped back, and the skinny tabby scrambled to his paws and shook his ruffled fur.

Leafpaw bounded across the marshy ground to stand beside Cinderpelt, half afraid that Russetfur might still attack the medicine cat. ShadowClan's deputy was not likely to take orders from the leader of a rival Clan.

Russetfur flicked her tail towards the dark grey tom. "Cedarheart, get back to camp. Warn Blackstar that we have been invaded, and fetch more warriors."

The grey warrior streaked off into the bushes.

"There's no need for that," Firestar pointed out, keeping his voice mild. "We're not invading your territory, and we're not trying to steal prey."

"Then what *do* you want?" Russetfur demanded bad-temperedly. "What are we supposed to think when you trespass on our territory?"

"I'm sorry about that." Firestar leaped down from the tree trunk and padded across to her. "I . . . I know we shouldn't be here. It's just that I have to speak to Blackstar. Something has happened, something that's too urgent to wait for the next Gathering."

Russetfur sniffed disbelievingly, but sheathed her claws. Leafpaw felt her racing heart begin to slow down. The ShadowClan deputy was too badly outnumbered to launch another attack, especially when she had sent away the grey tom, Cedarheart.

"What's so urgent then?" she growled.

Firestar gestured with his tail through the sparse trees, towards the swath of destruction that the Twoleg monster had left on this side of the Thunderpath. "Isn't that enough?" he asked desperately.

Russetfur silenced him with a furious hiss. "If you think ShadowClan is weakened . . ."

"I didn't say that," Firestar protested. "But you must have seen that we've had the same trouble in our territory. Now, are you going to drive us off, or are you going to let us talk to Blackstar?"

Russetfur narrowed her eyes, then gave a curt nod. "Very well. Follow me."

She led the way through the bushes. The ThunderClan cats bunched together behind her, and the tabby ShadowClan warrior brought up the rear. Leafpaw's heart began to pound again as the scents of the strange territory flowed around her. Even the day had grown darker, clouds covering the sun so that their path was shadowed. She tried to stop herself from jumping at every sound, or staring around as if there might be a ShadowClan warrior lurking behind every tree.

Soon Leafpaw became aware of a stronger ShadowClan scent coming from up ahead. Russetfur led the way around a thick clump of hazel; following her, Leafpaw stopped dead in front of a long line of cats—lean warriors with their muscles tensed and the light of battle in their eyes. Behind them rose a tangled wall of brambles.

"That's the ShadowClan camp," Cinderpelt muttered close to Leafpaw's ear. "It doesn't look as if Blackstar is going to invite us in."

The ShadowClan leader stood in the middle of his warriors. He was a huge white cat with black paws; his pelt showed the scars of many battles. As the ThunderClan cats appeared he stepped forward and faced Firestar with narrowed eyes.

"What's this?" His voice was rough. "Does the great Firestar think he can go where he likes in the forest?"

Firestar ignored the contempt in Blackstar's tone, simply dipping his head in the courteous greeting of one leader to another. "I have come to talk to you about what the Twolegs are doing," he began. "We have to decide what we're going to do if it carries on."

"We? What do you mean, we? ShadowClan does not talk with ThunderClan," Blackstar retorted. "We make our own decisions."

"But the forest is being destroyed!"

Leafpaw heard the exasperation in her leader's tone, and knew how hard it was for Firestar to stay calm when the ShadowClan leader insisted on treating him like an enemy.

The ShadowClan leader shrugged his powerful shoulders. "Firestar, you're panicking over nothing. Twolegs are mad. Even the smallest kit knows that. True, they knocked down a few trees—but now they've gone away again. Whatever was going on, it's over."

Leafpaw wondered if Blackstar really believed that. Surely he couldn't be such a fool? Or was this just a show of bravado to convince Firestar that ShadowClan had nothing to worry about?

"And if it's not over?" Firestar asked steadily. "If it gets worse? Prey has been frightened away from where the Twolegs have been. What if the Twolegs claw up more of our territories? What will you do in leaf-bare, Blackstar, if you can't feed your Clan?"

One or two of the ShadowClan warriors looked uneasy, but their leader stared defiantly at Firestar.

"We have no reason to fear leaf-bare," he meowed. "We can always eat rats from Carrionplace."

Cinderpelt twitched her ears impatiently. "Have you forgotten what happened last time you tried that? Half your Clan died from sickness."

"That's true." A small tabby tom, crouched at the end of the line, spoke up boldly. Leafpaw recognised Littlecloud, the ShadowClan medicine cat. "I was ill myself. I would have died if it hadn't been for you, Cinderpelt."

"Be quiet, Littlecloud," Blackstar ordered. "The sickness was a punishment from StarClan because Nightstar was not a properly chosen leader. There's no danger in eating food from Carrionplace now."

"There's danger if a leader silences his medicine cat," Cinderpelt retorted tartly. "Or pretends to know more than they do about the will of StarClan."

Blackstar glared at her, but said nothing.

"Listen to me," Firestar began again desperately. "I believe that great trouble is coming to the forest, trouble that we'll survive only if we work together."

"Mouse dung!" Blackstar snarled. "Don't try to tell me what to do, Firestar. I'm not one of your warriors. If you have any-thing to say, you should do what we have always done, and bring it to the next Gathering at Fourtrees."

Part of Leafpaw felt that the ShadowClan leader was right. The warrior code dictated that the business of the forest should be discussed at Gatherings. There was nowhere else that cats could meet under the sacred truce of StarClan. At the same time, she knew that the Twolegs wouldn't wait until after the next full moon to continue their destruction of the forest. What else might happen by the time of the next Gathering?

"Very well, Blackstar." Firestar's voice was hollow with defeat. *It's happening,* Leafpaw thought in panic. *He's giving up. The forest is going to be destroyed.* "If that's the way you want it. But if the Twolegs come back, you have my permission to send a messenger into ThunderClan territory, and we will talk again."

"Generous as always, Firestar." Blackstar meowed scornfully. "But nothing's going to happen that we can't handle ourselves."

"Mouse-brain!" Greystripe hissed.

Firestar shot Greystripe a warning glance, but the ShadowClan leader did not reply. Instead, he swept his tail towards Russetfur.

"Take some warriors and escort these cats off our territory," he ordered. "And in case you were thinking of paying us another uninvited visit," he added to Firestar, "we'll be increasing our patrols along that border. Now go."

There was nothing to do but obey. Firestar turned and signalled to his own cats to follow him. Russetfur and her warriors gathered around them in a threatening semicircle, letting them walk away but keeping them bunched tightly together. Leafpaw was glad when the tunnel under the Thunderpath came into sight, and more relieved still to be through it and heading for their own part of the forest.

"And don't come back!" Russetfur spat as they crossed the border.

"We won't!" Greystripe hurled a parting shot over his shoulder. "We were only trying to help, you stupid furball."

"Leave it, Greystripe." Now that they were back in their own territory, Firestar let his disappointment show. Leafpaw felt a sharp stab of compassion for him; it wasn't his fault that ShadowClan had refused to listen to reason.

"Maybe we should try talking to WindClan?" she suggested quietly to Cinderpelt as the patrol headed for camp. "Perhaps they've had trouble too. That could be why they've been stealing fish from RiverClan." She was referring to the furious accusations made by Hawkfrost, a RiverClan warrior, at the last Gathering.

"*If* they have. It was never proved," Cinderpelt reminded her. "All the same, Leafpaw, you might have a point. Ravenpaw said there were more Twolegs than usual on that part of the Thunderpath."

"Then perhaps Firestar should talk to Tallstar?"

"I don't think Firestar will be talking to any more Clan leaders for a while," Cinderpelt meowed, with a sympathetic glance at the flame-coloured tom. "Besides, Tallstar is a proud leader. He'd never admit that his Clan is starving."

"But Firestar has to do *something*!"

"Perhaps Blackstar was right, and he should wait for the Gathering. But if I get the chance"—Cinderpelt interrupted her apprentice's protest—"I'll have a word with him." She lifted her blue gaze to the cloud-covered sky. "And let's just pray that StarClan has mercy on us, whatever happens."

"Sorreltail, are you there?"

Leafpaw stood outside the warriors' den and tried to peer through the branches. It was early the following morning; a thick fog covered the camp and misted her fur with tiny droplets of water.

"Sorreltail?" she repeated.

There was a scuffling sound inside the den, and Sorreltail poked her head out, blinking sleep from her eyes.

"Leafpaw?" Her jaws gaped wide in a yawn. "What's the matter? The sun's not up yet. I was having this terrific dream about a mouse. . ."

"Sorry," Leafpaw mewed. "But I want you to do something with me. Are you due to go out with the dawn patrol?"

"No." Sorreltail squeezed out between the branches and gave the fur on her shoulders a quick lick. "What's all this about?"

Leafpaw took a deep breath. "I want to go and visit WindClan. Will you come with me?"

Sorreltail's eyes stretched wide, and her tail curled up in surprise. "What if we meet a WindClan patrol?"

"It should be OK—I'm a medicine cat apprentice, so I'm allowed to go into the territories between here and Highstones. Please, Sorreltail! I really need to know whether WindClan is having trouble too." Though she couldn't tell Sorreltail, Leafpaw knew that a cat from every Clan had been chosen by StarClan for the journey. Because of that, she suspected that every Clan would be invaded by the Twolegs, but she wanted to be sure.

The light of adventure was already sparkling in Sorreltail's eyes. "I'm up for it," she declared. "Let's get a move on, before any cat catches us and starts asking questions."

She darted across the clearing and into the gorse tunnel. Leafpaw followed, with a last glance back at the silent, sleeping camp. The fog hung thickly in the ravine, deadening the sound of their pawsteps. Everything was grey, and though the dawn light was strengthening, there was no sign of the sun. The bracken was bent double with the weight of water drops, and soon the two cats' pelts were soaked.

Sorreltail shivered. "Why did I ever leave my warm nest?" she complained, only half joking. "Still, if it's like this on the moor, the fog will help to hide us."

"And muffle our scent," Leafpaw agreed.

But before she and Sorreltail reached Fourtrees, the mist had begun to thin out. It still lay heavy on the stream, but when they climbed the opposite bank they broke out into sunlight. Leafpaw shook the moisture from her fur, but there was little heat in the sun's rays; she looked forward to a good run across the moor to warm herself up.

As they skirted the top of the hollow at Fourtrees, Leafpaw felt a breeze blowing directly off the moorland. She and Sorreltail paused for a moment at the far side of the hollow, their fur blown back and their jaws parted to scent the air.

"WindClan," Sorreltail meowed. She put her head to one side, uncertainly. "There's something odd about it, though."

"Yes. And there's no sign of any rabbits," Leafpaw added.

She hesitated for a couple more heartbeats, then led the way across the border. The two cats darted from one clump of gorse to the next, making what use they could of the scant cover on the moorland. Leafpaw's fur prickled; her tabby-and-white pelt would show up starkly against the short grass. In the ThunderClan camp she had been confident that as a medicine cat she would not be challenged; now she felt small and vulnerable. She wanted to find out what she could, then hurry back to the safety of her own territory.

She headed for the crest of a low hill that looked down over the Thunderpath, and flattened herself in the grass to peer down. Beside her, Sorreltail let out a long hiss.

"Well, there's not much doubt about that," she mewed.

Leading from the Thunderpath on the far side of the territory was a long scar where the moorland grass had been torn away. The track was marked by short stakes of wood like the ones Leafpaw had seen in ShadowClan territory the day before. It gouged a path across the moor and came to an abrupt halt at the foot of the hill where she and Sorreltail were crouching. A glittering monster sat silent where it ended. Leafpaw's breath came in short gasps as she imagined it scanning the moorland, ready to leap on its prey with a roar.

"Where are its Twolegs?" Sorreltail muttered.

Leafpaw glanced from side to side, but everything was quiet; an air of menace lay thick as fog on the scarred landscape. There was still no scent of rabbits—had they been frightened away, Leafpaw wondered, or had the Twolegs taken them? Perhaps they had moved to a different part of the moor when the monster dug up their burrows.

"Yuck!" Sorreltail exclaimed suddenly. "Can you smell that?"

As she spoke, Leafpaw picked it up too, a harsh tang like nothing she had ever scented before. Instinctively her stomach churned and she curled her lip. "What is it?"

"Probably something to do with the Twolegs," Sorreltail meowed disgustedly.

A distant yowl interrupted her. Leafpaw sprang to her paws and spun around to see three WindClan warriors racing towards them.

"Uh-oh," murmured Sorreltail.

Before Leafpaw could decide whether to run or stay to talk, the WindClan cats had surrounded them. With a sinking heart she recognised the aggressive deputy Mudclaw, with the tabby warrior Tornear and another tabby tom she did not know. She would rather have dealt with the Clan leader, Tallstar, or Firestar's friend Onewhisker, who were both more likely to listen to her explanations.

"Why are you trespassing on our territory?" the WindClan deputy demanded.

"I'm a medicine cat apprentice," Leafpaw pointed out, bowing her head respectfully. "I came to—"

"To spy!" That was Tornear, his eyes blazing with anger. "Don't think we don't know what you're up to!"

Now that the WindClan cats were up close, Leafpaw could see how thin they were. Their bristling pelts hardly covered their ribs. Fear-scent came off them in waves, almost drowning the scent of their fury. They were obviously short of food, but that didn't explain why they were so much more hostile than ShadowClan had been.

"I'm sorry, we were only—" she began.

Mudclaw interrupted with a frenzied shriek. "Attack!"

Tornear hurled himself at Leafpaw. The ThunderClan cats

were outnumbered and outclassed; besides, she and Sorreltail had not come to fight.

"Run!" Leafpaw yowled.

She leaped back from Tornear's outstretched claws. Spinning round, she fled for the border, her belly close to the ground and her tail streaming out behind her. Sorreltail raced along at her side. Leafpaw dared not look over her shoulder, but she could hear the shrieks of the pursuing cats hard on their paws.

The border was in sight, but she barely had time to realise that they were bearing too far towards the river when scent markers flooded over her, WindClan and RiverClan scents mixed together.

"Oh, no!" she exclaimed. "We're in RiverClan territory now."

"Keep going," Sorreltail panted. "It's only a narrow strip between here and ThunderClan territory."

Leafpaw risked a glance to see if the WindClan patrol was still pursuing them. They were—they must be so furious that they hadn't noticed the border, or did not care.

"They're gaining on us!" she gasped. "We'll have to fight. We can't lead them on to our territory."

She and Sorreltail whirled to face their attackers. Leafpaw braced herself, wishing desperately that she had never thought of entering WindClan territory, and especially that she had not brought Sorreltail into danger with her.

As Mudclaw leaped at her, Leafpaw saw a streak of golden fur shoot out from a nearby bush. It was Mothwing, the medicine cat apprentice from RiverClan. Then Mudclaw's body crashed against her and she was rolling on the ground, squirming to escape the flurry of raking claws. She tried to twist round and sink her teeth into his neck, but there was a wiry strength in the deputy's lean body that trapped her helplessly like a piece of prey. Leafpaw felt his claws rake across her side and bury themselves in her shoulder. With a massive effort she shook him off, trying to bring her hind paws up to attack his belly.

Suddenly the weight lifted and Mudclaw was scrabbling for a foothold beside her. Leafpaw staggered to her paws to see Mothwing cuffing him hard over both ears. "Get off our territory!" she spat. "And take your mangy friends with you."

Mudclaw aimed a final blow at her, but he was already backing away. Sorreltail sprang up from where she had Tornear pinned down and bit hard on his tail before releasing him. He fled, yowling after the Clan deputy; the other tabby warrior had already vanished.

Mothwing turned back to the ThunderClan cats. Her golden tabby fur was hardly ruffled and her amber eyes gleamed with satisfaction. "Having trouble?" she murmured.

Leafpaw fought for breath and shook leaves and scraps of twig from her pelt. "Thanks, Mothwing," she replied. "I don't know what we'd have done without you." Turning to her friend, she added, "Sorreltail, have you met Mothwing? She's Mudfur's apprentice, but she was trained as a warrior first."

"A good thing she was," Sorreltail mewed, with a nod of thanks to the RiverClan cat. "We bit off more than we could chew there."

"I'm sorry we're on your territory," Leafpaw went on. "We'll go right away."

"Oh, there's no hurry." Mothwing did not try to question them about why they were there, or what they had done to annoy WindClan. "You look pretty shaken. Rest for a bit and I'll find you some herbs to calm you down."

She vanished among the bushes, leaving Leafpaw and Sorreltail with nothing to do but sit and wait for her.

"Is she always this careless about the warrior code?" Sorreltail muttered. "She doesn't seem to understand that we shouldn't be here!"

"I think it's because I'm a medicine cat apprentice too."

"Even medicine cats have to stick to the warrior code," mewed Sorreltail. "And I can't see Cinderpelt being so welcoming to other Clans! Of course, Mothwing's mother was a rogue, wasn't she? That could explain it."

"Mothwing is a loyal RiverClan cat!" Leafpaw fired up in defence of her friend. "It doesn't matter who her mother was."

"I never said it did," Sorreltail soothed her, touching Leafpaw's shoulder with her tail-tip. "But that might be why she's more relaxed about Clan boundaries."

Mothwing returned at that moment with a wad of herbs in her jaws. The ThunderClan apprentice drank in the scent of thyme; she remembered Cinderpelt telling her how good it was for calming anxieties.

"There," Mothwing meowed. "Eat some of that and you'll soon feel better."

Leafpaw and Sorreltail crouched down and chewed up some of the leaves. Leafpaw imagined the juices soaking into every scrap of her body, healing the shock of their terrifying encounter with WindClan.

"Are you hurt at all?" Mothwing asked. "I can fetch some cobwebs."

"No, there's no need, thanks," Leafpaw assured her. She and Sorreltail both had a few scratches, but they would stop bleeding by themselves without need for a poultice of cobwebs. "We really ought to be going."

"So what was all that about?" Mothwing queried, as Leafpaw and Sorreltail swallowed the last of the herbs. She wasn't quite as uninterested as the ThunderClan cats had thought. "What were you doing on WindClan territory?"

"We went to see what the Twolegs are up to," Leafpaw explained. When Mothwing still looked mystified, she described how she had seen the monster roaring into the forest two days before, tearing up the ground, and then found evidence that WindClan and ShadowClan were being destroyed in the same way. She was aware of a doubtful glance from Sorreltail; the young warrior was clearly unhappy about revealing ThunderClan's problems to a cat from a rival Clan. Leafpaw shook her head impatiently; there could be no harm in taking another medicine cat into her confidence.

"Firestar wants to ask the other Clans what they think," she finished. "But ShadowClan won't admit anything is wrong, and—well, you've seen how WindClan reacted."

"What can you expect?" Sorreltail broke in. She passed her tongue over her lips as if she didn't much like the taste of the herbs. "No Clan is going to be in a hurry to tell us they're starving and losing their territory to Twolegs."

"We've seen nothing of these monsters in RiverClan," Mothwing meowed. "Everything's fine here. But it explains one thing. . . ." Her amber eyes widened. "I've sensed panic over WindClan territory. Their scent markers on the border are filled with fear."

"I'm not surprised," Sorreltail mewed. "They're thin as anything, and there's no scent of rabbits anywhere."

"Everything's changing," Leafpaw murmured.

"And inside the Clans, as well. An ambitious cat might take the chance of—" Mothwing spoke quickly, urgently, and then broke off awkwardly.

"What do you mean?" Leafpaw prompted.

"Oh . . . no . . . I don't know." Mothwing trailed off and looked away.

Leafpaw stared at her, wondering what was going on inside that beautiful golden head. She was too young to remember Tigerstar, the bloodthirsty cat who had plotted to make himself leader of ThunderClan. When his murderous plans failed, he had been prepared to destroy the whole Clan for vengeance. She shivered. Did Mothwing know of another cat with ambition like this? Surely the forest could never produce another Tigerstar?

Her thoughts were interrupted when Mothwing sprang to her paws, her head turned towards the river. "A patrol is coming!" she exclaimed. "Come this way—quickly!"

She slipped between two bushes; Leafpaw and Sorreltail followed. A few moments later they came into the open and found themselves on the slope that led up to the ThunderClan border.

"If your Clan is short of prey, come and see me," Mothwing mewed. "We can always spare a few fish. Now run!"

Leafpaw and Sorreltail streaked up the slope and plunged for cover into more bushes. Though Leafpaw braced herself for accusing snarls behind her, they reached the border unseen.

"Thank StarClan for that!" Sorreltail exclaimed as they crossed into their own territory.

Leafpaw looked back through the branches. Mothwing was standing where they had left her; a moment later the undergrowth parted and a large, sleek-furred tabby warrior emerged. Leafpaw recognised Mothwing's brother Hawkfrost; two other warriors followed him. Hawkfrost stopped to talk to his sister, but never once glanced in the direction of the ThunderClan cats.

Looking at the warrior's massive shoulders and strong muscles, Leafpaw was relieved that he had not caught them trespassing. Unlike Mothwing, he kept strictly to the warrior code, and he was unlikely to listen to explanations. Not for the first time, Leafpaw felt that he reminded her of some other cat, but however hard she stared at him, she could not remember who.

"Come on," Sorreltail meowed. "Are you going to stare at those RiverClan warriors all day? It's time we were getting back, and then you can decide how much you're going to tell Firestar."

CHAPTER 5

Stormfur's paws scrabbled on smooth grey rock. Heaving himself
upwards, he reached the top of the boulder and turned to look
down at his friends, his fur buffeted by the icy breeze.

"Come on," he meowed. "It's not so bad if you take a leap
at it."

Following the rising sun, he and the other cats had left the
moorland behind and begun to climb. Now, as sunhigh
approached on the second day of their homeward journey, the
mountains they had seen from a distance stretched up in front
of them even bigger than they had imagined, their sheer
slopes black and forbidding, with wisps of cloud floating
around their peaks. The soil beneath the cats' paws was rough
with pebbles, and little grew there except sparse grass and
twisted thorn trees. There was no clear path; instead they
followed winding narrow clefts and often had to turn back
when they came up against rock walls with no way through.
Thinking wistfully of the river sliding through deep, cool
grasses at home, Stormfur half wished they had decided to
return through Twolegplace instead.

Squirrelpaw bunched her hind legs and launched herself in a

massive leap, following Stormfur up the boulder that blocked their path. "Mouse dung!" she gasped as she missed the top and began to slide back. Stormfur leaned over and sank his teeth into her neck fur, steadying her until her scraping claws propelled her up the last tail-length to sit beside him.

"Thanks!" Her green eyes glowed at him. "I know my name's Squirrelpaw, but I never thought I'd wish that I *was* a squirrel!"

Stormfur let out a *mrrow* of laughter. "We'll all wish we were squirrels if we get much more of this."

"Hey!" Crowpaw's voice rose aggressively from below. "Stand back, will you? How can I get up there with you two furballs standing in the way?"

Stormfur and Squirrelpaw stepped back from the top of the boulder, and a moment later Crowpaw joined them, his long limbs managing the jump easily. Ignoring the others, he turned back to help Feathertail, who scrambled up with a muttered curse as one of her claws snagged on the rock.

Stormfur was worried that the rat bite in Tawnypelt's shoulder would stop her from climbing the boulder, and wondered if they would have to try finding a way round it, but to his relief her leap brought her almost to the top, where Crowpaw grabbed her by the scruff and hauled her up. Brambleclaw joined them last of all, shaking his ruffled tabby fur as he stood on top of the boulder and looked around. This close to sunhigh, there were few shadows to point them in the right direction and nothing but a sheer precipice in front of them, hiding what lay ahead.

"I suppose we go that way," he meowed, flicking his tail towards a narrow ledge leading across the face of the rock. "What do you think?" he asked Stormfur.

Stormfur felt his pelt prickle as he looked at the ledge. A few straggling bushes had rooted themselves in cracks, but apart from that the rock was bare and if they slipped there would be nothing to hold on to.

"We can try," he mewed doubtfully, rather surprised that Brambleclaw had asked his opinion. "There's nowhere else, unless we go back."

Brambleclaw nodded. "Bring up the rear, will you?" he asked. "We don't know what might be lurking around here, and we need a strong cat to watch our back."

Stormfur murmured agreement, feeling a warm glow that spread from his ears to his tail-tip at the ThunderClan cat's praise. Brambleclaw was neither his leader nor his mentor, but Stormfur couldn't help feeling strong admiration for the young warrior's courage and the way he had taken the lead on this difficult journey.

"I've changed my mind," Squirrelpaw announced as Brambleclaw squeezed his way along the ledge. "I don't want to be a squirrel anymore. I'd rather be a bird!"

Stormfur brought up the rear as Brambleclaw had asked, his ears pricked for danger while he tried to hide his nervousness about the sheer drop, which tugged at him like an invisible weight. He hugged the rock face, placing each paw carefully and using his tail for balance. After a little while the breeze grew stronger, and Stormfur's mind filled with terrifying images of himself or one of his friends blown right off the ledge and down to the ground below.

After a short while the ledge curved around the rock face, out of sight. Before Stormfur reached the turn, Tawnypelt, who was just in front of him, stopped abruptly, and from further ahead he heard Feathertail exclaim, "Oh, no!"

"What's the matter?" Stormfur asked.

Tawnypelt edged forwards more slowly, and Stormfur followed until he could see what was ahead. His belly lurched. A gap had opened up between their ledge and the rock face; the ledge became a spur of rock, jutting out from the side of the mountain and narrowing to a point. On both sides was a dizzying drop to a valley below where a mountain stream flowed, looking thin as a mousetail.

"Do you want to go back?" he called to Brambleclaw.

"Hang on a minute," the ThunderClan warrior replied. "There might be a way. Look over there."

Stormfur looked where his tail was pointing: On the mountainside beyond the gap the rock face had broken away, and a narrow rift had opened up between two steep slopes. Bushes were growing there and one or two small trees. A stream trickled down one side, overhung by grasses.

"The going looks easier there," Feathertail meowed. "But can we get across?"

Squirrelpaw lifted her head and tasted the air. "I can smell rabbits," she mewed longingly.

Stormfur measured the gap. It was wider than he liked, especially from a standing start. He thought he could manage it, but what about Tawnypelt? The ShadowClan warrior had started to limp again since they had started their climb, and even though she hadn't said anything, it was obvious the wound hadn't healed properly yet.

Before he could voice his doubts he heard Crowpaw mew, "What are we waiting for? Are we going to stand around here until we grow wings?"

Without any more hesitation the WindClan apprentice launched himself across the gap. For a heartbeat his grey-black body seemed to hang in the air; then he was across, landing lightly on the loose stones at the edge of the drop.

"Come on!" he called. "It's easy."

Catching Brambleclaw's eye, Stormfur knew that the tabby warrior shared his annoyance that the apprentice hadn't waited for the rest of them to agree. Now they all had to try the leap, whether they wanted to or not, because Crowpaw would never manage to jump back on to the narrow spur of rock, and they could not leave him on his own over there.

He was even less pleased when he saw Feathertail crouching at the edge of the rock with the wind buffeting her fur. Crowpaw was waiting to steady her at the other side, and she waved her plumy tail with pleasure as she realised that she had made it safely.

The remaining cats bunched together on the rock. Stormfur's pelt pricked with fear as he felt the breeze grow stronger.

"OK, who's next?" Brambleclaw asked steadily.

"I'll go," Squirrelpaw meowed. "See you over there."

She pushed herself off from the rock in a tremendous leap, landing a tail-length from the edge on the other side.

"She's quite something," Brambleclaw murmured, then looked confused, as if he hadn't meant to speak his thoughts aloud.

"She certainly is," Stormfur agreed.

"Tawnypelt, are you ready?" Brambleclaw asked, turning away. "Is your shoulder OK?"

"I'll be fine," Tawnypelt mewed grimly.

She measured the distance with a glance and then took off. For one horrible instant, Stormfur thought she had jumped short. Her body slammed into the edge of the rock and her front paws scrabbled frantically for a grip among the loose stones. A heartbeat later Feathertail was on one side of her, and Squirrelpaw on the other, sinking their teeth into her neck fur and pulling her up the rest of the way.

"Well done!" Brambleclaw called, his voice high-pitched from worry.

Tawnypelt did not reply. Her tail had fluffed out with terror; Stormfur saw Feathertail coaxing her over to the stream and encouraging her to drink.

"You next?" Brambleclaw asked Stormfur.

"You go; I'm fine."

But as Stormfur watched the strong tabby warrior leaping the gap, he couldn't help wishing he hadn't waited to go last. He was just about to jump when Squirrelpaw shrieked, "Stormfur! Look out!"

At the same instant a dark shadow fell over him and he

heard the beating of wings thudding through the air. Without pausing to look up, he launched himself across the gap, catching a glimpse of his friends on the other side scattering to the sides of the valley.

He hit the ground awkwardly, falling to one side, and froze with horror as he looked up to see an enormous bird swooping down on top of him, talons extended.

A cat yowled his name. Rolling away from the claws and stabbing beak he felt the draft from the beating wings and smelled a reek of carrion. Then he was aware of Brambleclaw and Feathertail hurtling towards him, hissing and spitting with their fur standing on end. The bird veered to one side; Stormfur had a couple of heartbeats to scramble away. Then the talons hit the ground, throwing up spurts of dust. The bird let out a frustrated screech. Its wings beat strongly, carrying it up again. All three cats streaked into the shelter of a bush where Squirrelpaw and Tawnypelt were waiting.

"What in StarClan's name was *that*?" Stormfur gasped, watching the bird climb higher until it was no more than a dot in the sky. "I've never seen such a big bird."

"An eagle." Crowpaw wormed his way under the lower branches to join them. "We see them in WindClan territory now and then. They prey on lambs, but the elders say they've taken cats before."

"In another heartbeat it would have taken me," Stormfur muttered. "Thanks, both of you," he added to Brambleclaw and Feathertail.

Feathertail shuddered. "Imagine what would have happened

if it had spotted us a bit earlier, when we were all stuck out on that rock!"

"I don't *want* to imagine it!" Squirrelpaw retorted.

"I think we need to take a break after that," Brambleclaw meowed. "What about finding some prey? I scented rabbits out there."

"I'll go," Crowpaw offered. "*I* don't need to rest. Coming, Feathertail?"

Stormfur opened his mouth to object as his sister pushed her way out of the bush behind Crowpaw. In the end, all he said was, "Watch out for that eagle!"

When they had gone, Tawnypelt closed her eyes with an exhausted sigh and within a couple of heartbeats she was asleep. Stormfur curled up beside her, but he found it hard to rest. He could hear Brambleclaw and Squirrelpaw murmuring quietly together, and found he was straining his ears to make out what they were saying, envying their closeness and wishing not for the first time that Squirrelpaw was in his Clan and not Brambleclaw's. He was worried about his sister too, out there alone with that apprentice. They should keep moving while they could; if they delayed too long, darkness would overtake them and they would be forced to spend the night here.

At last he drifted into an uneasy doze; a paw prodding him in the ribs brought him back to consciousness. He blinked up into Squirrelpaw's green eyes and his senses were flooded by the scent of rabbit.

"They're back," Squirrelpaw meowed. "And they've

brought enough fresh-kill for every cat. Of course," she added, her eyes glinting with amusement, "I can eat yours if you don't want it."

"Don't you dare!" Stormfur growled, flicking her ear with his tail as he scrambled up.

Crouching over his share of rabbit, he saw Feathertail and Crowpaw sitting close together as they ate. He suppressed a growl as he wondered yet again how Feathertail could possibly forget what happened when cats from different Clans tried to be together.

Once all the journeying cats were relaxing with full bellies, he managed to edge his sister away from the rest. "Listen, Feathertail, you and Crowpaw—" he murmured.

"What about Crowpaw?" Feathertail's blue eyes flashed and her voice was uncharacteristically sharp. "You others are so unfair to him!"

Stormfur wanted to point out that the young cat asked for trouble with the way he argued about everything, but he had enough sense not to say so to Feathertail. "That's not the point," he mewed. "What's going to happen when we get back home? Crowpaw's in a different Clan."

"We don't even know if there will be Clans any more," Feathertail pointed out. "We'll be leaving the forest, remember?"

Stormfur snorted. "Do you think all the Clan boundaries will vanish, just because we have to leave? I doubt it."

He was surprised by the flash of anger in Feathertail's eyes. "Have you forgotten already what Midnight said?" she spat. "The Clans won't *survive* if they can't work together."

"And have you forgotten what happens when cats from different Clans get together?" Stormfur growled. "Look at the way our own father has been torn between two Clans. You and I nearly *died* because we're half-Clan! Tigerstar would have killed us if the ThunderClan cats hadn't rescued us."

"But Tigerstar's gone now," Feathertail mewed stubbornly. "There won't be another cat like that in the forest. And Midnight said all the Clans will have to find somewhere else to live. Everything will be different."

"But you and Crowpaw . . ."

"I'm not going to talk about me and Crowpaw." Feathertail's anger died. "I'm sorry, Stormfur, but this doesn't have anything to do with you."

Stormfur started to deliver a stinging reply, then realised that she was right. Awkwardly he stroked her shoulder with the tip of his tail. "I worry about you, that's all."

Feathertail gave his ear a quick lick. "I know. But there's no need. Really."

Even though he did not agree with her, Stormfur said nothing. She was his sister and he would do anything to make her happy. He wished Crowpaw could make her happy too, if that was what Feathertail really wanted, but he couldn't believe that all the rivalry between the Clans would vanish, whatever happened, and let them be together.

When the cats emerged from the shelter of the bush to continue their journey they saw that the sky had grown darker. The wind had dropped but there was a chill in the air and clouds surged around the mountaintop, hiding the sun.

"Rain on its way," Tawnypelt commented. "That's all we need."

"Then let's push on while we can," meowed Brambleclaw.

They set off up the rift in the side of the mountain, keeping close to the sides and making what use they could of the cover from bushes, in case the eagle returned. Stormfur kept an eye on the sky; once, he saw a tiny dot, drifting lazily above the mountainside, and knew that the fierce bird was still on the watch.

They passed the source of the tiny stream, bubbling up from a crack between two rocks, and took a last drink before they pressed on. Stormfur gazed up the slope ahead, scanning it for something familiar that would show him the next source of food or shelter, and saw nothing but lifeless, grey rock.

The valley grew narrower and there was even less vegetation. Stormfur felt uncomfortably exposed, but the eagle did not return. As twilight gathered, a thin, cold rain began to fall. The cats' fur was soon soaked, and there was nowhere to shelter.

"We've got to stop soon," Squirrelpaw announced loudly. "My paws are falling off."

"Well, we can't stop here." Brambleclaw sounded irritable. "We need to get out of the rain."

"No, Squirrelpaw's right," Stormfur objected, facing up to

the ThunderClan warrior. "We can't go on in the dark; we risk falling."

Brambleclaw's neck fur rose and he fixed Stormfur with a furious glare. Behind him, Stormfur heard a faint murmur of distress from Feathertail. He realised they were within a couple of heartbeats of fighting among themselves. His growing respect for the ThunderClan cat meant that a fight was the last thing he wanted, but he could not back down and let Brambleclaw lead them on to slip over some precipice in the darkness.

Then he saw Brambleclaw's fur begin to lie flat again as the tabby seemed to understand Stormfur's concerns. "You're right, Stormfur. Let's shelter under the rock over there. It's better than nothing."

He led the way to an overhanging rock, open on one side to the wind and rain that grew heavier still as the cats settled down, huddling together in an attempt to keep warm and dry.

"Shelter?" Crowpaw muttered. "If this is shelter, then I'm a hedgehog!"

You're just as prickly, Stormfur thought, but he kept the words to himself.

That night he slept only in brief, uncomfortable snatches, and whenever he woke, he could feel his friends shifting uneasily around him. When at last the darkness began to lift he heaved himself to his paws, feeling stiff and bleary-eyed, and peered out of the overhang to see dense white mist swirling around them.

"We must be in the clouds," Brambleclaw murmured, coming to join him. "I hope it lifts soon."

"Do you think we should go on?" Stormfur asked hesitantly, wanting to avoid another confrontation with the ThunderClan cat. "If we can't see where we're going, we could walk straight over a cliff."

"We manage when the mist comes down on the moors," Crowpaw pointed out, yawning as he staggered to his paws. Then he added doubtfully, "But we know our own territory by scent as well as sight."

"And what about fresh-kill?" Squirrelpaw mewed. "There's no rabbit scent up here. I'm starving!"

Stormfur tried to ignore his own growling belly while Brambleclaw ventured out of their shelter and stood looking upwards. "I can see for a few fox-lengths," he reported. "This cleft seems to go on and on. I think we'll be safe if we follow it."

He glanced at Stormfur as he spoke, a questioning look in his eyes, as if he regretted their recent argument and wanted to be sure that the RiverClan cat agreed with him.

Stormfur stepped out to join him, shivering as the mist began to soak into his fur. "OK," he meowed. "Lead the way. It's not like we have much choice."

Reluctantly the other cats followed Brambleclaw out into the cold, clinging mist and padded after him up the rift. Stormfur noticed that Tawnypelt was limping worse today, as if her leg had stiffened in the night. Midnight's burdock root had cured the infection, but Stormfur suspected her muscles had been damaged. She needed a medicine cat to look at it, but that was impossible out here.

Daylight gradually grew stronger, and the swirls of cloud became paler, as if somewhere above them the sun was rising. The rift grew steadily narrower, with walls of rock closing in on either side.

"I hope this isn't a dead end," Feathertail mewed. "We can't go back to that ledge."

She had hardly spoken when the clouds began to thin out and the cats could see further ahead. Stormfur found himself staring up at a sheer rock face where the sides of the valley came to a point. There didn't seem any way of climbing up, not unless they all grew wings and flew. His fur was plastered to his body by the mist and he felt hollow with hunger.

"Now what?" Tawnypelt meowed, sounding as defeated as Stormfur felt.

The six cats stood looking upwards, a fine rain drifting around them as if the drops were light enough to be blown by the wind. Stormfur struggled with black despair. What was the point of all this? Even if they reached home, the forest was going to be destroyed. Their hopes of helping their Clans rested on the word of a badger—a creature whom the cats had always regarded as an enemy. Stuck here among rain-wet rocks, it was hard to remember his trust in Midnight's wisdom. And if Stormfur doubted her, what would his Clanmates say when he tried to pass her message on? They had never completely trusted him or Feathertail because of their half-Clan heritage, so why should they listen now?

Then Stormfur realised that he could hear a steady roaring sound. It reminded him of the river pouring through the ravine in his home territory.

"What's that?" he meowed, lifting his head. "Can you hear it?"

"Over here, I think," Brambleclaw called.

Stormfur followed him up to the valley's point, and discovered a split in the rock winding upwards, just wide enough for one cat at a time. Brambleclaw led the way into it, gesturing with his tail for the others to follow. Stormfur waited to bring up the rear, his fur brushing the rock on either side, with unpleasant thoughts going through his head of what would happen if the path became so narrow that they got stuck.

The roaring grew louder, and after a little while the path came out on an open ledge. Broken rocks lay in front of them, rising to a ridge above their heads. A stream poured over the ridge, foaming down past the place where the cats were standing until it vanished behind a jutting boulder.

"Hey, at least we can have a drink!" Squirrelpaw mewed.

"Be careful," Brambleclaw warned her. "One slip, and you'll be crowfood."

Squirrelpaw shot him a glare, but said nothing. She crept forward cautiously to the edge of the stream and crouched to lap. Stormfur and the other cats followed her. The water was ice-cold, refreshing Stormfur and giving him new courage. Perhaps their scramble over these hostile mountains would soon be over.

Rising to his paws again, he glanced downstream and froze

in shock. Just below where the cats were drinking, the rocks fell away into a precipice. Padding warily a few paces towards it Stormfur stretched his neck to peer over the edge and saw the stream pounding down in a waterfall until it crashed into a pool many tail-lengths below. The sound of thundering water filled his ears, making him dizzy, so that he instinctively tried to dig his claws into the rain-wet rock.

The rest of the cats gathered around him, their eyes wide and horrified.

"Awesome!" Squirrelpaw murmured. Peering over, she added, "There's prey down there, I bet."

Through the mist of spray that rose from the pool Stormfur caught a glimpse of another valley like the one they had just left, where grass grew up between broken rocks and bushes lined the rock walls. Squirrelpaw was right—if there were any other living things to be found around here, it would be down there.

"But we need to go up," Brambleclaw pointed out, flicking his ears toward the place far above their heads where the stream poured over the lip of the rock. "It doesn't look too difficult to climb. If we go down, we might never get back again."

"Big deal, if it meant we got something to eat," Squirrelpaw muttered, but so softly that Stormfur wondered if her Clanmate had heard.

With Brambleclaw in the lead again, they began the scramble upwards. They were all exhausted, their soaked fur making them clumsy. Tawnypelt in particular found the going tough, hauling herself painfully over every rock as if she had hardly any strength left.

The stream bubbled up beside them, splashing over the rocks that were already wet and slippery with rain, which was falling more heavily again. Stormfur kept a wary eye on the stream, half expecting it to overflow and sweep them off the rocks. He stayed to the back of the group, trying to watch every cat, well aware that if any of them slipped they could be washed into the pool below the waterfall.

Almost as soon as that thought crossed his mind he saw Feathertail's paws skid from under her. She slid sideways into the stream; water surged around her as she clung to the rocks by a single paw, her jaws wide in a silent wail of shock.

Stormfur bounded towards her, pushing past Tawnypelt, but before he reached her, Crowpaw had leaned out precariously over the foaming water, sunk his teeth into the scruff of Feathertail's neck, and dragged her back on to the path.

"Thank you, Crowpaw," she gasped. Stormfur saw with annoyance that her blue eyes were glowing with gratitude—and something more.

"You should be more careful," Crowpaw meowed gruffly. "Do you think you're a Clan leader, with nine lives to throw away? I saved you this once—don't make me save you again."

"I won't." Feathertail blinked and pressed her nose against Crowpaw's muzzle. "I'm sorry for not watching out."

"So you should be," Stormfur snapped, not sure whether he

was more annoyed by his sister's carelessness or by the fact that Crowpaw had been the one to save her. He shouldered the apprentice away so that he could examine Feathertail more closely. "Are you OK?"

"Yes, fine," Feathertail replied, trying to shake water from her fur.

A louder rumbling from farther up the mountain interrupted her, drowning even the roar of the waterfall below. Stormfur looked up and froze in horror at the sight of a wall of mud, branches, and water hurtling down on them. His worst fears had come true: The mountain stream was in flood. Squirrelpaw let out a terrified yowl and Brambleclaw sprang back towards her.

But the water was upon them before they could do anything. It struck Stormfur like a blow, carrying him off his paws. His legs flailed as the flood carried him down, driving him against rocks where he clawed in vain for a grip before the water swept him on again. He choked as water filled his mouth and one of his paws caught painfully against a rock. Then there was nothing beneath him at all, and he knew he was plunging over the waterfall.

There was a moment of eerie silence, broken by the whisper of rushing water. Then the roaring and pounding started up again, waiting to swallow him as he plummeted into the pool. Whirled around in the icy water, he caught a brief glimpse of Crowpaw floundering wildly before the surge closed over his head. Then more water crashed down on him, driving him under and filling his senses with churning white foam, a deafening roar, and then nothing.

I'm sorry, StarClan, Stormfur thought desperately as his senses faded. *I know it wasn't my mission, but I tried so hard. Please look after our Clans. . .*

CHAPTER 6

Leafpaw burst up through the surface of the water, gasping for air as she scrambled to find solid ground. Managing to stand in spite of the river flowing strongly around her legs, she shook icy drops of water from her pelt. The riverbank was only a couple of tail-lengths away. She shivered in the pale sun of leaf-fall as she looked up to see Mothwing peering down at her from an overhanging rock.

The RiverClan cat's amber eyes were narrowed in amusement. "You don't fish by jumping in the river," she pointed out.

"I know that!" Leafpaw retorted crossly. "I slipped, that's all."

"I believe you," Mothwing purred, giving her golden chest fur a quick lick. "Now come out, and we'll have another go. I'll teach you to fish if it's the last thing I do."

"I'm still not sure we should be doing this," Leafpaw meowed as she waded back to the bank.

"Of course we should. The rabbits and squirrels are starting to disappear, thanks to the Twolegs, but there's still plenty of fish for every cat."

"But I had to come onto RiverClan territory to get it," Leafpaw pointed out anxiously. "What would Leopardstar say if she knew?"

Mothwing blinked. "We're both medicine cats, so Clan boundaries don't matter for us like they do for other cats."

Leafpaw didn't think that was how the warrior code worked. Her friend had said much the same a couple of days earlier, when she had rescued Leafpaw and Sorreltail from the pursuing WindClan warriors. This morning she had called to Leafpaw while she was gathering herbs near Sunningrocks, and offered to give her a fishing lesson. Leafpaw had felt very nervous about crossing the Clan border, but her hunger had driven her on now that prey was becoming even scarcer in ThunderClan territory. All the same, her ears and nose were alert for the first signs of a RiverClan patrol.

"OK," Mothwing went on, "crouch here beside me, and look down into the water. When you see a fish, scoop it out with your paw. It's easy."

A couple of glittering fish lying on the bank showed just how easy it was for Mothwing. Leafpaw gave them a longing glance, wondering if she would ever learn.

"Want some?" Mothwing offered, following her gaze.

Leafpaw felt guilty at the thought of being full-fed while the rest of her Clan went hungry. But she had not tasted fresh-kill since the night before, and that had been only a stringy vole. "I shouldn't . . ." she murmured, trying to convince herself that it wouldn't help her Clan if she starved as well.

"Of course you can. Where's the harm?"

Leafpaw did not wait to be asked again. She crouched down in front of the fish, tucking her paws in, and sank her teeth into the cool flesh. "Delicious," she mumbled.

Mothwing looked pleased. "Learn how to do it, and you can take lots more for your Clan." She took a few dainty bites, as if she were full-fed already and didn't care whether or not she ate.

Gulping down the rest of the fish, Leafpaw told herself that she would find food for her Clan to make up for it. As soon as she had finished, she settled down on the rock beside Mothwing and concentrated on the water just below, to wait for a fish of her own.

An unfamiliar scent swept over her at the same instant as Mothwing hissed, "Hawkfrost!" Leafpaw felt a paw jab hard into her ribs, tipping her over the edge of the rock and back into the river. She thrashed wildly, wondering why Mothwing was trying to drown her. Then as her head broke the surface she saw the huge tabby shape of Hawkfrost approaching the bank, and realised that Mothwing had done the only thing she could to hide her quickly.

Her paws working gently to keep her nose just above the water, Leafpaw let herself drift downriver for a few tail-lengths until she came to a clump of reeds where she could crawl out on the ThunderClan side of the river and hide.

Hawkfrost had stopped to talk to his sister, and Leafpaw realised that she would have to crouch where she was, soaked and shivering, until he went away and she could make a break across open ground to the ThunderClan border.

". . . keeping my eyes open for WindClan," she heard him meow when her ears were clear of water. "I know very well they're stealing fish, and one day I'll catch them at it."

"Not down here, surely?" Mothwing replied innocently. "WindClan would fish closer to Fourtrees—if they're fishing at all."

"WindClan *and* ThunderClan," Hawkfrost growled. He added, "I can scent a ThunderClan cat now."

Leafpaw shivered and shrank down in her clump of reeds.

"So? The border's over there," Mothwing pointed out. "It would be odd if you *didn't* scent ThunderClan."

Hawkfrost grunted. "There's something not right in the forest. Cats have gone missing from all the Clans, for one thing. Do you remember what the other leaders said at the last Gathering? That's four more cats, beside Stormfur and Feathertail. I don't know what's going on, but I'll find out."

Leafpaw tensed. She had told Mothwing about the Twoleg monsters, but obviously Mothwing had not passed on the news to the rest of her Clan. Chilled by the hunger in Hawkfrost's voice, Leafpaw prayed to StarClan that she would say nothing about it now. To her relief, her friend meowed calmly, "There's nothing wrong in RiverClan, so why should we care?"

"Have you got bees in your brain?" Hawkfrost snapped. "This could be our chance to make RiverClan great. If the other Clans are weak, we could rule over the whole forest."

"*What?*" Mothwing sounded disgusted. "You're the one with bees in your brain. Who do you think you are— Tigerstar?"

"There are worse cats to imitate," Hawkfrost meowed.

Pure icy fear lanced through Leafpaw. Tigerstar had been prepared to kill any cat who opposed him in his quest for supreme power. And now another cat was preparing to follow in his pawsteps.

Another thought sprang into her mind. This was what Mothwing must have meant when she talked about a cat with ambitions, on the day she rescued Leafpaw and Sorreltail from WindClan. She had been worried about her own brother! A few days before, Leafpaw had been sure that the forest would never produce another Tigerstar; now she could only strain her ears, horrified, to make out what Hawkfrost would say next.

"Have you forgotten what happened to Tigerstar?" Mothwing snapped. "He failed, and now he's just a name to frighten kits with."

"I shall learn from his mistakes." Hawkfrost's voice rumbled deep in his chest. "Our mother told us enough about him, after all. He broke the warrior code, and he deserved to fail. I shall know better."

Leafpaw stared at the reeds in front of her, puzzled. Hawkfrost's mother, Sasha, the rogue cat, had told them about Tigerstar? How did she know? Leafpaw had never met Sasha—the Clanless she-cat had stayed in RiverClan for only a short while, long enough to decide that she wanted her kits to be raised as part of the Clan. No cat knew where she had been before then.

In her bewilderment Leafpaw had not noticed that the

wind had changed, and that a playful breeze, twisting its way upriver, had carried her scent with it.

"I *can* smell ThunderClan," Hawkfrost declared suddenly. Leafpaw's heart nearly jumped out of her chest. "The scent's fresh too. If one of their warriors is on our territory, I'll claw his fur off."

Above her head, Leafpaw heard Mothwing scramble to her paws. "You're right!" she exclaimed. "It's this way. Come on!"

Leafpaw heard her voice growing fainter as she bounded away in the opposite direction. "Mouse-brain!" Hawkfrost argued. "It's *downstream*. . ."

Leafpaw didn't wait to hear any more. While he was following Mothwing, she broke out of the reeds and streaked up the bank towards the ThunderClan border. She plunged thankfully into thick bracken just on the ThunderClan side of the border.

Turning to peer out again, she saw Hawkfrost padding downstream, stopping to give the clump of reeds where she had just been hiding a good sniff before turning back to Mothwing with a frustrated growl. Once again Leafpaw was struck by the powerful tabby's resemblance to some other cat; the thought bothered her like a tick she couldn't reach, because she still couldn't remember who.

She was too far away to hear what the two RiverClan cats said to each other, but after a few moments, they both continued downstream to the stepping-stones and crossed to the RiverClan side of the river. When they finally disappeared into the reeds, Leafpaw drew a huge breath of relief and started trotting back to camp.

The guilt she felt about her full belly was almost forgotten amid pricklings of unease about what Mothwing had said. Hawkfrost sounded as ambitious as Tigerstar—and there was no place for that when the forest was on the brink of destruction.

A gleam of dying sunlight pierced the clouds and lay like a streak of blood on the forest floor. Leafpaw guessed that Cinderpelt would be wondering where she was, but she needed time to figure out how Hawkfrost and Mothwing knew so much about Tigerstar. She sat down and began to groom her drying fur.

Sasha had been a rogue cat wandering the forest, until she had come to RiverClan with her kits and settled briefly there. She might have visited ShadowClan when Tigerstar was leader. It was possible. . .

Leafpaw froze. She realised which cat Hawkfrost resembled so strongly. Brambleclaw! And every cat knew who Brambleclaw's father was. Could it be possible that *Tigerstar* was Hawkfrost's and Mothwing's father as well? If he was, that would make Hawkfrost and Brambleclaw half brothers.

She was staring into the trees as if she could see the answer there when her thoughts were interrupted by the frantic beating of wings. She looked up to see a magpie fluttering out of the bushes to land on a branch above her head. At the same time a loud voice exclaimed, "Mouse dung!"

The bushes just ahead of her rustled violently and Greystripe appeared, glaring up at the magpie with frustration in his yellow eyes. "Missed it," he muttered. "I don't know what's the matter with me."

Leafpaw rose to her paws as the deputy approached, dipping her head respectfully and letting out a sympathetic purr. She hoped that her pelt was dry enough for Greystripe not to notice that she had been swimming.

"Hello, Leafpaw," he meowed. "Sorry if I startled you. Actually, I do know what's wrong with me," he went on, the tip of his tail twitching uneasily. "I can't get Feathertail and Stormfur out of my head. I wish I knew where they've gone. Brambleclaw and Squirrelpaw too."

Leafpaw felt another pang of guilt. She could save Greystripe so much worry if she told him what she knew about the prophecy, but she had promised the journeying cats that she would keep silent.

"I feel that they're all safe," she ventured, "and that they'll come back to us."

Greystripe looked up with a flicker of hope in his amber eyes. "Has StarClan told you that?"

"Not exactly, but—"

"I can't help wondering if it has something to do with the Twolegs," Greystripe interrupted. "Cats go missing—Twolegs invade us. . . ." His paws worked against the ground, tearing up the grass with his claws.

"Greystripe, can I ask you something?" Leafpaw meowed, desperate to change the subject.

"Sure, go ahead."

"Did you ever meet Sasha—Hawkfrost and Mothwing's

mother?"

Greystripe looked at her in surprise. "Once. At a Gathering."

"What was she like?" Leafpaw asked curiously.

"Nice enough," Greystripe told her. "Quiet and ready to be friendly. A lot like Mothwing to look at. But it was clear that being among a lot of cats spooked her. I wasn't surprised when she left the forest as soon as Mothwing and Hawkfrost were old enough to do without her."

"Does any cat know who their father was?"

The deputy shook his head. "No. I always assumed it was another rogue."

"Rogues?"

There was the sound of pawsteps behind them, and Leafpaw spun around to see Firestar approaching from the direction of the camp.

"Have you seen rogues?" he demanded, tension clear in every hair on his flame-coloured pelt. "For StarClan's sake, that's the last thing we need right now."

"No, no, not at all." Greystripe meowed quickly. "Leafpaw was just asking about Sasha, and which cat fathered Mothwing and Hawkfrost."

Firestar turned to look at Leafpaw, his green eyes puzzled. "Why do you want to know?"

Leafpaw hesitated. She wasn't about to admit that she had been spending time with Mothwing in RiverClan territory. "Oh, I just saw Hawkfrost," she meowed. "He was patrolling on the border." Well, she comforted herself, that was not entirely a lie. There was no way she was going to mention her suspicions that Tigerstar had fathered Hawkfrost and Mothwing, not when he and Firestar had been such bitter enemies.

Firestar nodded. "Well, I've no idea. Sasha might have told some cat in RiverClan, I suppose."

He padded across to Greystripe and touched noses with his old friend as if he guessed the thoughts that were troubling him. Both cats had lost children among the six cats that had vanished from the forest. They stared up into the trees, where a chilly wind was tugging leaves from the branches until they drifted down to join the other dead leaves on the forest floor.

"They must be cold, with no Clan to shelter them each night," Greystripe murmured.

"At least they have one another," Firestar mewed, pressing himself against Greystripe's side.

For a moment both cats remained silent; then Firestar turned to his daughter. "Leafpaw, you sometimes know what Squirrelpaw is thinking, don't you? You told us she was with the RiverClan cats. Have you any idea where they are now?"

Leafpaw blinked. She couldn't deny her father the chance to know if Squirrelpaw was alive—and she wanted to know just as fiercely. She shut her eyes and summoned up her old rapport with her sister. Emptying her mind, she concentrated fiercely. She gasped to feel a surge of cold and wet, shuddering as a blast of cold wind probed her drying fur. But there was no sign of Squirrelpaw anywhere—just water, blasting air, and endless rock.

Opening her eyes, Leafpaw blinked in confusion as she realised that her fur was dry and the forest was still. She had made contact with her sister after all!

"She's alive," she murmured. Beside her, Firestar's eyes lit up. "And wherever she is, I think it must be raining. . ."

CHAPTER 7

Stormfur opened his eyes and blinked in light that was sharp as a claw. His breath rasped in his throat and every muscle in his body ached. He felt too exhausted even to move.

As his vision cleared he saw that he was lying on rain-wet rock, beside a pool of churning black water. His ears were ringing; when he raised his head feebly he saw a waterfall thundering down into the pool in a whirl of foam and spray, and realised that what he could hear was the roar and crash of falling water.

At once he remembered the flood that had swept him down from the rocks and plunged him into the pool. How had he survived? He remembered the roar, the foam, the darkness. . . Fear for his friends stabbed through him.

"Feathertail? Squirrelpaw?" he mewed hoarsely.

"Over here."

The reply was so faint, it was nearly lost in the endless pounding of the waterfall. Stormfur turned his head to see Squirrelpaw splayed out on the rock beside him, her dark ginger fur sodden.

"Got to sleep . . ." she muttered, closing her eyes.

Just beyond her, Stormfur could see Brambleclaw, stretched limply on his side. The ThunderClan warrior was staring up at the sky, his breathing fast and shallow. Crowpaw was on Stormfur's other side; with a feeling of horror, he thought the WindClan apprentice was dead until he saw the faint rise and fall of his flank.

What about Feathertail and Tawnypelt? Beginning to panic, Stormfur struggled to sit up. At first he could not see either his sister or the tortoiseshell she-cat. Then a movement farther around the pool caught his eye. Near the waterfall, Feathertail was helping Tawnypelt out on to the rock. The ShadowClan warrior was tottering on three legs, and as soon as she reached solid ground she collapsed and lay without moving. Feathertail hauled herself out, her grey fur plastered to her sides so it looked almost black. She settled down beside Tawnypelt and gave her shoulder a couple of feeble licks.

"Thank StarClan!" Stormfur rasped aloud. "We all made it."

He vaguely knew they had to find shelter, that if they went on lying here they were vulnerable to predators like the eagle, but he was too exhausted to move. He gave his drying fur a few licks, but even that was too much effort. He lay still, his senses drifting, his gaze fixed unseeingly on the rocks beside the pool.

As his senses gradually returned he noticed that they were lying in a curved bowl of rock, open on the side where the stream surged out of the pool and headed down the valley. Boulders covered the ground on either bank, a couple of spindly trees rooted among them. Light shivered on the water; the rain had almost stopped and the clouds were thin-ning out. Above Stormfur's head, rainbows danced in the spray thrown up by the waterfall. A thin beam of sunlight splashed on the rocks a tail-length away from him; he dragged himself painfully into it and sighed with pleasure at the warmth on his fur.

A few heartbeats later he thought he saw a flash of move-ment. He blinked, straining to focus his eyes. For a moment all was still; then he caught another flicker on the far side of the pool. His fur prickled. They were being watched!

Stormfur narrowed his eyes, gazing hard at the boulders near the waterfall. "Brambleclaw," he whispered. "Look over there."

"What?" The ThunderClan warrior raised his head, peered around, and lay down again. "Can't see anything."

"There!" Stormfur hissed as movement flickered again, this time a tail-length closer. He flexed his claws, knowing how helpless he and his friends were to defend themselves.

Then a grey-brown shape detached itself from the rock and began padding toward him around the edge of the pool. It was a cat! Before Stormfur could move, another cat appeared and then another, a whole group of cats moving silently away from the rocks where they had been hidden, camouflaged against the boulders, as if they were carved from stone themselves. They sat on the edge of the pool, staring unblinkingly at the group of half-drowned travellers.

Stormfur swallowed hard. These cats were like none he had ever seen before, uniformly grey-brown with dull, flattened fur. Then one moved into the sunlight and he realised that their fur was covered with thick streaks of mud, helping them to blend into the rocks and hiding the real colour of their pelts.

Stormfur sat up, his muscles shrieking a protest. He prodded Squirrelpaw with one paw and whispered hoarsely, "Sit up very slowly. Whatever you do, don't say anything out loud."

Squirrelpaw lifted her head, then saw the watching cats and tried to scramble up with alarm flaring in her green eyes. Her movement disturbed Brambleclaw, who jumped up at once. Stormfur managed to get to his paws and stand beside him, thankful to have the strong ThunderClan warrior with him as they faced danger.

Brambleclaw glanced around for the other cats. "Feathertail, Tawnypelt—over here, now." There was a commanding rasp in his voice, even though it shook with exhaustion. "You too, Crowpaw."

Crowpaw struggled up, for once not arguing, and went to help Feathertail. Tawnypelt was leaning against her shoulder, hardly able to move. The three of them limped around the pool until they could bunch together with Stormfur and the others, their eyes wide and scared as they watched the strange cats.

Stormfur knew they were too shaken and exhausted to defend themselves. But in spite of his fear a pang of curiosity stabbed him. He wanted to know more about these strangers who looked so different from any other cats he had known.

The thought even flashed through his mind that they might help with food and shelter—then he reminded himself that he and his friends were unlikely to be made welcome after trespassing on the strange cats' territory, and the best they could expect was to be driven off.

He hardly dared to breathe as the first cat approached and studied them all carefully. Padding close to Stormfur, he gave him an especially long scrutiny, barely sparing a glance for the cats on the other side of him. Stormfur tried to meet the staring yellow eyes, wondering uneasily what it was about him that interested the mud-clad cat so much.

"Is this the one?" A tabby she-cat stepped forward eagerly. She spoke in the same language as the Clan cats, though the sound of the words was strange to Stormfur's ears, and the question more confusing still. He watched her as she drew closer, her lithe body balancing easily on the slippery stones at the edge of the pool. "Is this what we've hoped for?" she persisted, reaching her Clanmate's side.

The first cat's head whipped round and he glared at the speaker. "Silence, Brook!" Turning back to Stormfur he asked roughly, "Who are you? Have you travelled far?"

Stormfur heard Tawnypelt mutter, "What are these—mud warriors? We're more than a match for them," and felt heartened by the ShadowClan cat's abrasive courage.

"Yes, we've come a long way," Squirrelpaw answered. "Can you help us?"

"Careful," Brambleclaw interrupted with a warning look. To the strange cat he added, "We are travellers trying to cross the mountains. We're not looking for trouble, but if you are enemies, we can fight."

The cat narrowed his eyes. "We have no wish for fighting. Your journey has brought you to the Tribe of Rushing Water."

"You are welcome if you come in friendship," the tabby she-cat added, a glow in her amber eyes as she looked at Stormfur.

Stormfur remembered that Midnight the badger had spoken of cats who lived in Tribes instead of Clans. These must be the cats she meant, though she had said nothing to suggest the Clan cats would encounter them on their journey home. Surely she must have known that they would come across the Tribe as they crossed the mountains. Stormfur reminded himself that he had instinctively trusted Midnight; if the Tribe had been dangerous, she would have warned them, or told them to go the other way. Instead she had implied that this route had been laid down for them. Did that mean she thought that they were destined to meet the Tribe?

As the she-cat spoke, another of the strangers came padding up to look at Stormfur with a gleam in his eyes. "Come on, Crag," he meowed to the first cat. "We should take this one to Stoneteller."

"What?" Brambleclaw stepped forward to confront Crag, while Stormfur tensed his muscles in readiness for a fight. "You're taking him nowhere without us. We want to talk to your leader." As Crag motioned the other cat back with an angry flick of his tail, the ThunderClan warrior relaxed slightly. "We only want to travel in peace," he went on. "My name is Brambleclaw of ThunderClan."

Crag bowed his head while stretching out one paw, an odd but polite gesture. "My name is Crag Where Eagles Nest," he announced.

"And I am Brook Where Small Fish Swim," the tabby she-cat added, stretching out a paw as Crag had done.

Crag gave her a disapproving look, as if he was not happy that she had put herself forward. His gaze flicked past Brambleclaw and rested again on Stormfur. "What is this one's name?"

"I'm Stormfur." He tried to push down the uncomfortable feeling that these cats' fascination gave him. "I come from RiverClan."

"Stormfur," Crag repeated.

"I'm Squirrelpaw." The tense moment was broken as the ThunderClan apprentice spoke up.

"And I'm Crowpaw."

"I'm Feathertail, and this is Tawnypelt." Stormfur's sister fixed anxious blue eyes on Crag. "Please, can you help her? Her shoulder is badly injured."

Brambleclaw glared at Feathertail with a hiss of disapproval; this was no time to be admitting weakness to strangers.

Instantly Crowpaw stepped forward. "She's right," he defended Feathertail. "This Clan might have a medicine cat who can help."

"Your words are strange to us," Crag responded. "But we will help. Come with us now and our leader will speak with you."

"Hang on," Crowpaw meowed. He was still shaky on his legs but he was obviously trying hard to sound fit to defend himself. "How far are we going?"

"Not far," meowed Brook.

Stormfur glanced at the watching cats around the edge of the pool. "What else can we do, except go with them?" he murmured to Brambleclaw. "We need to rest."

He said nothing of his own misgivings about Crag's penetrating gaze. After all, any cat would stare if he found six half-drowned strangers in his territory.

Brambleclaw nodded. "All right," he meowed to Crag. "We'll come."

"Good." Crag led the way along the edge of the pool, leaped up the first few rocks beside the waterfall, and then vanished behind the sheet of foaming water.

Stormfur stared in astonishment, half expecting the strange cat to come hurtling down into the pool again, knocked off his paws by the waterfall.

Then Brook stepped forwards, gesturing with her tail. "This is the Path of the Rushing Water. Come—it is safe."

The rest of the cats had risen to their paws and gathered around them; Stormfur felt uneasy that he and his friends were being herded after Crag as if they were prisoners. But he had no choice but to follow the mud-covered cats and scramble up the rocks. It was a hard climb after their fall, especially for Tawnypelt, who was limping heavily. Halfway up, she stumbled and almost slipped back into the pool, until Brook darted forward to steady her.

The ShadowClan warrior flinched away from her. "I'm fine," she growled.

As Stormfur hauled himself up to where Crag had disappeared, he saw the Tribe cat waiting for him on a narrow ledge of rock leading behind the waterfall. A dark hole gaped at the end of it.

"I'm not going in there!" Squirrelpaw exclaimed.

"You'll be fine." Brambleclaw spoke reassuringly behind her.

"There is no danger," Crag meowed, padding confidently along the path and standing at the mouth of the hole.

Stormfur swallowed. They had to trust these cats—there was no way they could make it through the mountains without food and rest. "Come on."

Taking the lead, he edged along the path, pressing himself against the rock as far as possible from the sheet of thundering water. It was barely a tail-length away from him; spray misted his fur, and the rock underneath his paws was cold and slippery. Too tense to turn round, he could not be sure that the other cats were following him. He felt as if he were walking alone into endless, thundering darkness.

But the gaping hole led into a cave with steep rocky walls, stretching nearly to the top of the waterfall. Stormfur paused on the threshold, peering past Crag at soaring walls that ran with water. The scent of many more strange cats drifted out to him, hidden in the shadows around the edge of the cave.

"What's in there?" Feathertail murmured nervously, trying to peer inside. She was shivering, her pelt so sodden that it looked almost as dark as Crowpaw's.

Crowpaw brushed against her flank. "Whatever happens, we'll be there together," he murmured.

Stormfur suspected he was not supposed to hear that; he had to stop himself from spitting at Crowpaw or shooting an angry glare at his sister. There were far more pressing things to think about right now.

Crag waved his tail once again and padded into the cave, turning back to check that the others were behind him.

"I don't like this," Squirrelpaw muttered. "How do we know what we're going to find in there?"

"We don't," Brambleclaw replied. "But we've got to face it. Everything on this journey happens for a reason. We owe it to the Clans to see this through."

"We never thought it would be easy," Stormfur agreed, trying to shake off the deep sense of dread that overcame him at the thought of setting paw inside the cave.

"Well, if we have to do it, let's get on with it." Crowpaw pushed forward and led the way inside.

Stormfur followed, the other cats crowding behind him. As he gazed around he heard Tawnypelt mew quietly, as much to reassure herself as the rest of them, "StarClan will be with us, even here."

CHAPTER 8

"*If a cat leaps at you,* roll on to your back," Cinderpelt instructed. "Then you can attack his belly with your claws. Try it."

Leafpaw waited as her mentor crouched in front of her and then leaped into the air. Rolling over as Cinderpelt had told her, she dug her hind paws into the medicine cat's belly and flung her off to one side.

"Good," Cinderpelt meowed. She scrambled to her paws, awkward because of her injured leg. "That's enough for now."

The two cats had been training all morning in the sandy hollow, and though thick, grey clouds covered the sky Leafpaw's rumbling belly told her it must be close to sunhigh. She had enjoyed the session with her mentor. The exercise had been a good distraction from her worries about the Clan and the Twolegs, not to mention Squirrelpaw and the other cats who were travelling with her.

She followed Cinderpelt down into the ravine. Before they reached the entrance to the gorse tunnel, Leafpaw heard a patrol returning close behind them. Turning, she saw Firestar, Dustpelt, and Sorreltail. Firestar looked more worried than ever, while Dustpelt's brown tabby fur was bristling and his tail lashed furiously from side to side.

Cinderpelt limped over to meet Firestar, while Leafpaw hurried to Sorreltail's side. "What in StarClan's name is going on?"

"WindClan," Sorreltail mewed, with a glance at the older warriors. "They've been stealing prey from us."

Leafpaw remembered the thin, desperate cats who had chased them out of their territory, and knew that she was not surprised at the news.

"We found scraps of rabbit fur and bones by the stream near Fourtrees," Sorreltail went on. "They reeked of WindClan scent."

"It's because their rabbits have vanished," Leafpaw meowed. She pushed aside a guilty memory of how she had taken fish from RiverClan.

"It's still against the warrior code," Sorreltail pointed out. "Dustpelt was furious."

"So I see," meowed Leafpaw.

She followed her friend down the gorse tunnel to find Firestar and Dustpelt standing beside the fresh-kill pile. Her belly lurched when she saw how small it was.

"Look at it!" Dustpelt gestured with his tail. "How is that going to feed the Clan? You'll have to do something about WindClan, Firestar."

Firestar shook his head. "We all know that Tallstar wouldn't allow his warriors to steal prey unless his Clan was in real trouble."

"Tallstar might not know what's going on. Besides,

ThunderClan is in trouble too. It's not as if we have prey to spare."

"I know," Firestar sighed.

"I'm worried about Ferncloud," the brown warrior added. "She's already lost a lot of weight, and she still has three kits to feed."

"If this goes on, I'll have to start rationing," Firestar decided. "But meanwhile, we *will* do something about Wind-Clan, I promise."

Whirling round, he bounded across the clearing and leaped to the top of the Highrock. As he yowled out the summons, the rest of the Clan began to appear at once. Leafpaw was shocked to see how lean they were; she had never really noticed before the gradual change from day to day as prey got harder to find. But now they looked more like skinny WindClan cats than sturdy, forest-born ThunderClan warriors. Dustpelt was right that Ferncloud in particular looked gaunt and exhausted; her kits were thinner, too, and they trailed after their mother as if they had no energy left to play. Were all the Clans—apart from RiverClan—slowly going to starve?

Leafpaw listened anxiously as Firestar told the rest of the Clan what the patrol had discovered. Wails of indignation broke out at the news that WindClan cats had trespassed on to ThunderClan territory and stolen prey.

"WindClan needs to be taught a lesson!" Cloudtail called out. "I haven't had the sniff of a rabbit for days."

"We should attack now," Mousefur put in, her brown fur bristling.

"No," Firestar meowed firmly. "Things are bad enough without us looking for a battle."

Mousefur didn't argue, though she muttered something under her breath, and Cloudtail lashed his tail. Leafpaw saw Brightheart meow a few words to him, trying to calm him down.

"What are you going to do?" Speckletail called out from the entrance to the elders' den. "Go and ask them nicely not to steal our food? Do you think they'll take any notice?"

More voices were raised in protest, with more than one cat echoing Mousefur's demand to attack.

"No," Firestar repeated. "I'm going to talk to Tallstar. He's a noble, trustworthy cat; maybe he doesn't know that his warriors have been stealing prey."

"And what good will talking do?" Cloudtail snorted. "Blackstar didn't listen when you went to talk to *him*."

"If you ask me," Speckletail rasped, "you're crossing Clan boundaries far too often. The last cat to ignore borders like that was Tigerstar."

Leafpaw winced at the old she-cat's suggestion that their leader was anything like the murderous Tigerstar. She wasn't the only cat to be shocked. Several cats turned on Speckletail, hissing fiercely, but when Firestar replied, his voice was calm.

"Tigerstar wanted to satisfy his greed for power. All I want is to make peace. And as for Blackstar," he added to Cloudtail, "Tallstar has always been more reasonable."

"That's right." Greystripe supported his leader from where he sat at the base of the Highrock. "Remember when Bluestar wanted to fight WindClan? Tallstar was ready to make peace then."

"But there wasn't a shortage of prey back then," Thornclaw reminded him.

"Right." Mousefur's tail lashed again. "Some cats will do *anything* if their bellies are empty."

Leafpaw listened in dismay as yowls broke out around her, agreeing with Mousefur. She spotted her mother, Sandstorm, exchanging an anxious glance with Greystripe.

Firestar signaled with his tail for silence. "That's enough! My mind's made up. All the Clans are in trouble together now. This is no time to start fighting one another."

"Be careful, Firestar," Sorreltail warned him, as the yowls of protest died into discontented muttering. "You may go in peace, but the other clans might not see it that way." She glanced at Leafpaw, reminding her of their of their narrow escape from WindClan only a few days ago.

Firestar nodded. "WindClan will have to respect a patrol that looks strong enough to fight back," he meowed. "I'll make it clear to Tallstar that there'll be trouble if he can't control his warriors and keep them on their own side of the border. But we won't be looking for a fight. With StarClan's help we can avoid that."

Leafpaw's mind filled with images of the scarred moorland she had seen when she visited WindClan territory, and the desperation of the warriors who had chased her. Every hair on her pelt shrank from the idea of attacking WindClan and making their plight even worse.

"This is a bad time for all of us," she began hesitantly. "We should be trying to help one another. Why don't we all share the fish in the river? There are still plenty of those."

"That's for RiverClan to say, not us," Greystripe pointed out, while Ashfur added, "Fishing's too difficult."

"No, it's not," Leafpaw protested. "We can learn how."

She noticed that some of the other cats were giving her suspicious looks, as if they were wondering what she knew about fishing. Embarrassed, she scuffled her forepaws on the ground. "It was just an idea," she mumbled.

"But not one we can use," Firestar mewed decisively.

Anxious not to draw any more attention to herself, Leafpaw bowed her head, and sat looking at her paws while Firestar chose the cats who would make up the patrol going to WindClan.

"Greystripe, of course," he began. "Sandstorm, Dustpelt, Thornclaw. Ashfur. And you, Cinderpelt. Tallstar will listen to a medicine cat if he won't listen to me."

Leafpaw realised that he had not chosen any of the cats who had been arguing for an attack straight away, though he had included some formidable fighters. This patrol would not need to run!

She stayed where she was while the meeting broke up. With her eyes still fixed on the ground, she was aware of Firestar leaping from the Highrock and padding over to her.

"Well, Leafpaw," he began. When she lifted her head, she was relieved to see warm affection in her father's eyes, and felt even more ashamed of herself. "What's all this about fishing?"

Leafpaw knew she would have to tell the truth. "Mothwing taught me how," she explained. "She said it was ok, because we're both medicine cats. . ."

"You are medicine cat *apprentices*," Firestar meowed. "And it sounds as if you both have a lot to learn. You know that it's against the warrior code to take prey from another Clan. Even medicine cats have to respect that."

"I know." Guilt swept over Leafpaw again, making her feel like a naughty kit. She just hoped that RiverClan had not found out what Mothwing had done, and punished her for her generosity. "I'm sorry."

"I shall have to punish you, you realise that?" Firestar went on. His tail-tip touched her shoulder gently as he added, "I can't have any cat saying I favour you because you're my daughter."

"Oh, come on, Firestar." Cinderpelt had limped up to join them, and was regarding her Clan leader with amusement in her blue eyes. "I remember a couple of cats who took ThunderClan prey across the river to RiverClan, when the Twolegs poisoned the fish. Surely you haven't forgotten?"

"No. And Greystripe and I were punished for it," Firestar retorted. Then he sighed. "Leafpaw, I know it's hard to see other cats hungry and do nothing about it. But the warrior code is what makes us what we are. If cats can break it when they feel like it, where does that leave us? Whatever is going to happen to the forest—whatever is happening now—we can't forget everything we believe in."

"I'm sorry, Firestar," Leafpaw repeated. She managed to stand up straight and look her father in the eye.

"Let her come with the patrol to WindClan," Cinderpelt meowed before Firestar could speak. "It'll be good experience for her."

Leafpaw looked hopefully at her Clan leader.

"Honestly, Cinderpelt." Firestar sounded exasperated. "There are cats who would say that's a *reward*, not a punishment. Oh, very well," he added. "We're leaving right away. I'll just go and get the others."

He touched Leafpaw's shoulder once more before padding away with his tail high.

"Thanks, Cinderpelt," Leafpaw meowed. "I know I was stupid. It's just that . . . well, when Mothwing said it, it sounded ok to take the fish."

Cinderpelt snorted. "Like Firestar said, you've both got a lot to learn."

"I don't know if I *ever* will!" Leafpaw burst out. "There are warrior rules, and medicine cat rules, and it's all so confusing!"

"It's not just about rules," Cinderpelt murmured sympathetically, touching her nose to Leafpaw's muzzle. "Your sympathy for other Clans, and your willingness to see that sometimes rules have to be ignored, will make you a great medicine cat in the end."

Leafpaw's eyes widened. "Really?"

"Really. 'Medicine cat' means nothing on its own, without an understanding of what should be done—which isn't always what you first think. Remember what I've told you about Yellowfang? She never followed the rules, but she was one of the best medicine cats the forest has ever seen."

"I wish I'd known her," Leafpaw murmured.

"So do I. But I can pass on to you what she taught me. To truly *be* a medicine cat lies in a cat's heart, and all its five senses. You must be braver than warriors, wiser than a Clan leader, humbler than the tiniest kit, more willing to learn than any apprentice. . ."

Leafpaw gazed up at her mentor. "I'm not sure I can be all that," she whispered.

"Well, I *am* sure." Cinderpelt's voice was low and intense. "For we do not achieve this by ourselves, but by the strength of StarClan within us." Suddenly the intensity was gone and the humour back in Cinderpelt's eyes. She swatted Leafpaw lightly with her tail. "Come on. Firestar will never forgive us if we aren't ready for the patrol on top of everything else."

Sunhigh was long gone and a brisk wind was breaking up the clouds by the time Firestar led his patrol towards Fourtrees. Before they were very far from the camp Leafpaw could hear the roar of Twoleg monsters as they forced their way even further into ThunderClan territory. In contrast, the usual forest sounds—the calling of birds, the rustle of prey in the undergrowth—were silent. Even though leaf-fall had well and truly arrived, Leafpaw knew there should be much more prey than this. The small creatures that the cats depended on for their survival were gone, frightened away by Twolegs or even killed as the monsters tore up their forest homes.

As they drew closer to Fourtrees the roar of the monsters died away, and Leafpaw could make out the faint scrabblings of prey among the bushes, but it was still much less than usual. She swallowed nervously as she imagined a harsh and hungry leaf-bare.

A yowl from Thornclaw jerked her out of her thoughts. "Look!"

There was a flash of movement in the thick undergrowth beside the stream. Two cats—a dark brown tom and a tabby— leaped across the stream and streaked up the slope towards Fourtrees. One of them had a small piece of prey, a vole or a mouse, in its jaws.

"WindClan cats!" Sandstorm meowed, her pale ginger fur bristling. "That was Mudclaw and Tornear, I'm sure of it."

Dustpelt and Ashfur sprang after the fleeing warriors, but Firestar called them back sharply. "We mustn't look as if we're attacking WindClan," he told them. "I'm coming in peace, not fury, to speak with Tallstar."

"You mean you're letting them go?" Ashfur asked disbelievingly. "With our fresh-kill in their mouths?"

"It's more proof that they're stealing prey," Firestar pointed out. "Tallstar won't be able to ignore what we have to tell him now."

"But they'll warn Tallstar," Dustpelt protested. "WindClan could ambush us before we get anywhere near their camp."

"No. Tallstar isn't like that. If he fights us, he'll do it in the open."

The two warriors exchanged doubtful glances before falling in behind Firestar. Leafpaw could see that Dustpelt was still smouldering with anger, but he expressed it with no more than an irritable twitch of his tail-tip.

The patrol crossed the stream, the water still churned and muddy from the WindClan warriors' paws, and climbed the slope to Fourtrees. Leafpaw's heart started beating uncomfortably as Firestar led them around the top of the hollow. Remembering her doomed visit with Sorreltail, she wondered whether they would be able to speak to Tallstar at all.

As they approached the border, the breeze carried a strong scent of cats towards them. Leafpaw looked out over the windblown grass to see a ragged group of WindClan warriors racing over the crest of the moorland. In the lead she recognised the Clan leader, Tallstar, by his black-and-white pelt and long tail. He must have spotted the ThunderClan patrol, for he slackened his pace and signalled with his tail. His warriors slowed to a walk and spread out to form a long line facing the ThunderClan cats.

"See?" Dustpelt hissed. "They're ready for us."

On an unspoken command, the WindClan cats stalked up to the border and halted a couple of tail-lengths from the ThunderClan patrol. They were even thinner than Leafpaw remembered, the sharp lines of their ribs plainly visible. Hostility burned in their eyes, and it was clear that not one of them wanted the ThunderClan visitors to set paw on their territory.

"Well, Firestar?" Tallstar growled. "What do you want with us this time?"

CHAPTER 9

❧

Stormfur stared in amazement. The cave was at least as broad as the waterfall that screened it from the outside world, and stretched far back into the mountainside, until the furthest recesses were lost in shadow. He could just make out a narrow passage leading off on either side of the wall opposite the sheet of water. The roof, far above his head, was shadowed too; here and there, stones like fangs emerged to point straight down at the cave floor.

The only light came through the rushing water, pale and wavering, so that it was like standing in the depths of a pool. As the cats ushered them further into the cave, Stormfur heard more running water beneath the roar of the falls, and saw a stream trickling over a mossy rock to fall into a shallow pool on the floor of the cave. Two or three cats—a skinny elder and a couple who looked young enough to be apprentices—were crouched beside it to drink. All of them looked up warily at the arrival of the newcomers, as if they were expecting danger.

Just beyond the pool was a pile of fresh-kill and, as Stormfur watched, a couple more of the mountain cats came in and deposited prey. It was the first thing he had seen that looked at all familiar, and his belly growled with hunger at the sight of the rabbits.

"Do you think they'll let us eat?" Squirrelpaw muttered close to his ear. "I'm starving!"

"For all you know, they think *we're* fresh-kill," Crowpaw hissed from Squirrelpaw's other side.

"They haven't done anything to harm us yet," Brambleclaw pointed out.

Stormfur tried to share his optimism, but Crag and Brook had vanished, and for a few moments none of the other cats came up to speak to them. Instead, the cats who had been drinking sidled over to their guards, and the elder whispered something, all the while darting glances at him. The two apprentices murmured excitedly to each other. The roar of the waterfall drowned their voices, though Stormfur noticed that the mountain cats seemed to have no trouble hearing one another.

Trying to ignore the muttering—most of which seemed to be directed at him, though he told himself to stop being so paranoid—Stormfur identified what looked like sleeping places beside the cave walls: shallow scoops in the earth floor, lined with moss and feathers. One cluster of sleeping places lay close to the entrance and the other two were further back, at opposite sides of the cave. He wondered if one set was for warriors, one for apprentices, and one for elders. Spotting a couple of kits scuffling outside the entrance to one of the passages, he guessed that led to the nursery. Suddenly he saw the dark, noisy, frightening cave in a different way: This was a camp! The Tribe shared some of the ways of the Clans in the forest; Stormfur began to feel much more hopeful of getting food and rest, and help for Tawnypelt, who had sunk shivering to the floor.

Then he spotted Crag again, emerging from the far passage and padding across the cave floor towards the tight group of forest cats. He was followed by another cat, long-bodied and skinny as a WindClan warrior. So much mud plastered his fur that Stormfur couldn't make out what colour it was underneath, but his eyes were a deep and glowing green, and a few white hairs around his muzzle betrayed the fact that he was older than the cats they had seen so far.

"Greetings," he meowed in a deep voice that seemed to echo around the cave. He made the odd gesture with one paw extended that Crag and Brook had used outside. "My name is Teller of the Pointed Stones, though you will find it easier to call me Stoneteller. I am the Healer of the Tribe of Rushing Water."

"Healer?" Brambleclaw glanced uncertainly at his friends. "Do you mean the medicine cat? Where is the leader of your Clan—I mean, Tribe?"

Stoneteller hesitated for a moment. "I am not sure what you mean by a medicine cat, and there is no other leader of this Tribe. I interpret the signs of rock and leaf and water, and that shows me what the Tribe should do—with the help of the Tribe of Endless Hunting."

Stormfur picked out the bit of Stoneteller's speech that he

understood. "Then he's medicine cat *and* leader," he muttered to Brambleclaw. "That's pretty powerful!"

In reply, Brambleclaw dipped his head politely. "We come from a forest a long way from here," he began, repeating his own name and the names of his friends. "We have a difficult journey ahead of us, and we need food and shelter before we can go on."

More of the Tribe cats crowded around as he spoke, openly curious. Stormfur picked out kits and apprentices by their sizes, and noticed that the warriors seemed to divide into two groups, one with massive shoulders and powerful muscles, the other more slender, with wiry strength and long limbs for speed. He noticed too how anxious they all looked; they seemed to be on edge, as if they were poised to flee.

A brown tabby she-cat, her eyes fixed on Stormfur, murmured, "Yes! This is the one—it must be!"

Stormfur started. Brook had said something similar, when they first met beside the pool. He opened his mouth to ask what she meant, but the Tribe's Healer had turned to the young brown tabby. "Be silent!" he hissed. More smoothly he went on to the Clan cats, "You are welcome to our cave. Here is caught-prey in plenty." He flicked his tail towards the fresh-kill pile. "Eat your fill, and rest. We have much to say to one another."

Brambleclaw looked at the other Clan cats. "We might as well eat," he meowed quietly. "I don't think they're going to hurt us now."

As Stormfur followed him towards the pile, he felt once

more dozens of eyes burning into his fur. It wasn't his imagination—they were definitely watching him more closely than the others. His fur prickled from nose to tail-tip as he settled down to eat.

As he bit into the rabbit he had chosen, he heard a gasp from somewhere behind him and a shocked voice whispering, "They don't share!"

Glancing up, he saw a young grey cat giving him a hostile stare, while an older tabby bent her head to him and murmured, "Shh. It's not their fault if they haven't been properly taught."

Stormfur didn't know what they meant. Then he spotted two of the Tribe cats who were eating side by side; each of them took a bite from the piece of fresh-kill they had taken, then exchanged pieces before they settled down to finish it off. Embarrassment flooded over him as he realised how rude he and his friends must look to the cats of the Tribe.

"We don't do that," he meowed directly to the young cat who had spoken at first. "But we *do* share." He flicked his tail towards Feathertail, who was gently coaxing Tawnypelt to eat a mouse. "None of us would let our friends go hungry, and the hunting patrols always feed the Clan before taking food for themselves."

The grey cat backed away a pace or two, looking confused, as if he hadn't intended the newcomers to hear his comments. The tabby dipped her head with a friendlier look. "Your ways are strange to us," she meowed. "Perhaps we can learn from one another."

"Perhaps," Stormfur agreed.

He began gulping down his rabbit again. After a few moments one of the bolder kits pattered right up to the group of Clan cats, urged on by his littermates. "Where do you come from?" he asked.

"A long way away," Squirrelpaw mumbled with her mouth full. Swallowing the bite of prey she added more clearly, "Across these mountains and lots of fields and then a forest."

The kit blinked. "What are fields?" Before Squirrelpaw could reply, he added, "I'm going to be a cave-guard."

"That's nice," Feathertail mewed.

"'Course, I've got to be a to-be first."

"Tooby? What's a tooby?" asked Crowpaw.

Stormfur hid his amusement at the scornful look the kit gave the WindClan apprentice. "To-be a cave-guard, of course. You know, training and stuff. Don't you new cats know *anything?*"

"He means an apprentice," Stormfur explained, and couldn't resist adding, "Like you."

Crowpaw curled his lip as the kit stared at him and exclaimed, "You're only a to-be? You're *way* old!"

"It sounds as if they have some of the same traditions as us," Tawnypelt murmured.

"I wonder if they believe in StarClan?" Squirrelpaw whispered.

"It's too far for them to go to Mothermouth," meowed Stormfur, "and no cat has ever seen them there."

"Stoneteller mentioned the Tribe of Endless Hunting,"

Feathertail remembered. "Perhaps that's what they call StarClan." Her blue eyes stretched wide and her voice was uneasy as she added, "Or do you think they have different warrior ancestors?"

"I don't know," Brambleclaw replied. "But I guess we'll find out."

When he finished eating, Stormfur had not felt so comfortably full since they left the woods where they said goodbye to Midnight and Purdy. He would have liked to sleep, but as he swallowed the last mouthful and swiped his tongue around his jaws he spotted Stoneteller making his way towards them with three other cats. One of them was Crag; the others were she-cats, though neither of them was Brook. Stormfur felt faintly disappointed. The young she-cat had shown courage and friendliness when they first met, and he had looked forward to seeing her again.

"You have eaten well?" Stoneteller asked as he approached.

"Very well, thanks," Brambleclaw replied. "It's good of you to share prey with us."

"Why wouldn't we?" Stoneteller sounded surprised. "The prey is not ours—it belongs to the stones and the mountain."

He sat down in front of the forest cats, wrapping his tail neatly round his paws. The other three cats gathered round him, but remained standing. Brambleclaw looked expectantly at them.

"Crag you already know," meowed Stoneteller, introducing his companions. "He is the leader of our cave-guards, the cats who protect this place," he added, when the Clan cats looked confused. "This"—he flicked his tail towards the younger of the two she-cats—"is Mist Where Sunlight Shimmers. She is one of our best prey-hunters."

Mist dipped her head and blinked with friendly interest at the forest cats.

"And this," Stoneteller went on, indicating the other she-cat, "is Star That Shines on Water. For now she is a kit-mother, though when her kits are grown she will go back to being a cave-guard."

"You all have different duties, then?" Tawnypelt questioned, as the other forest cats murmured greetings.

"We do," Stoneteller replied.

"Do you choose the best fighters to be cave-guards, and the fastest cats to be prey-hunters?" Stormfur asked, fascinated in spite of his wariness.

Stoneteller twitched his whiskers in disagreement. "No. All the cats in our Tribe are born to their duties. That is our way. But tell us something more of yourselves," he went on, interrupting Squirrelpaw as she was about to ask another question. "Why are you making this long journey? We have never seen cats like you before."

Brambleclaw gave Stormfur a sideways glance and muttered, "What do you think? Do we tell them?"

"I think we have to tell them we were sent by StarClan." Stormfur breathed his reply close to the tabby warrior's ear, aware of how acute the mountain cats' hearing was. "Otherwise they might think we're outlaws. But don't tell them why we had to make the journey in the first place," he added. "We don't want to sound weak."

Brambleclaw nodded. Clearing his throat self-consciously he began to explain about the dreams each of the four chosen cats had received from StarClan, and the saltwater signs that had led them to the sun-drown place where they had met Midnight.

More of the Tribe cats gathered warily around to listen. Stormfur spotted admiring glances from them as Brambleclaw spoke of the dangers they had faced, but there were a few suspicious mutterings too, as if some of them found it hard to trust the strangers.

"Don't worry," he put in, when Brambleclaw paused in his story. "StarClan hasn't sent us to fight you. They didn't say anything about meeting you, in fact."

"StarClan?" Mist echoed, glancing at Stoneteller in bewilderment. "What is StarClan?"

Stormfur heard Tawnypelt stifle an exclamation of surprise. Feathertail was right after all; these cats were not guided by StarClan. His fur prickled as he suppressed a shiver at the thought that perhaps StarClan was not watching over him and his friends in this strange place.

"Do not be troubled," Stoneteller meowed, touching Mist's shoulder with the tip of his tail in a reassuring gesture. "Not all cats believe as we do, and we must respect that which we do not know. Ignorance is nothing to be afraid of. Please"—he gestured toward Brambleclaw with one paw—"continue."

"So at last we came to the sun-drown water and discovered

that Midnight is a badger," Brambleclaw explained. "She told us the meaning of StarClan's prophecy, and now we're going home to tell our Clans."

"A prophecy?" Stoneteller meowed. His green gaze was fixed on Stormfur in a stare of eerie intensity. "Then you too have visions of what is hidden?"

"Well, sometimes we have dreams," Tawnypelt explained. "But mostly our medicine cats interpret signs for us—clouds, the flight of birds, the fall of leaves. . ."

"This I do also," Stoneteller mewed.

He broke off as a group of cats appeared in the cave entrance. Rising to his paws, he murmured, "Forgive me. These are cave-guards, returning from patrol. I must hear what they have to tell me." Dipping his head, he walked off to meet the leader of the group.

Mist and Star stayed with the forest cats. Stormfur was struck again by how anxious the Tribe cats looked, and he realised that so far he had not seen any of them enjoying themselves: no apprentices play-fighting, no warriors sharing tongues, or elders gathering to exchange gossip and stories. The whole Tribe seemed to live in an atmosphere of suppressed fear.

"Are you OK?" Tawnypelt meowed to Mist, echoing Stormfur's thoughts. "You look worried. Is something wrong?"

"Are you being attacked by another Tribe?" Squirrelpaw added.

"No, there are no cats to attack us," Star replied. "There are no others in the mountains that we know of. How could there be another Tribe when we guard the Cave of the Pointed Stones?"

"What's that?" meowed Crowpaw.

His question was ignored.

Mist exchanged a swift glance with Star and murmured, "Should we tell them?" Stormfur barely caught the words and realised that he had not been meant to hear.

A hiss came from one of the Tribe cats who had crept closer to listen to the conversation. More than one of them looked scared or angry with Mist.

"What are you afraid of?" Stormfur persisted, his fur beginning to prickle with dread of the unknown.

"Nothing," Star replied. "Or nothing we may speak of." Rising to her paws, she dipped her head and began to walk away, gesturing with her tail for Mist to follow her. Mist gave the forest cats a backward glance, her eyes filled with fear, before she vanished into the shadows at the back of the cave. The other cats too began to creep away.

Mystified, Stormfur turned to Brambleclaw, and saw his own apprehension reflected in the ThunderClan cat's amber eyes. "What was all that about?" he muttered.

Brambleclaw shook his head. "StarClan knows. But whatever it is, it's obvious that something is frightening them. I wonder why they don't want to tell us what it is."

CHAPTER 10

Leafpaw gazed along the line of hostile WindClan cats, and locked eyes with a bracken-coloured apprentice. The young cat drew its lips back in a snarl; Leafpaw's fur prickled. She was a medicine cat and supposed to be outside normal Clan rivalries. But she found her claws instinctively flexing into the soft moorland grass; if it came to a fight, that apprentice would soon discover that she was not lacking in warrior skills.

"Well?" When Firestar did not immediately answer his question, Tallstar repeated it. "Why have you come? Do you think we're so weak that you can drive us out as Brokenstar did?"

Defiant yowls and hisses broke out from the warriors behind him, and it was a moment before Firestar could make himself heard.

"Tallstar, you have known nothing but friendship from me since the time that Greystripe and I found you and brought you home," he replied. "Have you forgotten that? I think you must have, or you wouldn't accuse me of being like Brokenstar."

Leafpaw thought she detected a flash of guilt in the older

cat's eyes, but there was still a challenge in his voice as he meowed, "Then why have you come here with so many warriors?"

"Don't be absurd, Tallstar," Firestar growled. "I haven't enough warriors to take on your whole Clan. We want to talk to you, that's all. WindClan have been stealing prey from ThunderClan territory, and you know as well as I do that that's against the warrior code."

Tallstar looked taken aback, as if he genuinely hadn't known what his warriors were up to. Before he could reply, his deputy Mudclaw called out, "Prove it! Prove that WindClan has stolen so much as a sniff of prey!"

"*What?*" Leafpaw saw Greystripe's whole body stiffen. "We saw you ourselves just now! And we found prey bones reeking of WindClan scent."

"So you say," Mudclaw sneered. "If you ask me, it's just an excuse to attack us."

Furious, Greystripe launched himself across the border, his claws reaching out as he bowled over the WindClan deputy. Mudclaw let out a screech and the two cats rolled on the short moorland grass.

Tallstar gazed down at the two battling warriors with a look of contempt, as if he had found maggots in his fresh-kill. Warriors on both sides were poised to spring, their teeth bared and the light of battle in their eyes. Leafpaw's heart beat faster as she tried to remember the fighting moves her mentor had taught her.

Firestar stepped forwards with a fierce hiss. "Stop!"

At once Greystripe broke away from Mudclaw's raking claws and stood back, breathing heavily. Mudclaw scrambled to his paws and glared at him.

"Greystripe, I told you we were not here to fight," Firestar meowed.

The deputy's yellow eyes were smouldering. "But did you hear the lies he told?"

"Yes. But that doesn't change my orders. Get back on to our side of the border. Now."

His tail twitching angrily, Greystripe obeyed. Leafpaw understood how he must feel, especially when he was still worrying about his missing children, but she could also guess how uncomfortable it must be for Firestar when his friend and deputy disobeyed a direct order, and in full view of WindClan. She stifled a sigh. Was this part of being a medicine cat, to understand every cat so clearly and want to sympathise with them all?

Cinderpelt limped forwards to stand beside Firestar. "You know that medicine cats do not lie," she meowed to Tallstar. "You know, too, that it is not the will of StarClan for warriors to trespass on the territory of other Clans and steal their prey."

"And is it the will of StarClan for my Clan to starve?" Tallstar asked bitterly. "Yesterday one of our elders died, and he will be the first of many if we don't do something."

"If we could help you, we would," Cinderpelt replied with feeling. "But ThunderClan is short of prey too. The whole forest is suffering because of the Twolegs."

"We should work together," Firestar added. "I swear to you by StarClan that if ThunderClan finds an answer to these problems, we will share it with WindClan."

Tallstar met his gaze with a long, thoughtful look, his bitterness dying away and leaving deep sorrow behind it. "An answer? Firestar, I don't think that even you can find an answer to our troubles. Unless you let us hunt on your territory." Even while he was speaking, he shook his head, to show Firestar he did not make that suggestion seriously. "No, you are right to keep your own prey. The warrior code demands that you feed your own Clan first. WindClan does not look to you for help."

Firestar dipped his head to the WindClan leader. "Tallstar, we promise you that ThunderClan has not lied to you. There will be no fighting now, but if the prey-stealing doesn't stop, you know what to expect."

He turned and walked away, gesturing with his tail for his warriors to follow him. As they withdrew, yowls of derision rose from the WindClan warriors, as if they had fought a battle and driven invaders away from their territory.

Leafpaw felt her neck fur rise, half expecting the rival Clan to pursue them like the warriors had pursued her and Sorreltail a few days before. But the sounds died away behind them as Firestar led the way around the top of the hollow at Fourtrees and down the slope towards the stream.

"Why didn't we fight it out?" Dustpelt demanded. "We could have taught them a lesson that they wouldn't forget in a hurry!"

"I know," Firestar sighed. "But as I said before, the Clans cannot afford to turn on one another."

"And when our patrols catch WindClan stealing prey again?" Dustpelt's tail twitched; he was short-tempered at the best of times, and Leafpaw knew how anxious he was about Ferncloud and their kits.

"We'll see them off if we catch them trespassing," Firestar promised. "But let's pray to StarClan that Tallstar sees sense and keeps his warriors on their own territory. I don't think he knew what was going on until today."

"Maybe not. But he'll back his own warriors now." Dustpelt paused, his brown tabby fur bristling as if he could see his enemy in front of him.

"Why don't you go and hunt for a bit?" Firestar suggested. "See if you can find a bit of fresh-kill for Ferncloud."

Dustpelt glanced at him, his neck fur beginning to relax. "OK, I will." In a reluctant growl he added, "Thanks." Swiftly he turned and disappeared into the thicker vegetation beside the stream.

Firestar watched him go, his expression full of sorrow. Leafpaw could hardly bear to see his frustration and hope-lessness. She knew he would never give up, not before the monsters had destroyed every last tree in the forest. But it looked like the time when that might happen was drawing near, and what would Firestar do then?

As she followed him across the stream towards the ThunderClan camp, she struggled yet again with the guilt she felt about not telling her father what she knew about

Squirrelpaw and Brambleclaw. Perhaps now was the time to speak up, to relieve some of his anxieties about them, and to assure him that StarClan knew about the suffering in the forest and had their own plan to relieve it. But what would Firestar say to her, when she had kept silent for so long? Leafpaw shrank at the thought of his anger.

Seeing that Cinderpelt had dropped a little way behind the other cats, she wondered if her mentor might have the answer. She could tell Cinderpelt; the medicine cat would understand, and perhaps help her to pass the news on to Firestar.

Leafpaw waited for her mentor to catch up to her. "Cinderpelt . . ." she began, anticipating the medicine cat's usual sensible, no-nonsense advice.

But when Cinderpelt turned to her, her blue eyes were clouded with pain. "I've heard nothing from StarClan," she mewed without giving Leafpaw the chance to speak first. "Have they abandoned us? It *can't* be their will for the Twolegs to destroy us all."

As if to emphasise her desperation, the roar of the Twoleg monsters thundered in the distance. Though she couldn't see them from here, Leafpaw could picture all too clearly the garish, glittering pelts and the vast black paws that tore up the forest as easily as Dustpelt's claws had torn the grass moments before.

She brushed comfortingly against her mentor. "Suppose StarClan spoke to us in another way?" she suggested, feeling her heart begin to pound. The whole forest was turned upside down, if apprentices knew about prophecies that had not been sent to older cats.

"What other way? They haven't sent me a single dream or a sign."

"They might have sent it to another cat."

"To you?" Cinderpelt rounded on Leafpaw with her blue eyes blazing. "Have they?"

"No, but—"

"No, StarClan are silent." Cinderpelt's brief flash of energy vanished and her tail drooped. "They must want something from us, but what?"

Leafpaw found it impossible to go on. Perhaps this wasn't the right time to speak after all. How would Cinderpelt feel if she found out that StarClan had chosen to speak to inexperienced warriors, and send them on the journey instead of the medicine cats? She felt so lonely and confused that she instinctively tried to reach out to Squirrelpaw and share her sister's thoughts. But she found no comfort there. All she could sense was darkness, and the noise of rushing water.

"Leafpaw! Are you coming?"

With a jump, Leafpaw realised that Cinderpelt was several tail-lengths ahead of her.

"Sorry!" she called back, and plodded on at the rear of the patrol, her head bowed down by her fears for StarClan's chosen cats and for all the forest. And, most of all, for Squirrelpaw—wherever she was.

CHAPTER 11

Moonlight shone into the cave, turning the waterfall into a sheet of rippling silver. Stormfur felt as though the day had lasted for a moon, and now even the shallow, sandy dips in the cave floor were looking as comfortable as his nest among the reeds back home.

Stoneteller had returned and shown the forest cats to sleeping hollows at the side of the main cave, their curved sides lined with a sparse layer of moss and feathers. "You may rest here," he meowed. "Stay many days—for as long as you want. You are all welcome."

Once he had gone, Brambleclaw beckoned with his tail for all his friends to gather round. "We need to talk," he mewed. "How long do you think we should stay here?"

Crowpaw's tail lashed from side to side. "I don't know how you can ask that!" he rasped. "I thought we were on a mission. What about taking Midnight's news to the forest?"

"Crowpaw's right," Stormfur meowed, stifling a brief stab of annoyance that he had to agree with the WindClan apprentice. "I think we should leave right away."

"Me too," mewed Tawnypelt. "Leaf-bare's coming, and

there'll be snow up here."

"But what about your shoulder?" Brambleclaw reminded her. Since their plunge over the waterfall, she'd been limping on three legs, and a trickle of dried blood ran down her shoulder, seeping between her claws. "We've got to stay until the rat bite is better. We'd all get on faster after that."

Tawnypelt's neck fur bristled. "I knocked it again, that's all. If you think I'm holding you back," she spat, "then just come out and say so."

"Brambleclaw didn't mean that." Feathertail brushed her side comfortingly against Tawnypelt's flank, taking care to avoid the injury. "That's more than just a knock. It looks like you've done as much damage as before, and it won't heal if you don't rest."

Squirrelpaw looked thoughtful. "It sounded as if the Tribe cats don't think we should leave at all. What are they all so frightened of? Are we going to meet more danger further on?"

The other cats looked uneasily at one another. Stormfur admitted to himself that the thought had crossed his mind too. Part of him wanted to stay safely in the cave for as long as they could, if the alternative was unknown terror among the rocks and precipices of the mountains.

"It'll be risky whenever we leave," Crowpaw pointed out. "OK, I agree about Tawnypelt, but let's get Stoneteller to fix her shoulder, and then go."

"That's all very well," Squirrelpaw broke in, her green eyes sparkling in the moonlight. "But we're all assuming we can leave whenever we want."

"What do you mean? They wouldn't dare stop us!" Crowpaw exclaimed.

Squirrelpaw snorted. "I'll bet you my next piece of freshkill that they *would*. Look over there."

She flicked her ears toward the cave entrance. A caveguard was seated on either side, making no secret of the fact that they were keeping an eye on the newcomers.

"Perhaps they're guarding the cave from enemies outside," Feathertail meowed.

"We could always try leaving," Crowpaw suggested, the tip of his grey-black tail twitching. "Then we'd see what happened."

"No." Brambleclaw's voice was firm. "It would be mousebrained to leave right now. We're all tired out, and we need to sleep. Tomorrow we'll see how Tawnypelt's shoulder is, and figure out when we can leave."

There was a murmur of agreement. Not even Crowpaw wanted more trouble just then, and it was not long before the forest cats were settling into their sleeping hollows, huddled together against the curious stares that darted at them from all around the cave.

As Stormfur prodded his bedding into place, he heard a pawstep behind him, and turned to see one of the mountain cats padding across the cave toward him. Warm recognition swept through his pelt as he recognised Brook by her soft tabby fur and lithe walk. She carried a wad of feathers in her jaws.

Dropping them in the sleeping hollow Stormfur had chosen,

she dipped her head to him. "Stoneteller sent me to make sure you're comfortable."

"Er, thanks," Stormfur replied. Did Brook mean that Stoneteller had sent her to all the cats, or to him in particular? She showed no signs of going to fetch more feathers for the rest of them. True, Stormfur still felt battered from the fall into the pool, but so did all his friends. He was not their leader either, who would get special treatment.

"I . . . I hope you'll be happy here," Brook went on hesitantly. "This must be very different from what you're used to. Do you have caves for sleeping in your forest?"

"No, we sleep in nests of reeds and bushes. RiverClan's camp—that's my Clan—is on an island." A pang of homesickness stabbed Stormfur as he spoke, and he wondered if he would ever again lie curled up in the warriors' den, listening to the soft sighing of the wind in the reeds. If Midnight was right, and all the Clans had to leave the forest, he might never find another home that was so peaceful.

Brook's eyes shone in the moonlight. "Are you a cave-guard or—" She broke off, scuffling her paws in embarrassment. "No, of course not, if you have no caves there will be no cave-guards. Do you guard your camp, or are you a prey-hunter?"

"Our Clans don't work like that," Stormfur told her. "We all guard and hunt and patrol."

"That must be hard," Brook meowed. "We are born to our duties, so we know exactly what we have to do. I am a prey-hunter," she added. "If Stoneteller allows it, perhaps you would like to hunt with me tomorrow?"

Stormfur swallowed. It sounded as if Brook assumed that the forest cats would be staying for a while. He was not sure either that he liked the idea of asking Stoneteller's permission for everything; they would respect the Tribe's leader while they stayed in his territory, but he had no right to give them orders. All the same, it would be fun to hunt with Brook.

He wondered whether to ask her outright if they were prisoners, but before he could speak, the pretty young tabby dipped her head in farewell. "You're tired; I'll leave you alone now," she mewed. "Sleep well. I hope we will hunt together soon."

Stormfur said goodbye to her and watched her retreat across the cave before he settled into the feathers. All around him were the soft murmurs of his sleeping friends. But although his muscles ached and his head spun with exhaustion, it was some time before sleep claimed him as well.

The sound of pawsteps padding past his sleeping hollow woke Stormfur the next morning; he opened his eyes to see sunlight spilling through the cascade of water and into the cave. It reminded him of how they should be following the rising sun back to the forest, and he scrambled out of his hollow, shaking off a feather that clung to his pelt.

Brambleclaw was already up, standing a few tail-lengths away and watching a patrol of cave-guards leaving through the main entrance. Their quiet sense of purpose reminded Stormfur of the patrols at home. He padded over to

Brambleclaw, who twitched his whiskers in greeting.

"Tawnypelt's shoulder started bleeding in the night. I think the muscles have torn open again," the ThunderClan warrior meowed. "I told her to get some more sleep, but it means we'll have to stay here for a day or two at least."

Stormfur glanced back to where he could see the smooth curve of Tawnypelt's tortoiseshell fur as she lay curled in her sleeping hollow. Feathertail was anxiously bending over her, examining her injured shoulder, while Crowpaw looked on. Squirrelpaw was still sleeping.

The sight of his sister so close to the WindClan apprentice did nothing to improve Stormfur's temper. "Well, if we must, we must," he muttered. "But sooner or later we'll have to find out why these Tribe cats have been quite so welcoming. We know there's something they're not telling us."

"True." Brambleclaw was calm, his amber eyes meeting Stonefur's in a level stare. "But we'll learn more if we co-operate with them—to begin with, anyway."

"You could be right," Stormfur grunted.

Movement at the back of the cave caught his eye, and he spotted Stoneteller emerging from one of the tunnels and heading towards them. Crowpaw and Feathertail spotted him too; Crowpaw prodded Squirrelpaw to wake her, and all three cats came bounding over to Stormfur and Brambleclaw.

Tawnypelt raised her head as Feathertail moved away. "Are we leaving?" she meowed; Stormfur could hear the pain grating in her voice. "I can go on if I have to."

Feathertail glanced back at her. "No, we're not going anywhere yet. Try to get some sleep."

"Are you going to ask Stoneteller to let us out of here?" Crowpaw hissed to Brambleclaw. "If he thinks he can keep us prisoner, I'll claw his ears off!"

"No, you won't," Brambleclaw said swiftly. "You know very well Tawnypelt needs to rest until that rat bite is better. Besides, the last thing we want to do is offend any of these cats. Let me do the talking."

Crowpaw shot the tabby warrior a glare, but said nothing more.

"I'm sure we're not prisoners." Stormfur spoke more confidently than he felt, trying to convince himself that he had imagined the eerie interest the Tribe cats took in him. "Why should we be? We've done them no harm."

"Maybe we have something they want," Squirrelpaw suggested.

That idea was so close to what Stormfur himself had been thinking that he found nothing to say in reply. Besides, Stoneteller was approaching; there was no more chance to talk among themselves.

"Good morning," the Healer meowed. "Have you slept well?"

"Very well, thank you," Brambleclaw replied. "But Tawnypelt's shoulder is badly hurt, so we'd like to stay for a day or two until she's better, if that's all right with you."

"Good." Stoneteller's head swivelled towards Stormfur as he spoke, and the glow in his green eyes made Stormfur even more apprehensive. "I will look at your friend's shoulder, and find some herbs to heal her."

"The rest of us would like to go hunting," Brambleclaw continued. "We need to stretch our legs, and we'd like to catch our own prey. You can't go on feeding six of us while we sit around doing nothing."

Stoneteller's ears pricked forwards, and his eyes narrowed. Stormfur got the idea that he was not pleased by Brambleclaw's request.

However, the Healer scarcely hesitated. "Of course," he meowed. "We will be glad for your help. Some prey-hunters are about to leave, so you can go with them."

As he spoke, Stormfur saw several of the Tribe cats gathering beside the cave entrance; Brook was among them, and Mist, the prey-hunter they had met the day before. Stoneteller led the Clan cats over to them.

"Our new friends want to go hunting," he announced. "Take them with you, and teach them the way we hunt."

The order given, he padded away again. Stormfur glanced after him, slightly stung that he thought Clan warriors would need to be taught how to hunt. Then he realised that Brook was beside him again.

"Greetings," she mewed. "There are so many of us, we'd better split into two groups. Will you hunt with me?"

"Yes, I'd like that," Stormfur replied, slightly surprised at how pleased he felt that Brook had remembered her invitation of the previous night.

Quickly the Tribe cats divided into two groups. One of them, with Mist in the lead, took Crowpaw and Feathertail, while Stormfur joined Brook's group, along with Brambleclaw and Squirrelpaw.

Tawnypelt watched them go with a brief flash of fear in her eyes, but as Stormfur left the cave, he spotted the kit-mother Star padding over to her with a piece of fresh-kill.

"She'll be fine," Brambleclaw murmured. "With any luck, she'll sleep until we get back. It doesn't look like the Tribe cats mean her any harm."

Seeing the friendliness with which Star spoke to Tawnypelt, Stormfur realised that the tabby warrior was right. He stepped cautiously along the ledge behind the waterfall, shivering as the spray soaked into his fur, and out on to the rocks beside the pool.

As he shook off most of the moisture, he noticed that Crag and a number of other cats were already waiting, their fur streaked with fresh mud. They were strong cats with massive shoulders, unlike the lithe prey-hunters. Stormfur guessed they were all cave-guards.

Catching Brambleclaw's eye, he muttered, "What are they doing here?"

Brook heard his low-voiced comment. "We take cave-guards with us on our hunts," she explained. "We need them to watch for eagles, and—"

She broke off with a nervous glance at Stormfur, who wondered what she had been about to say. Still, he felt relieved at her explanation. The thought had crossed his mind that the cave-guards might be there to keep an eye on him and his friends, and make sure that they did not try to escape. Of course, they would never leave Tawnypelt, but Stoneteller didn't know that.

When Brook had explained to Crag that the visitors were joining them for the hunt, the cave-guards joined the two groups. One of them, with Crowpaw and Feathertail, began to climb the rocks where Stormfur and the others had fallen the day before, while Brook led Stormfur's group further down into the valley.

The ground here was hard earth, where a few scanty clumps of grass poked up among broken rocks. A few bushes straggled here and there beneath the steep rock walls. Though the rain had stopped, the boulders gleamed wet in the morning light. The prospects for prey looked meager to Stormfur's eyes, and he wondered how the Tribe cats had managed to find the fresh-kill they had shared so generously. He tasted the air, and picked up only the faintest traces of prey-scent.

Brook led her group along one side of the valley, in the shadow of the bushes. Now Stormfur could see why they streaked their pelts with mud; it made them blend into the rock so that when they were still it was hard to see them at all. In contrast Squirrelpaw's dark ginger fur looked like a splash of blood, though Stormfur's grey pelt and Brambleclaw's dark tabby were inconspicuous enough. All the Tribe cats moved silently; Stormfur had to concentrate to make sure his paw-steps were just as quiet.

Before long he saw Squirrelpaw halt, her ears flicking up in excitement. "Look—a mouse!" she whispered.

Stormfur spotted it too, nibbling on a grass-seed a few tail-lengths ahead. Squirrelpaw dropped into the hunter's crouch, but instantly Brook swung her tail in front of her, barring her way. Her jaws formed the word, "Wait."

Stormfur expected Squirrelpaw to make an indignant protest, but the ThunderClan apprentice obviously figured that if she did she would frighten the prey. She glared at Brook instead, but the young she-cat didn't notice. Her eyes were fixed on the mouse.

A shadow flicked over Stormfur. A heartbeat later a falcon swooped down from the sky and gripped the mouse in its powerful talons. At the same moment Brook launched herself forward. She sprang onto the bird's back, sinking her claws into its shoulders. Its wings beat furiously; for a couple of heartbeats it lifted Brook off the ground, only to fall back under her weight. A second prey-hunter ran up, and helped Brook finish the falcon off. Its wings stopped beating and it lay limp on the rocky ground.

"And we get the mouse too," Crag pointed out to Stormfur, swiping his tongue around his jaws.

Stormfur's eyes stretched wide with admiration at Brook's hunting skills. What a warrior she would make, if she'd been forest-born! Briefly he imagined her in RiverClan, teaching them this new way of hunting, but he banished the picture almost at once. Brook belonged here in the mountains, and within the next day or two he would have to part from her. He felt a strange stab of regret at the thought and was surprised. How could he already feel attached to a cat he barely knew?

Squirrelpaw was staring in disbelief at the dead falcon, all her indignation forgotten. "That was *brilliant!*" she meowed. "I want to try it." To Brambleclaw she added, "Could we hunt like this at home, do you think?"

"There aren't as many hawks," Brambleclaw pointed out. "WindClan might try, I suppose—Crowpaw said he'd seen eagles on the moors."

Stormfur noticed that instead of scraping earth over her prey until she was ready to collect it, Brook hid the mouse and the falcon by dragging both of them into a crevice in the rock. Then she set off again at the head of her group.

This time she led them up the wall of the valley, bounding over some loose rocks and then along a ledge. Stormfur couldn't think what prey she hoped to find out here, but by now he was content to wait and see, aware that these mountain cats had tricks he and his friends had never heard of.

They came to a flattened heap of twigs and dried grass, blocking the ledge. There was a strong reek of stale prey. Brook sprang nimbly over it, and the rest of the cats followed.

"This is a hawk's nest," she explained. "In the freed-water season, we can sometimes find hawk chicks."

"'Freed water'?" Squirrelpaw echoed.

"I expect she means newleaf," Brambleclaw replied in a low voice. "When the water's freed from ice, I guess. That's when there would be chicks in the nest."

"Very good they are, too," Crag added, coming up from behind. "And it means there are fewer hawks to grow up and prey on us. Like this one," he added, with a massive leap into the air.

Stormfur jerked his head up with a gasp. Just above him a huge hawk had swooped down, its talons extended, but as Crag leaped upward it veered off, shedding air from under its wings as it slid sideways.

Crag came down perilously close to the edge of the rock, regaining his balance with the ease of long practice. Stormfur's respect for him increased; the courage and speed with which the cave-guard had attacked the fierce bird matched any skills possessed by the best Clan warriors.

"Thanks," he gasped as he crouched on the ledge and watched the falcon swoop away, many tail-lengths below.

Crag turned to him, amber eyes gleaming. "That's the first thing a to-be learns," he meowed with a purr of amusement. "Never forget to look up!"

CHAPTER 12

❧

Stormfur crouched on a jutting spur of rock and looked down into the valley a couple of tail-lengths below. The sun was going down on the fourth day since he and his friends had come to the cave of the Tribe cats. Although the thought of what was happening in the forest hung over their heads like a swollen rain cloud, they had been unable to move on. Tawnypelt's shoulder was healing again, thanks to the herbs Stoneteller had given her, but it was still too stiff for her to walk.

Meanwhile, Stormfur was beginning to think he had gotten the hang of the Tribe cats' way of hunting. It depended much more on keeping still and silent than on stalking prey, for among the rocks there was not as much cover as in the forest or even by the river where he used to fish.

His ears pricked as he caught the faint sound of fluttering wings, and he peered down into the shadows. A bird had landed just below him and was pecking at the ground. Bunching his muscles, Stormfur sprang. His claws met feathers, and the bird's frantic alarm call was cut off as he killed it with one blow of his paw.

Stormfur stood up, his prey in his jaws, and saw the dim

shape of one of the mud-covered cave-guards approaching up the valley. The fresh-kill in his mouth masked the scent, and he did not recognise Crag until the cat spoke.

"Good catch! You'll make a great prey-hunter."

Stormfur nodded his thanks, but Crag's words made him slightly anxious; did he really mean "you *will* make a good prey-hunter," or had he meant to say "you *would*"? The cave-guard sometimes seemed to assume that Stormfur intended to stay with the Tribe for good. But there was no opportunity to ask him what he meant; Brook and the rest of the prey-hunters had just appeared, and the whole patrol set off back to the cave, collecting the prey they had caught earlier on their way.

When they reached the pool, Stormfur set down his load for a brief rest before climbing the rocks and negotiating the ledge behind the waterfall. The sun had set and the peak was outlined against a sky the colour of blood. Stormfur shivered, trying not to picture blood being shed back home in the forest. However happy he felt to be hunting with the Tribe, they had to move on as soon as they could.

Brook padded up beside him, her eyes shining in the evening light. "A good day's hunting," she purred. "You have learned our ways well, Stormfur."

A warm glow spread through him from ears to tail-tip. Even more than before, he knew how much he would miss her when he had to leave. In these last few days she had become a friend; even her strange accent had begun to sound familiar. He guessed she felt the same; at least, she always asked him to go hunting with her, while the rest of the forest cats, if they hunted at all, went with other groups. Stormfur wondered what Brook really thought of him. Would she miss him when he had to go?

He opened his jaws and picked up a strong rank scent. It was like nothing he had ever smelled before: a bit like a cat's, but harsher and tinged with carrion. He felt his neck fur rise with a premonition of danger.

"What's *that*?"

Brook's eyes stretched wide with fear, but she did not reply. Already the rest of the hunting patrol were gathering up their prey, hurrying for the safety of the cave. Crag bounded over and almost pushed Stormfur up the rocks. Glancing up, Stormfur thought he spotted a shadowy movement near the top of the waterfall, but he wasn't sure. Then he had to concentrate on keeping his footing on the slick, wet stones of the ledge, struggling to see around the half-grown falcon in his jaws. No cat tried to explain the reason for the sudden panic, and Stormfur had learned by now that there would be no point in asking.

In the cave, he carried his prey over to the fresh-kill pile and went to find his friends. Spotting them near their sleeping hollows, he headed towards them, dodging around a couple of to-bes who were training with one of the cave-guards. They were using unfamiliar fighting moves; Stormfur's pelt itched to join in and learn, and teach the Tribe cats a few RiverClan tricks too. *Maybe later*, he promised himself.

The other Clan cats were all gathered around Tawnypelt, who was on her paws, twisting her head to examine her shoulder. Feathertail's tongue rasped busily over her fur.

"It's much better," she meowed. "There's no swelling at all, and the wound's healing cleanly. How does it feel, Tawnypelt?"

The ShadowClan warrior flexed the injured shoulder, then dropped into the hunter's crouch and crept a few tail-lengths along the cave floor. "Stoneteller certainly knows his stuff," she reported. "I don't know the herbs he used, but they're just as good as burdock root. The shoulder's a bit stiff, that's all," she added, springing up again. "It'll be fine if I keep exercising it. I just wish I could get my claws on that rat!"

"Then it's time we were leaving," Brambleclaw mewed. "I'll have a word with Stoneteller, and we'll set off first thing tomorrow."

"Right!" Crowpaw's eyes flashed. "And they'd better not try to keep us here."

"They won't." Feathertail pressed her muzzle against his side. "I'm sure you're worrying about nothing. The Tribe cats have been nothing but kind to us ever since we got here."

"They'll probably be glad to see the back of us," Squirrelpaw agreed cheerfully. "They're bound to be short of prey when leaf-bare comes."

"It's nearly here," mewed Feathertail. "The rocks were white with frost this morning."

"Right." Squirrelpaw waved her tail. "So they won't want us sitting here stuffing ourselves."

Stormfur could see from the look Brambleclaw gave his Clanmate that he was still worried, but he said nothing.

Instead, it was Crowpaw who spoke, noticing for the first time that Stormfur had padded up to join them.

"There you are!" he exclaimed, his lip curling unpleasantly. "Decided to join us, have you? Getting bored with your new friends in the Tribe?"

"Don't," Feathertail murmured, flicking him with her tail.

Stung, Stormfur stalked up to the young WindClan apprentice. "If he's got something to say, let him say it."

"Only that you spend all your time with them. Maybe you'd like to stay with them for good. After all, things are going to be pretty tough when we get back to the forest."

"Don't be stupid," Stormfur retorted. Turning his back on Crowpaw, he saw that all the others were looking at him gravely, as if they half agreed with what the WindClan cat had said. "Come on," Stormfur went on, alarmed. "What have I done? Gone out hunting a couple of times, that's all. You said yourself, Brambleclaw, that we should catch our own prey while we're here. What makes you think that I care any less than you about what happens to the forest?"

"No cat thinks that," Feathertail mewed soothingly.

"*He* does." Stormfur twitched his ears at Crowpaw. "This isn't about the dreams, is it? Just because I wasn't chosen by StarClan . . . You haven't had more dreams, have you, and not told me?"

He unsheathed his claws, hating that they scraped against stone rather than soft riverside earth or a tangle of reeds. Crowpaw he could understand; the apprentice had always been difficult, and he would fight with StarClan themselves.

But that the others might think him less than loyal—even his own sister . . . It was almost as bad as the time when Tigerstar had merged two Clans together, and he and Feathertail had nearly been killed for being half-Clan. Feathertail at least should remember that and understand. Stormfur stifled a flash of guilt as he remembered how comfortable he felt among the Tribe, but he was determined to remain loyal to RiverClan.

"No, we haven't had any more dreams," Brambleclaw replied. "Settle down, Stormfur, and Crowpaw, stop annoying him. We have problems enough without that."

"It's that waterfall," Tawnypelt meowed unexpectedly. "The noise of it, day and night, is driving me mad. StarClan could be sending us every sign under the sun, but we'd never hear them. I'll be glad when we're out in the open again, and well away from this place."

There was a soft snarl in Crowpaw's voice. "We need to go back to the forest, and defend it like warriors should. Stormfur can come or not."

"Shut up, mouse-brain," Squirrelpaw snapped. "Stormfur's just as loyal as you."

Stormfur blinked gratefully at her. "Of course I'm coming with you," he meowed.

"Then let's eat, and get a good night's sleep," Brambleclaw growled. "It might be our last chance for a while."

Stormfur looked up and flinched, surprised to see that while they had been talking several of the Tribe cats had gathered and were watching them with serious faces.

Crag stepped forwards. "Why do you talk about leaving?" he meowed. "You'll never make it through the mountains in the season of frozen-water. Stay with us until the sun returns."

"We can't do that!" Squirrelpaw exclaimed. "There's trouble back home—we told you that when we arrived."

"We're grateful for the offer," Brambleclaw meowed more diplomatically, brushing his tail across Squirrelpaw's mouth to silence her. "But we have to go."

The Tribe cats glanced at one another, their neck fur starting to bristle. Suddenly they looked threatening. Several of the powerful cave-guards moved to stand between them and the entrance, and two or three of the kit-mothers began anxiously herding their kits towards the nursery tunnel. The meaning was clear; Stormfur knew that if they tried to leave now they would have a fight on their paws.

Spotting Brook near the back of the group, he thrust past a cave-guard to stand in front of her. "What's going on?" he demanded. "Why are you treating us like prisoners?"

Brook would not meet his eyes. "Please . . ." she murmured. "Are you so unhappy here that staying is such a terrible thing?"

"'Unhappy' isn't the point. We're on a mission; we don't have any choice." Stormfur whirled around to question Crag, but the cave-guard avoided his gaze, and he knew that their friendship was being brushed aside out of loyalty to the Tribe, for reasons he could not begin to guess. He had believed that the Tribe cats liked him for himself, and pain at their betrayal tore him like an eagle's talons.

"Fox dung to this!" Crowpaw muttered, trying to force his way past the cave-guards.

Crag raised his paw, and another cave-guard thrust Crowpaw back with a furious hiss. The WindClan apprentice's bristling fur and lashing tail showed that he was ready to attack both of them at once.

"Wait," Feathertail murmured, pushing between Crowpaw and the guards. "Let's find out what all this means."

"It means trouble," Crowpaw snarled. "No cat is going to stop me from leaving."

He shouldered his way past Feathertail and leaped on Crag, bowling the huge cave-guard over. Crag's hind paws battered his belly, but before the fight could go any further, Brambleclaw fastened his teeth into Crowpaw's scruff and dragged him off.

The apprentice spun around to face him, eyes blazing. "Get off me!" he snarled.

"Then stop being so mouse-brained!" Brambleclaw hissed, just as furious. "These guards could turn you into crowfood. We have to find out what they want."

Stormfur hated to admit defeat, but if they fought their way out tonight—even supposing they could—they would have to face a cold night on an unfamiliar mountainside. And looking around at the lean, well-muscled cave-guards, barely out of breath from the tussle with Crowpaw, Stormfur knew they could not hope to survive a fight without injury, and that would make their journey harder than ever. *Why didn't Midnight foresee this?* he wondered desperately. Or had she foreseen it, and kept it hidden from them?

He saw that Stoneteller had emerged from his tunnel. *Now perhaps we'll get some answers,* he thought.

The cave-guards stepped back to allow their leader to come closer to the Clan cats; Brambleclaw padded forwards to face him. "I think there must be some misunderstanding," he began. Stormfur could see his efforts to stay calm. "We have to leave tomorrow, and your Tribe doesn't seem to want us to go. We're grateful for your help and shelter, but—"

He broke off; Stoneteller wasn't listening. His eyes glimmered like pebbles on a streambed as he gazed around the group of cats. Raising his voice, he meowed, "I have received a sign from the Tribe of Endless Hunting. It is time for a Telling."

"A Telling? What's that?" Squirrelpaw mewed.

"Maybe it's like a Gathering," Stormfur murmured.

"But there aren't any other Tribes to meet with."

"Then maybe it's something to do with the Tribe of Endless Hunting." In spite of his fears that they would not be allowed to leave the cave, Stormfur couldn't help feeling curious about discovering more of the Tribe's strange beliefs.

The cave-guards gathered more closely around the Clan cats and began to herd them towards the tunnel from where Stoneteller had just emerged.

"Back off!" Tawnypelt snapped at one of them. "Where are you taking us?"

Stormfur wondered that too. Until now he had assumed

that the second tunnel just led to Stoneteller's private den.

"To the Cave of Pointed Stones," Stoneteller replied. "There, many things will be made clear to you."

"And what if we don't want to go?" Without waiting for a reply, Crowpaw launched himself at the nearest cave-guard, a cat almost twice his size. The cave-guard casually swatted him with a huge paw, sending him half stunned to the floor of the cave. Feathertail spat at the guard and lashed out a paw, claws extended.

Stormfur felt his neck fur stand on end, but before a real fight could break out Brambleclaw hissed, "No! If we're going to get an explanation, we'll listen to it. Then we'll decide what to do. Do you hear me, Crowpaw?"

The apprentice, scrambling to his paws with his fur torn and his tail fluffed out, glared at him but said nothing.

"Get a move on," growled one of the guards.

Stormfur stumbled, almost losing his balance as the nearest guard butted him towards the tunnel. It took all his self-control to move on quietly. Then he realised that Brook was beside him. There was something like relief in her eyes as she mewed, "Don't worry. Everything will become clear soon."

"I'm not worried." Stormfur's voice was cold. He had thought they were friends, and she had betrayed him. "You can't keep us here forever."

He was almost pleased when she winced. "Please . . ." she whispered. "You don't understand. It's for the sake of the Tribe."

Stormfur curled his lip and turned away. He padded after

Tawnypelt into the passage, with a couple of cave-guards close behind.

In the darkness he heard Stoneteller's voice raised in a soft chant. "When the Tribe of Endless Hunting calls, we come to listen."

More voices answered him from behind Stormfur, not just the cave-guards but more of the Tribe cats pressing into the tunnel. "In rock and pool, in air and light on water, through fall of prey and cry of kit, through scrape of claw and beat of blood, we hear you."

The voices echoed through the shadows. Stormfur saw moonlight filtering in from somewhere ahead, and Tawnypelt's pricked ears outlined in grey. He stepped out into another cave, and for a moment all his fears and frustrations vanished and he stood with his mouth dropped open in awe.

This cave was much smaller than the one they had just left. A jagged rift high in the roof let in a shaft of moonlight that bathed the floor in watery grey light. Stormfur was standing amid a forest of pointed stones, many more than in the main cave; some of them grew up from the floor while others hung down above his head. A few of them had joined together as if they were propping up the roof, pale yellow and rippled with tiny streams of water trickling down to pool on the hard stone floor.

Earlier that day rain had fallen through the hole to leave a pattern of puddles around Stormfur's paws. The roar of the waterfall, so loud in the outer cave, had sunk to a whisper, faint enough that he could hear drops of water falling from the roof.

All the Clan cats were silent, the same awe, which Stormfur felt, shining in their eyes. The place reminded Stormfur of Mothermouth; as well as being in a moonlit cave, there was the same sense of being in the presence of something greater than himself. But this was not the home of StarClan, but of the Tribe of Endless Hunting, and would they even care about cats from territories far away? A shiver went through him and in his mind he formed a prayer to StarClan. *Guard us and guide us, even here.*

The cave-guards nudged the Clan cats farther into the cave, while Stoneteller stalked ahead of them until he stood in the centre of the forest of stones. There he turned to face the rest of the cats. "We stand in the Cave of Pointed Stones," he meowed; his voice was high and expressionless. "Moonrise is here, caught in rock and in water as it has always been and always will be. It is time for a Telling. We call on the Tribe of Endless Hunting to show us their will."

"Show us your will," the other Tribe cats responded in chorus. Almost all of them had pushed into the cave behind the Clan cats; the air was growing warm with their bodies and damp, misty breath.

Moving like a shadow, Stoneteller padded to and fro, peering into the puddles. His eyes shone in the moonlight, and the mud on his fur looked more sinister and stonelike than ever. Brook had told Stormfur that her leader had been given nine lives by the Tribe of Endless Hunting, just as the Clan leaders were given nine lives by StarClan, but he had found it hard to believe until now. Outlined in watery light and surrounded by strange points of rock, Stoneteller looked in possession of more power than all the forest cats put together.

At last the leader of the Tribe paused beside one of the biggest pools, and murmured, "We greet you, Tribe of Endless Hunting, and we thank you for your mercy in saving us at last from Sharptooth."

"We thank you," the Tribe cats murmured in response.

Stormfur tensed. Exchanging glances with his friends, he saw his own confusion reflected in their eyes. What did Stoneteller mean? What was Sharptooth, and why did the Tribe need to be saved from it?

"Why is—" Squirrelpaw began, only to be reduced to silence by a hiss from a nearby cave-guard.

Stoneteller went on. "Tribe of Endless Hunting, we thank you for sending the promised cat."

"We thank you," the Tribe cats responded again, their voices growing stronger.

Raising his head, Stoneteller commanded, "Let him stand forth."

Before Stormfur could protest, two of the burly cave-guards thrust him forward. Taken by surprise, he slid side-ways into a puddle, shattering the moonlight into glittering splinters. A gasp of shock rose from the Tribe, and he heard a cat mutter, "An evil omen!"

Fighting to stay calm, he shook the water off his paws and walked forwards until he stood beside Stoneteller in the centre of the pointed stones.

"What are you doing?" he demanded.

Stoneteller raised a paw for silence. His eyes glowed in the moonlight with unconcealed triumph as he murmured, "Do not question. This is your fate."

Glancing around, Stormfur saw that all the Tribe cats were gazing at him with the same expectation in their eyes and a kind of joy, as if he were the most wonderful sight they had ever seen. "It is your fate," they repeated.

He had been right all along. The Tribe had singled him out as special, and now he was going to find out why.

"The time has come," Stoneteller intoned solemnly. "The promised cat is here, and at last we will be saved from Sharptooth."

"I don't understand!" Stormfur burst out. "I've never even heard of Sharptooth."

As if his words had broken a spell, his friends pressed forwards to stand beside him, only to be shoved back again by the cave-guards. Squirrelpaw spat, and both Crowpaw and Tawnypelt flexed their claws on the cold stone, but Brambleclaw held them back with a word of warning. The cave-guards clearly did not want a fight either; they kept their claws sheathed, only shouldering the forest cats into a tight group.

"Sharptooth is a huge cat," Stoneteller began, his voice hushed with fear. "He lives in the mountains, and makes the Tribe his prey. For many seasons now he has been picking us off, one by one."

"He looks like a lion," Crag added, and asked, "Do you know of lions?"

"We have legends of LionClan," Stormfur replied, still wondering what Sharptooth could possibly have to do with him. "Lions are known for their strength and wisdom, and they have a golden mane like the sun's warm rays."

"Sharptooth has no mane," Stoneteller meowed. "Perhaps he lost it because he is so evil. He is the enemy of our Tribe." His voice was bleak, his eyes shining cold with memories. "We feared that he would not rest until every cat of the Tribe had been killed."

"But then the Tribe of Endless Hunting sent us the promised cat." Stormfur's head whipped around as he heard Brook's voice. She had drawn close to him, and was gazing at him, her eyes filled with admiration. "Stormfur, you're the chosen one. You'll save us all. I know you will."

"How can I?" A slow anger had begun to burn inside Stormfur, replacing his bewilderment. "What do you expect me to do?"

"Before the last full moon, the Tribe of Endless Hunting sent a prophecy to us," Stoneteller explained. "They said that a silver cat would save us from Sharptooth. We knew as soon as we saw you by the pool that you must be the cat who was promised to us."

"But I *can't* be," Stormfur protested. "I come from a forest a long way away, and I've never even seen Sharptooth."

"That's true." Brambleclaw padded forward to stand beside Stormfur. "We're sorry that Sharptooth is threatening you, but our Clans at home are in danger too."

"Maybe even worse danger," Feathertail added anxiously.

"We have to go."

Stoneteller flicked his ears. Without a word, the cave-guards surrounded the forest cats and began thrusting them back towards the cave entrance—all except Stormfur, who was surrounded by a separate patrol. Feathertail desperately tried to break through to her brother, but the nearest cave-guard bowled her over with a swipe of his paw.

"Take your paws off her, you piece of fox dung!" Crowpaw spat, hurling himself at the cave-guard and raking his claws over the Tribe cat's ear. The two of them rolled on the ground in a flurry of claws until Brambleclaw hauled Crowpaw away.

"Not now," he commanded the furious apprentice. "It won't help any cat for you to get ripped to shreds."

"We should fight!" snarled Crowpaw. "I'd rather die fighting than be trapped here."

"Just say the word," Tawnypelt hissed at her brother. "I'll tear their pelts off and feed them to the eagles."

"StarClan, help us!" Feathertail cried out as she was forced back to the tunnel entrance. "Show us you haven't abandoned us!"

"Do not fear," Stoneteller meowed reassuringly. "This is the will of the Tribe of Endless Hunting."

Stormfur felt as though he were falling into deep, dark water as he saw his friends shoved away from him, back to the main cave. When he tried to follow, Crag and another cave-guard moved to block his way.

"Over there," Crag meowed, pointing with his tail to the other end of the Cave of Pointed Stones. "You'll find a sleeping hollow ready for you." As Stormfur faced him with burning eyes, Crag added awkwardly, "It won't be so bad. You'll kill Sharptooth for us—the Tribe of Endless Hunting says so—and then you can leave if you still want to."

"Kill Sharptooth!" Stormfur exclaimed, remembering the rank scent and the shadowy shape he had seen at the top of the waterfall. That must have been Sharptooth, prowling close to the cave entrance; no wonder Brook and the rest of the patrol had been so frightened. "How can I do that, if all of you have failed? This is a mouse-brained idea. You're all mad."

"No." That was Stoneteller again, padding up to stand at Stormfur's shoulder. "You must have faith in the Tribe of Endless Hunting. The sign was clear, and you came, just as they promised."

"My faith is in StarClan," Stormfur retorted, trying to hide how scared he felt inside. Had the spirits of his warrior ancestors really abandoned him?

"Go to your sleeping hollow," Stoneteller meowed. "We will bring you fresh-kill. Your coming has been long awaited, and you need have no fear that we will ill-treat you."

No, but you'll keep me prisoner, Stormfur thought desperately. He padded to the back of the cave to find the sleeping hollow Crag had indicated and found it warmly lined with dried grass and feathers. A couple of tail-lengths away was another scoop in the rock, also lined with bedding, where he guessed Stoneteller slept.

Stormfur lapped water from the nearest pool and then lay down with his head on his paws to try to figure out how to escape. But it was hard to think, with the pain of betrayal still throbbing through him. He had really believed that the Tribe cats liked him, without any of the questions that shadowed his RiverClan friendships about his parentage or his loyalty. Instead, they only wanted him to fulfil their prophecy.

A few moments later Brook appeared, a rabbit in her jaws, and set it down timidly in front of him. "I'm sorry," she whispered. "Is it really so bad, to stay with the Tribe? I . . . I want to be your friend, Stormfur, if you will let me." She hesitated, and then added, "I'll stay with you now, if you like. It is our way to groom each other's fur, especially in times of hardship. We call it the giving of close comfort."

She must mean sharing tongues, Stormfur realised. Not long before, he would have been delighted at the thought of sharing tongues with Brook. Now the idea outraged him. Did she really think he would want to be close to her, when she had betrayed him and lied to him?

"Stormfur . . . ?" Brook's eyes shone with compassion, but their glow was like a fire searing Stormfur to the heart. He turned his head away without saying anything.

He heard a faint gasp of pain from Brook, and then her pawsteps vanishing down the tunnel. When she had gone he turned the rabbit over with one paw. He had been hungry at the end of the day's hunting, but now the thought of eating made him feel sick. Still, he forced himself to choke down the fresh-kill, because he knew that whatever happened next, he would need all his strength.

He curled up in the sleeping hollow and lay staring at the

tunnel where his friends had disappeared. Crag and the other cave-guard were on duty at the entrance, and as Stormfur watched, Stoneteller emerged from the shadows and slipped between the guards, back to the main cave. Between them and Stormfur lay pools of shimmering water, lit by the cold moonlight. They reminded Stormfur of the river, but he missed its endless murmuring and the glitter and splash of moving water.

As he closed his eyes and tried to sleep he reflected sadly that he need never have come on this journey at all. He hadn't been chosen by StarClan, had never been summoned by a dream. But right now he would have given anything for the whole adventure to have been a dream, if only he could wake up in the morning to find himself back home in RiverClan.

CHAPTER 13

♣

Leafpaw shifted uneasily in a pool of moonlight and listened to the soft sighing of the wind in the oaks at Fourtrees. She and Cinderpelt were on their way to meet with the other medicine cats at Mothermouth, and already the half-moon was high in the sky.

"They're late," Cinderpelt meowed. "We're wasting moonlight."

Littlecloud, the ShadowClan medicine cat, settled himself more comfortably in a hollow in the grass. "They'll be along soon."

Cinderpelt's tail-tip twitched. "We need all the time we have at the Moonstone, especially tonight. We have to find out what we should do about the Twolegs."

Leafpaw tried to curb her own impatience with the RiverClan medicine cats, who should have met them long before now. Perhaps sharing tongues with StarClan wasn't so important to them, when their own territory hadn't been invaded by the Twoleg monsters. Everything was quiet now; the Twoleg monsters slept at night, but Leafpaw knew they were still there, squatting on the scarred ground among the trees they hadn't destroyed yet. The silence in the forest was unnatural, without the small sounds of prey that always seemed louder at night.

Her belly rumbled at the thought of prey. Cinderpelt had given her travelling herbs to quell her appetite before they set out, but they didn't help her hunger when she couldn't remember the last time she had been full-fed. All the Clan cats were suffering; lack of food had begun to weaken them so that they couldn't run as fast and catch what prey there was. With leaf-bare looming ever closer, crisping the leaves and sending them spiralling to the ground in the chill breeze, Leafpaw couldn't see what help StarClan might give.

To her embarrassment, her belly rumbled again, loud enough for the others to hear. Littlecloud shot her a sympathetic glance.

"Blackstar has sent warriors to fetch rats and crowfood from Carrionplace," he told Cinderpelt. His eyes darkened. "We haven't had any sickness yet, but it's only a matter of time."

"I hope you remember the herbs and berries I gave you when you were ill," Cinderpelt meowed.

"I've been collecting them. I know I'll need them soon."

"And tell your Clan not to touch any crowfood," Cinderpelt advised. "Fresh rats might be OK, but not carrion."

Littlecloud sighed. "I've tried, but what can I do when Blackstar gives the orders? Most of our cats are too hungry to care what they're eating."

Just then Leafpaw caught sight of Mudfur, the RiverClan

medicine cat, and his apprentice, Mothwing, climbing the slope from the river. She leaped to her paws, delighted to see her friend again, though she could not suppress a pang of envy that Mothwing looked so well fed, her long golden fur sleek with good health.

"At last!" Cinderpelt growled as the two cats came up. "I was beginning to think a fish must have jumped out of the river and swallowed you."

"Well, we're here now." Mudfur hardly paused for greetings, but led the way around the top of the hollow towards the WindClan border.

Cinderpelt and Littlecloud followed, while Leafpaw and Mothwing brought up the rear, side by side.

"I got into trouble about that fishing lesson," Leafpaw whispered. "I knew I should not have eaten your prey."

"Your leader's got no right!" Mothwing meowed indignantly. "We're medicine cats."

"Still, we shouldn't have done it," Leafpaw replied. "Medicine cats have to stick to the warrior code as much as any cat."

Mothwing just snorted. "I think I'm getting on really well," she mewed after a moment. "Mudfur taught me the herbs to use for greencough and blackcough, and the best way to get thorns out of pads. He said he'd never seen a cat do it so neatly."

"That's great!" Leafpaw purred. She didn't mind her friend boasting because she knew how insecure Mothwing felt. Because she was the daughter of a rogue, many of her own

Clan thought that she should never have been allowed to train as a medicine cat. Mothwing was desperate to prove them wrong.

As they approached the WindClan border, Leafpaw felt a twinge of nervousness. It was not long since the confrontation with WindClan, and she knew that their warriors would still be hostile. They seemed determined to keep their starvation a secret, even though it was horribly obvious from their scrawny frames and dull eyes. Would they be desperate enough to attack medicine cats if they found them on their territory? She said nothing; Firestar would be furious if she gossiped with Mothwing about that fateful encounter.

None of the medicine cats paused as they crossed the border. They hurried on, their pace set by Cinderpelt's limping gait. Coming to the top of a gentle rise, Leafpaw found herself looking down on the worst scene yet of Twoleg devastation. The scar on WindClan's territory was much longer and wider now than when she and Sorreltail had first seen it. A couple of Twoleg monsters squatted there, moonlight glinting off their shiny pelts. If a hill got in their way they just gorged a path through it, leaving earth piled high on either side. Were they going to devour the whole moor?

Shuddering, Leafpaw bounded on behind her mentor. Not far from the WindClan camp, Barkface, the WindClan medicine cat, emerged from behind a gorse bush. Even though Leafpaw had been prepared for him to look hungry, it was a shock to see how thin he was—barely more than a walking skeleton covered by his ragged pelt.

Cinderpelt went up and touched noses with him sympathetically. "StarClan be with you, Barkface," she mewed.

"And with all my Clan." Barkface heaved a great sigh. "Sometimes I think StarClan wants every one of us to join them, and not even a kit left to keep the warrior code alive."

"Perhaps they will show us what to do when we share dreams at the Moonstone," Cinderpelt tried to encourage him.

"It's getting worse for WindClan." Mothwing's amber eyes were wide as she murmured the words to Leafpaw. "They've been stealing fish from the river again, you know. Hawkfrost caught a couple of them, and chased them off."

"They have to find prey somewhere." Leafpaw knew that what the WindClan warriors were doing was wrong, but she couldn't blame them. Not when the river was full of fish, enough to feed all the Clans. Fleetingly, she realised that Firestar was right—the Twolegs were destroying the forest, but in doing so they were also destroying the invisible boundaries between the Clans as well. Maybe the cats would survive only by joining together after all.

Mothwing paused to scent the air. "Hang on, I can smell rabbit—at least, I think it's rabbit; it smells funny somehow. Yes, look, over there!"

She gestured with her tail at a dip in the moorland where a small stream chattered over stones. Lying beside it was a small, brown-furred body.

"It's dead," Leafpaw pointed out.

Mothwing shrugged. "So it's crowfood. I imagine

WindClan can't afford to be too fussy. Hey, Barkface!" she called. "Look what I found." She bounded down the slope towards the rabbit.

"Stop!" Barkface commanded. "Don't touch it!"

Mothwing skidded to a halt beside the limp bundle of fur and looked back up the slope. "What's the matter?"

Barkface padded down to join her, followed by Leafpaw and the other medicine cats. Warily he approached the rabbit and sniffed it. Leafpaw sniffed too, and recognised the harsh tang she had picked up when she and Sorreltail had visited WindClan territory. Her stomach churned and she swallowed to stop herself from gagging. Whatever had happened to this rabbit, it wasn't fit for food.

"Yes, I thought so," Barkface murmured, his eyes clouding. "There's that scent again. . ." Facing the other cats, he explained quietly, "Twolegs have done something bad to the rabbits in the territory. They all die. And if cats eat them, they die too. We have lost half our elders and nearly all of our apprentices."

There was a horrified silence. Compassion lanced through Leafpaw. Tallstar had said nothing of this when he confronted Firestar; the proud WindClan leader would rather let other Clans think his cats could not catch prey in their territory, than that their own fresh-kill was killing them, one by one.

"And you couldn't help them?" Mudfur asked.

"Do you think I didn't try?" Barkface sounded desperate. "I gave them yarrow to make them sick, just as we do for deathberries. Two of the strongest pulled through, but most of them died." His claws tore up the grass in front of him; his eyes burned with grief and frustration. "What hope is there for us when even our prey can kill us?"

Cinderpelt limped up to him and pressed her muzzle against his side. "Let's go on," she murmured. "We'll ask StarClan for guidance about this as well as everything else."

"Shouldn't we bury the rabbit?" Leafpaw suggested as the cats began to climb the slope again. "In case some other cat finds it?"

Barkface shook his head. "There's no point. No WindClan cat would touch it now." His lips stretched in a wry snarl. "We know better than to trust fresh-kill from inside our own borders." Head bowed, tail drooping, he plodded on across the moor toward Highstones.

Leafpaw blinked in the silver light from the Moonstone, letting it soothe her until she felt like a fish sinking into deep water. Here in the cavern, far below Highstones, it was easy to believe that StarClan ruled everything, and the troubles of the world above were too far away to matter. But medicine cats came to the Moonstone only so that they could learn the wisdom of StarClan and take it back to help their Clans. In these dark days, they needed that wisdom more than ever.

The other medicine cats were lying with her around the stone. Mothwing was next to her; the RiverClan cat's eyes were wide with wonder as she gazed at the shimmering crystal surface. Trying to focus her thoughts, Leafpaw pushed away the questions that nagged her about Mothwing and her aggressive brother, Hawkfrost. Mothwing had a right to be here; StarClan themselves had approved her with a moth's wing left at the entrance to Mudfur's den before she had finally been accepted as a medicine cat apprentice.

With a quick plea to StarClan for guidance, Leafpaw closed her eyes and pressed her nose against the stone. Cold instantly seized her like a claw, the hard surface of the cave floor vanished from beneath her, and she felt as though she were floating in darkness.

Squirrelpaw! Squirrelpaw, can you hear me? she called silently. She was desperate to make sure that her sister was still alive and safe, and more than that: If the chosen cats had discovered the answer to the trouble that had come upon the forest, then seeking out Squirrelpaw might give her some hope that she could share with the others.

But tonight something seemed to be blocking her thoughts. The silence was broken by the sound of rushing water, loud as thunder, and then the darkness shifted to show her a waterfall, crashing endlessly down into a pool below. Before Leafpaw could properly understand what she was seeing, clouds swirled over it. Out of them came a terrible snarling, and she caught a glimpse of sharp fangs. She sensed the presence of warrior ancestors and reached out for the comforting presence of StarClan. But she caught only a flickering vision of lean, prowling cats, their fur streaked with mud and blood. Their eyes glared with desperation, as if they stared at some terrible sight that was hidden from Leafpaw.

She thought she cried out to them, but they did not answer, and she was not even sure that they were aware of her.

A wind howled around her, sweeping all the visions away, and Leafpaw woke up with a jolt. She blinked in confusion, staring around the cavern that was dark now except for the faint glitter of Silverpelt. In the dim light she could just make out a cat crouched beside her, a beautiful tortoiseshell with a white chest and white paws. The sweet scent of herbs clung about her fur.

For a heartbeat Leafpaw mistook the cat for Sorreltail, until she remembered that her friend was back in the ThunderClan camp. And where were Mothwing and the medicine cats? Leafpaw realised that except for herself and the strange tortoiseshell, the cavern was empty.

The tortoiseshell cat opened her eyes and turned to blink at Leafpaw. "Greetings," she mewed softly. "Do not be anxious for your sister or your Clan. A time of great trouble has come, but the Clans are strong and have the courage to meet it."

Leafpaw froze. She had woken up in another dream. Her eyes widened as she realised who the tortoiseshell cat must be. She had heard many stories of the medicine cat who had befriended her father when he first came to ThunderClan, and guided him in dreams on his path to becoming leader.

"Are you . . . are you Spottedleaf?" she meowed.

The tortoiseshell cat bowed her head. "I am. I see that Firestar has told you about me."

"Yes." Leafpaw stared curiously at the she-cat. "He told me how much you helped him."

"I loved him as well as any cat," Spottedleaf purred. "Maybe even more than I should have done, as a medicine cat. If StarClan had not chosen me to walk their path, things might have been different." Her eyes narrowed with affection. "I never had kits of my own, Leafpaw, but I cannot say how happy it makes me that Firestar's daughter will be following the path of a medicine cat. I know that StarClan has great things in store for you."

Leafpaw swallowed. "May I ask you something?" she meowed hesitantly.

"Of course."

"Can you see Squirrelpaw? Is she all right?"

There was a long pause. "I cannot see her," Spottedleaf replied at last, "but I know where she is. She is safe, and on her way home to you."

"Why can't you see her, if you know where she is?" Leafpaw challenged.

Spottedleaf's gaze shone with gentleness and compassion. "Squirrelpaw is in the paws of different warrior ancestors now."

"What do you mean?" Leafpaw remembered the fearsome, blood-streaked cats she had sensed when she tried to make contact with Squirrelpaw. In her dream, her eyes flew wide and she sprang to her paws. "Whose warrior ancestors are these? There can't be more than one StarClan!"

Spottedleaf laughed softly. "The world is wide, dear young one. There are other cats who are guided by other spirits. There is always more to learn."

Leafpaw's head whirled. She stammered, "I thought—"

"StarClan does not control the wind or the rain, do they?" Spottedleaf prompted gently. "They do not command the sun to rise or the moon to wax and wane. Do not fear, little one," she went on. "From now on, wherever you walk, I will walk with you. . ."

Her voice began to fade; her fur paled and her shape seemed to melt into the darkness. For a heartbeat longer, Leafpaw could see her white front shining like a star and her glowing eyes. Then she was blinking awake, emerging from her dream into the cavern where Mothwing and the medicine cats were stirring around her.

Is it true? she wondered, too dazed to speak out loud. *Are Squirrelpaw and the others in the paws of another Clan? And are there really powers other than StarClan's—and does that mean that StarClan won't be able to save the forest after all?*

As she staggered to her paws, she could still catch a trace of Spottedleaf's sweet scent.

CHAPTER 14

❦

Feathertail gazed back helplessly at the tunnel entrance as the cave-guards thrust her out of the tunnel and back into the main cave. She felt unseen claws tearing into her heart with every step she took away from her brother.

What did Stoneteller mean, that Stormfur was the promised cat who would save the Tribe from Sharptooth? True, her brother was a strong and brave warrior, more skilled at fighting than any of the other cats on this journey. But if Sharptooth was as huge and terrible as the Tribe cats said, what could even the bravest warrior do?

"Please," she meowed to one of the cave-guards, a huge mud-coloured tabby whose name was Scree Beneath Winter Sky, "you *can't* keep Stormfur here. He belongs with us."

There was sympathy in the Tribe cat's eyes, but he still shook his head. "No. He is the cat sent here by the Tribe of Endless Hunting. They told us a silver cat would come."

"But—"

"Don't try to argue with them," Crowpaw growled into Feathertail's ear. "There's no point. If we have to fight to get Stormfur out, then that's what we'll do."

Feathertail looked at the WindClan cat's bristling fur and the fierce courage in his eyes. "We can't," she mewed sorrowfully. "There are too many of them."

"I don't see why the Tribe is so worried about Sharptooth." Crowpaw's voice was scornful. "We haven't seen a whisker of him since we arrived, so what's the big deal?"

"Be thankful you haven't seen him," Scree meowed.

Crowpaw bared his teeth, but this time he didn't spring at the guard, just turned away and touched his nose to Feathertail's muzzle. He would have fought the whole of StarClan for her, Feathertail knew that, but he had to see that this time fighting would do no good.

The cave-guards herded the Clan cats across the cave until they reached their sleeping hollows.

"What's going on?" Brambleclaw mewed in surprise. "Aren't you throwing us out?"

"Into the night?" The mud-coloured guard sounded indignant. "We're not cruel. It's cold out there and dangerous. You can eat and rest here, and leave in the morning."

"With Stormfur?" Tawnypelt challenged.

Scree shook his head. "No. I'm sorry."

The cave-guards left them, except for Scree and another who remained on watch a few tail-lengths away. A couple of to-bes trotted over with fresh-kill in their jaws.

"Isn't it great?" the first of them mewed excitedly, dropping the prey he carried. "No more Sharptooth!"

"Shut up, beetle-brain," growled his friend, giving him a sharp prod in the flank. "You know Crag told us not to talk to them."

They retreated quickly, glancing around to make sure no cat had spotted them disobeying orders.

"I'm not eating that!" Crowpaw spat, glaring at the small pile of fresh-kill. "I don't want anything from the Tribe."

"Great StarClan!" Tawnypelt let out a noisy sigh. "How's that going to help, you stupid furball? You need your strength twice as much now—to save the forest and to save Stormfur."

Crowpaw muttered something inaudible, but made no other protest as he dragged a falcon out of the heap.

"Well?" Squirrelpaw demanded when they had divided the rest of the fresh-kill and were crouched close together to eat. "We're not putting up with this, are we? What are we going to do?"

"There's not very much we can do," Brambleclaw pointed out. "There aren't enough of us to fight the cave-guards."

"You're not going to leave him?" Squirrelpaw's green eyes were wide with disbelief.

Brambleclaw paused; Feathertail could see an agony of indecision in his expression. She began to shiver. Since they left the forest she had come to respect the young warrior's skills as the unelected leader of their group; if he could not see what to do, then what hope was there for Stormfur?

"We should never have come into these mountains," growled Tawnypelt. "It's a hundred times worse than Twolegplace. Midnight mentioned cats in a Tribe, so she must have known about Sharptooth. Why did she send us this way?"

"It must have been a trick all along," Crowpaw hissed. "I

knew we should never have trusted that badger."

"But why would she trick us?" Brambleclaw objected. "StarClan sent us to her, and she warned us about the Twolegs destroying the forest. If we can't trust her, then nothing makes sense."

Feathertail wanted to agree with him, but she suddenly remembered something Purdy had said, when they were discussing which way to go at the edge of the wood. "Purdy tried to tell us not to come through the mountains," she meowed out loud. "And Midnight wouldn't let him speak. You're right. They both *knew*."

She looked around and saw her alarm reflected in the faces of her friends.

"Midnight said we would need courage," Brambleclaw reminded her after a heavy pause. "She said our path was laid out for us. So even if she knew about the Tribe and Sharptooth, there must be a way we can get through this. That makes me think that we must still be following the right path."

"So *you* say," Crowpaw sneered. "I don't suppose it matters to a ThunderClan warrior if a cat from RiverClan gets left behind."

"And what does it matter to WindClan?" Squirrelpaw fired up in defense of her Clanmate. "I'd have thought you'd be delighted if Feathertail's brother weren't here to keep an eye on you."

Crowpaw sprang to his paws, hissing a challenge. Squirrelpaw's green eyes blazed. Horrified, Feathertail forced herself to get up and shoulder Crowpaw away.

"Stop it!" she cried. "Can't you see you're making it worse?"

"Feathertail's right," meowed Tawnypelt. "What Clan we come from doesn't matter here. Four of us are half-Clan anyway—have you ever thought StarClan might have chosen us *because* of that? If we quarrel among ourselves, then we'll lose everything."

Squirrelpaw's gaze seared into Crowpaw for a moment longer before she stepped back and began to tear mouthfuls off a rabbit. Crowpaw looked into Feathertail's eyes and then ducked his head and muttered, "Sorry."

"So maybe we can discuss what to do without ripping one another's fur off?" Tawnypelt meowed tartly. When no cat answered, she went on, "Don't forget that StarClan didn't choose Stormfur in the first place. He's only here because he wouldn't let Feathertail come on this mission alone." She paused; her eyes grew troubled as she added, "What . . . what if the Tribe cats are right and he *is* the promised cat who's going to save them from Sharptooth?"

"That's mouse-brained!" Crowpaw exclaimed.

Feathertail was not so sure. Tawnypelt had put words to the fear that she had also felt squirming inside her ever since Stoneteller had first told them about the prophecy. Sure, Stormfur's fur wasn't what she would call silver—it was darker than that, more like Greystripe's—but he had come into the world of the Tribe cats just as their warrior ancestors had promised.

"Does that mean . . ." Her voice shook and she had to start

again. "Does that mean we're going to leave him here?"

"No, it doesn't." Brambleclaw sounded determined. "These are not our warrior ancestors. StarClan has nothing to do with this Tribe. But we can't get him out by fighting, so we'll have to do it another way. In the morning, when they tell us to leave, we'll go without trouble. Then we'll come sneak back and rescue Stormfur."

The cats were silent for a moment, glancing at one another as if they were weighing the idea. Feathertail began to feel the first faint stirrings of hope. Then she noticed that the cave-guards were watching them suspiciously; had they overheard? She flicked her ears, and the Clan cats, following her gaze, huddled more closely together.

Crowpaw spoke softly. "That's easy to say." He sounded doubtful, but he wasn't sneering anymore. "We'd still have to get into that inner cave, and the whole place is crawling with cave-guards."

"We could wait until it's dark," Tawnypelt suggested.

"And the noise of the waterfall will hide our pawsteps," Squirrelpaw added optimistically.

Crowpaw still looked uncertain. "I'm not sure—haven't you noticed the Tribe cats are so used to it that they can hear a kit squeak at the other end of the cave?"

Feathertail knew he was right. She looked around, wondering if the darkness or the crashing of the torrent would help them at all. Moonlight rippled into the cave through the sheet of thundering water, but shadows fell thickly around the walls. Perhaps it would be possible. But however hard it seemed, they had to try. Stormfur was her *brother*.

"I'm willing to give it a try," she announced. "You can leave me behind if you want."

"Well, I for one—" Crowpaw began.

"Don't try to stop me," Feathertail interrupted. "I know we have to get StarClan's message to the Clans before they're destroyed along with the forest, but they don't need all of us. I can stay here."

"Who said I was going to try to stop you?" Crowpaw demanded indignantly, his neck fur bristling. "I was going to say I'll help, but if you don't want me . . ."

"Don't be mouse-brained." Feathertail gave his ear a quick lick. "I'm sorry I misunderstood. Of course I want you with me."

"I don't think we should split up." Brambleclaw's eyes narrowed thoughtfully. "It's all of us or none. We came on this journey together and we'll finish it together—and that means Stormfur as well." More briskly he added, "Let's finish eating and get some sleep. We'll need all our strength."

Feathertail tried to obey him, forcing down the young hawk that the to-be had left for her, though she felt sick with apprehension. She tried to focus her thoughts on how loyal her friends from the other Clans were. It was hard to imagine that they would ever be able to separate back into their different Clans when they returned to the forest. How would she ever go back to her regular life without them?

She curled into her sleeping hollow, tired enough to sleep, then sat up again. *What was that?* She turned her head to one side and listened. She could hear voices whispering but there were no cats nearby, except for the Clan cats, and they were all asleep. Twitching her ears, Feathertail froze. The voices were coming from the *waterfall*, almost hidden among the rushing, hissing water. She strained to make out what they were saying.

The silver cat has come, they seemed to whisper. *Sharptooth will be destroyed.*

No, Feathertail argued silently, instinctively. She didn't stop to figure out who she was talking to. *You're wrong. Stormfur is not your cat. He must come with us.*

She waited for a reply, but the voices had vanished into the roar of the water, and Feathertail began to wonder if she had even heard them at all. A long time passed; moonlight crept across the floor of the cave and faded before exhaustion overcame her and she finally fell into a troubled sleep.

A paw roughly shaking her shoulder woke Feathertail, and she looked up into the stern face of Crag. "It's time to go," he announced.

Other guards were rousing her friends. As she stumbled drowsily out of her sleeping hollow, she saw Stoneteller standing at the entrance to the tunnel that led to the Cave of Pointed Stones. Two more cave-guards stood alertly beside him, and Feathertail thought she could make out more in the tunnel itself; the Tribe cats were making sure that Stormfur was too heavily guarded for any sort of rescue attempt.

"We will take you to the edge of our territory and show you

the best way through the rest of the mountains," Crag meowed.

"What about Stormfur?" Brambleclaw asked, shaking a feather from his pelt. "We can't go without him."

The ThunderClan warrior's last attempt to free his friend peacefully was doomed to failure; Crag was shaking his head before he finished speaking. "You can't take him with you," he meowed. "His destiny is to stay here and save our Tribe from Sharptooth. We will care for him and honour him."

"So that makes it all right, then?" Crowpaw muttered disgustedly.

The cave-guards gathered around the Clan cats and forced them towards the entrance. Feathertail noticed that Crowpaw was still limping from the blow he had taken from the cave-guard the night before.

"Are you OK to travel?" she murmured in his ear.

"I don't have much choice, have I?" he meowed disagreeably, only to turn to her a moment later and touch his nose to her muzzle. "Don't worry; I'll be fine."

Just before they reached the waterfall, Feathertail heard her name, and turned to see Brook bounding toward her.

"I . . . I wanted to say farewell," she mewed as she came up. "I'm sorry it turned out like this. But without your brother, Sharptooth will destroy the whole Tribe."

Feathertail gazed into the young prey-hunter's eyes. She knew Brook believed what she was saying, but she couldn't forget how Stormfur had thought that this cat was his friend. Stormfur didn't make friends easily—a legacy of being half-

Clan, always feeling as if he had more to prove than other warriors, as if he could never fight hard enough or catch enough prey. Feathertail had watched this she-cat win her brother's trust, but now she had betrayed him, and would probably see him die in a battle with Sharptooth for the sake of her Tribe.

"Come on." Crowpaw brushed his tail against Feathertail's flank, already damp from the spray of the waterfall. Feathertail turned away from Brook without another word. As she padded along the narrow path, she strained to hear the voices in the thundering water, but today she heard only the ceaseless pounding of foam.

Whoever you are, she vowed silently, *we will come back for my brother. He is ours, and his destiny lies far away from here.*

The forest cats travelled through the mountains until almost sunhigh. The cave-guards kept pace with them on either side, their gaze fixed on the path ahead. They did not even stop to hunt, and the tense silence made every hair tingle on Feathertail's pelt.

She tried to study every rock, every tree, every twist in the path, hoping that they would be able to follow their own scent trail back to the cave. The rocky slopes were more familiar to her now, but all the paths still looked the same. In contrast, the cave-guards seemed to know exactly where they were going, sometimes doubling back to avoid boulders or cliffs.

Once Crag led them down a slope of shifting scree to a mountain stream. "Drink," he ordered, flicking his tail at the tumbling water.

Crowpaw's eyes narrowed as he gazed at the slippery rocks by the waterside, and Tawnypelt exchanged a suspicious glance with her brother.

"We're not going to push you in," Crag mewed irritably. "You must learn to drink when you can in the mountains."

Still wary, the forest cats crouched down and lapped the icy water.

The air was crisp and cold, with the sun shining in a pale blue sky. Wind ruffled their fur, but there was no sign of rain to wash away the scent trail. To Feathertail's relief, Crowpaw's limp didn't seem to be bothering him, and grew less apparent as the young cat exercised his injured leg. Tawnypelt was also managing well; although Feathertail saw her flinch once or twice when she had to cope with a difficult leap, she did not complain.

After a scramble over steep rocks, Crag brought them to a halt.

"This is the edge of our territory," he announced, though there were no scent markers to indicate a border. "You must go on alone from here."

Relief stabbed through Feathertail. She couldn't wait to get away from the cave-guards and their stern, silent looks.

"Head for that mountain," Crag went on, pointing with his tail at a sharp peak, its upper slopes streaked with the white of snow. "A path winds round it to greener lands beyond. You should be safe from Sharptooth until night falls."

Feathertail thought he put too much stress on *Sharptooth*, as if there were other dangers lurking among the rocks. Her suspicions hardened when she saw one of the other guards give him a warning glance. "Go on," the Tribe cat meowed roughly, giving her no chance to ask any questions, "while there's still plenty of daylight."

He dipped his head to Brambleclaw. "Farewell," he meowed. "I wish we could have met in a happier time. Our Tribes have much to teach each other."

"There's nothing I want to learn from *you*," Squirrelpaw muttered, and for once Crowpaw looked as if he agreed with her.

"I wish that too." Brambleclaw shot an icy glance at his companions to silence them. "But there cannot be friendship between us while you keep our friend a prisoner."

Crag bowed his head again; he looked genuinely regretful. "That is our fate and his, as our warrior ancestors have promised. Just as yours have made a promise to you."

He called the rest of his patrol around him with a flick of his tail, and all the cave-guards waited while Brambleclaw led the Clan cats up a grassy slope. Soon the grass gave way to loose stones, leading upwards to a ridge of spiky rock.

Brambleclaw paused at the top. Feathertail glanced back to see that Crag and the other cave-guards were still watching them with unblinking stares.

"They're making sure we leave," Tawnypelt growled. "That means they'll probably be looking out in case we come back."

Crowpaw shrugged. "Their loss." He flexed his claws against the bare rock. "If we meet a patrol out here, they're crowfood."

Brambleclaw flashed him a glance. "We'll do this *without* fighting, if we can," he mewed. "Remember that we can't afford injuries this far from home. Meanwhile," he added, "let's keep going, and make them think we've given up."

He led the way between the rocks. On the other side the land fell away sharply into a grassy hollow. A spring of water bubbled out of a crevice and fell into a small pool. Two or three bushes grew beside it. The wind brought Feathertail the scent of rabbits.

"Can't we stop here?" Squirrelpaw pleaded. "Remember what they said about drinking when we can? We could hunt, and rest until it's time to go back."

Brambleclaw hesitated. "OK. But we'd better keep watch in case the cave-guards come to check on us."

"I'll take first watch," Tawnypelt offered. "My shoulder's fine," she added. "And I'll call you if there's any trouble."

Very cautiously, stepping as lightly as if she were stalking a mouse, she slid back between the rocks and disappeared. Squirrelpaw was already bounding down into the hollow, calling out, "Come on! I'm starving!"

"She'll frighten every scrap of prey from here to Highstones," Crowpaw grumbled as Brambleclaw took off after her.

Feathertail watched as Brambleclaw caught up to the younger cat, and the two of them went on together, their pelts brushing. They had become very close during the journey, even if they didn't quite realise it yet.

"Don't mind Squirrelpaw," she told Crowpaw. "Let's go and

see if there are any fish in that pool. I could give you a lesson, just in case you want to catch any fish when we get
home." She broke off and looked awkwardly down at the
ground. "It'll be a useful thing to know, whatever happens."

Crowpaw brightened. "OK." He paused as if he wanted to
say something more, then without a word bounded down the
slope after the two ThunderClan cats. Feathertail followed,
her mind buzzing with her feelings for Crowpaw as well as her
fears for her brother. She approached the pool and gazed
down into its blue depths. She and Crowpaw had plenty of
time to figure out what they would do when they got back
to the forest. She tried to push away the tiny, persistent voice
that kept telling her that cats from different Clans couldn't
be together without causing a whole heap of trouble. She
shook her head impatiently; right now, the only thing any of
them should be thinking about was finding prey to give them
strength for Stormfur's rescue.

A silver flash caught her eye and her paw shot out, claws
extended, to hook a fish.

"Come over here," she instructed Crowpaw, "so your
shadow doesn't fall on the water. And when you see a fish, be
quick!"

Crowpaw came to join her, picking his way with a grimace
around the muddy edge of the pool. He settled down at her
side, but instead of peering into the water he looked into her
eyes. "I know I shouldn't ask this, but . . . will you still see me
when we get home?" He glanced down at his paws and added,
"I want to be loyal to my Clan, but . . . there's never been

another cat like you, Feathertail."

Feathertail's pelt tingled with happiness and excitement. She touched his muzzle with her nose, sensing the uncertainty that made it hard for him to believe that she could like him enough to cross Clan boundaries for him. "I know how you feel. We'll have to wait and see. It might not be so bad. With everything that's happening in the forest, the Clans will *have* to come together."

To her surprise, Crowpaw shook his head. "I don't see how. There have *always* been four Clans."

"Well, maybe *always* is going to change," she meowed quietly. "Now, what about that fish?"

Crowpaw brushed her shoulder with his tail, and crouched down over the water. A few heartbeats later his paw shot out. A fish curved up out of the water and fell wriggling on the ground; Crowpaw grabbed it in his jaws before it could slide back into the pool.

Feathertail jumped up and pushed her nose against his shoulder. "Well done! We'll make a RiverClan cat of you yet." She broke off, confused, and Crowpaw blinked in understanding.

His eyes were shining; Feathertail wished their companions could see this side of him, eager and enthusiastic, instead of the defensive, difficult face he chose to show to them.

She was distracted by a movement at the top of the rocks and looked up to see Tawnypelt crouched on the smooth stone.

"The cave-guards have gone," the ShadowClan warrior

called down to them. "But I'll stay on watch."

Not long after, Brambleclaw and Squirrelpaw returned from their hunting expedition with a couple of rabbits and a few mice; along with Feathertail's and Crowpaw's fish there was enough fresh-kill for all of them.

They each took a turn on watch, but there was no sign of any Tribe cats. They spent the rest of the day in the shelter of the bushes. Feathertail felt more at home out here, in the silent open air, than in the stuffy, noise-filled cave.

Clouds gathered in the sky, grey and ominous, covering the sun. The wind dropped; the air became heavy and damp, as if there were a storm coming.

At last the daylight faded and shadows began to thicken in the hollow.

Brambleclaw rose to his paws. "It's time," he meowed.

He took a few pawsteps back up the slope; as the others followed, Feathertail suddenly noticed how easily they could be seen against the rocks, especially Squirrelpaw's dark ginger pelt and her own light grey fur.

"This is never going to work. They're bound to spot us coming," she mewed anxiously.

"Wait." Squirrelpaw narrowed her eyes. "Why don't we roll ourselves in the mud? Then we'd look like Tribe cats, especially in the dark. It would help to hide our scent too."

Tawnypelt gave her a look full of respect. "That has to be the best idea I've heard for a moon."

Squirrelpaw's green eyes glowed, and she hurried back to the pool and began nosing around the edge. "There's plenty of mud here!" she called, beginning to roll in a sticky patch to plaster her fur.

Crowpaw's whiskers twitched in disgust as he and the others followed. "Just the sort of idea *she* would dream up. Clever, though," he admitted grudgingly.

Feathertail winced as she padded to the edge of the pool and felt mud ooze around her paws. Cold seeped through to her skin as she lay down in the glutinous hollow, thinking that at least her thick RiverClan pelt was suited to getting wet. Crowpaw would be much more uncomfortable with his thin, wind-flattened fur, although for once he didn't complain. She blinked fondly at him, remembering what he'd said earlier about wanting to see her when they got home. Right now, she didn't want to ever let him out of her sight.

Their pelts streaked and spiky with the mud, the Clan cats climbed back to the ridge and down the slope on the other side, warily crossing back into the Tribe's territory. Feathertail pricked her ears, alert for the sound of other cats, and they all stopped every few paces to sniff the air. Even with Squirrelpaw's disguise, there was a huge risk that they would be spotted, and no cat was sure how far the Tribe cats would go to keep Stormfur. Feathertail knew how desperate they were that their ancestors' prophecy should come true. She and her friends could all be returning to their deaths.

Brambleclaw's nose was almost touching the path as he sniffed out their scent trail from that morning. Feathertail tried hard to remember the landmarks they had passed, but everything looked different in the gathering darkness. They were padding down a steep path between broken rocks when Crowpaw suddenly halted, his muzzle raised and his jaws parted. Then he whirled on Feathertail and pushed her behind a rock, signalling wildly with his tail for the other cats to hide too.

A heartbeat later, Feathertail caught the same scent: Tribe cats! Peering out cautiously, she saw a patrol of lithe prey-hunters bounding along the path in the same direction, their jaws filled with prey, their escort of cave-guards around them. She tensed, waiting for them to pick up the intruders' scent and turn to attack, but they passed her hiding place without pause and disappeared into the darkness. Squirrelpaw's mud must have masked their scent, as they'd hoped.

"That's twice I saved you," Crowpaw teased, stepping away to let Feathertail stand up straight.

She touched noses with him with a purr of amusement. "I know. I won't forget it; don't worry."

Brambleclaw emerged from among the rocks at the other side of the path, signalling to the others to move on. This time Tawnypelt brought up the rear, keeping a lookout behind in case more prey-hunters were on their way home. The moon was just rising over the topmost peaks, a fuzzy white glow behind the covering of clouds, when they came to the river. Still alert for the sound of other Tribe cats, they followed the rushing water until they heard the roar of the waterfall in the distance.

"Quiet now," Brambleclaw whispered. "We're getting close."

Silently they padded on until they reached the top of the

falls. Feathertail crouched at the edge of the river, watching the dark water slide over the lip of the rock. Then a flash of lightning split the sky overhead, and above the thunder of the water she heard a rumbling in the sky.

"Storm's coming," Crowpaw breathed into her ear.

A fat drop of rain landed on Feathertail's head, and she shook it off. The noise and confusion of a storm might help them, but then she wondered if it would drive more cats than usual into the cave. Stormfur was heavily guarded already—they couldn't hope to take on the whole of the Tribe.

"Let's *go*," Squirrelpaw muttered impatiently.

Lightning flashed and another roll of thunder crashed overhead as the cats peered down. Feathertail could just make out the foaming white of the water as it fell into the pool. Then she thought she saw a movement in the darkness at the end of the path.

"What's that?" Crowpaw had seen it too.

As if in answer, another claw of lightning crackled across the sky. Feathertail heard Tawnypelt gasp in horror. For a single heartbeat that seemed to last forever, the white flash lit up the shape of a huge tawny-coloured cat slinking along the path; it paused as the thunder pounded the sky, then padded on to disappear behind the waterfall.

Sharptooth!

CHAPTER 15

A terrible shrieking broke out in the cave, slicing through the sound of the rain pattering around them and even the noise of the falls. Feathertail sprang to her paws; every hair on her pelt told her to flee as far from the cave as she could. Only the thought of the danger that Stormfur was in made her stay where she was.

"Come on!" Brambleclaw's voice was tense.

The rest of the cats stared at him in disbelief.

"Down there?" Crowpaw demanded. "Are you mouse-brained?"

"Think!" Brambleclaw was already bounding towards the cave entrance; he paused and swung around to face the apprentice. "With Sharptooth in the cave, no cat will notice us. This might be our only chance to get Stormfur out."

Without waiting to see if the others were following he leaped down the rocks towards the path.

"I still think he's crazy!" muttered Crowpaw, but he followed all the same.

Feathertail scrambled down after them, her paws sliding on the wet rocks, her claws scraping painfully as she tried to keep her balance. She ran along the ledge behind the falls with barely enough time to be afraid of slipping and falling into the turbulent pool below. The screeching grew louder. Terror surged through Feathertail as she imagined what they would find inside the cave; Sharptooth might be sinking his fangs into Stormfur's neck at that very moment, clawing her brother's pelt and turning him into fresh-kill.

She skidded into the cave and halted just behind Brambleclaw. For a moment she could hardly make sense of what she was seeing. With the moon covered by clouds, the cave was almost dark; the huge shape of Sharptooth seemed to be everywhere at once, massive paws pounding on the floor as he sprang from wall to wall, blood spattered against his flanks and saliva dripping from his jaws. This was more terrible than Feathertail had ever imagined—there was no way Stormfur could challenge this beast and survive.

The Tribe cats scattered, scrambling blindly out of their sleeping hollows. Feathertail caught a glimpse of Brook, hustling a kit down the tunnel that led to the nursery, with another dangling from her jaws. Near the other tunnel, a cave-guard was clinging to the huge lion-cat's neck, only to be thrown off and flung against the wall with a sickening thud. The cave-guard slid to the floor and lay still, a trickle of blood running from its mouth. While Feathertail stared in horror, two or three cats fled past her with shrill cries, blundering against the Clan cats without realising who they were.

"This way!" Brambleclaw ordered. He looked at each Clan cat in turn, his gaze resting longest on Squirrelpaw. "We have to do this for Stormfur," he reminded them.

Sharptooth had pounded across to leap up the far wall of the cave, trying to reach a Tribe cat who cowered on a ledge just above the vicious claws. Skirting the cave walls, clinging to the darkest corners, Brambleclaw headed for the tunnel leading to the Cave of Pointed Stones. Feathertail and the others followed. In the blackness they stumbled against Tribe cats, some wounded, others frozen in fear, but the terror and blood-scent filling the cave were so strong that no cat recognised them.

At the tunnel entrance, two cave-guards still held their positions, their fur standing on end and their eyes stretched wide. Feathertail felt a flash of respect for their courage, to stay there when all their Tribemates were running for their lives.

"Now!" Brambleclaw and Crowpaw launched themselves at the cave-guards, their claws slashing and their teeth bared. Squirrelpaw was only a heartbeat behind them. Feathertail heard an exclamation of astonishment from one of the guards, and recognised Crag's voice. She saw Brambleclaw bowl him over and fasten his teeth in the cave-guard's neck fur, while Crowpaw cuffed the other guard on both ears, drawing him away from the tunnel entrance. Squirrelpaw sank her teeth into Crag's tail and held on.

With the entrance clear, Feathertail and Tawnypelt darted down the tunnel. Before they reached the Cave of Pointed Stones they met two other cats, barely visible in the darkness. With a surge of relief and joy Feathertail recognised Stormfur's scent. The other cat was Stoneteller; she glimpsed his blazing eyes as he pelted past her and launched himself into the outer cave.

"Quick!" the Tribe leader yowled to Stormfur. "Your time has come. Oh, Tribe of Endless Hunting, help us now!"

"Feathertail!" Stormfur exclaimed. "What's happening?"

For a moment Feathertail was content just to drink in his scent and twine her tail with his. She had been afraid they'd find the Cave of Pointed Stones empty, that Stormfur would have already been sent out to do battle with the lion-cat, and that his body had been one of those bleeding in the corners of the cave.

"There's no time for that!" Tawnypelt snapped. "Head for the entrance. Don't stop for anything."

She dashed back down the tunnel, and Feathertail and Stormfur followed. As they reached the outer cave, a shriek ripped through the darkness, louder than thunder. A flash of lightning revealed Sharptooth backing towards the entrance. His jaws were clamped around a Tribe cat; with a shudder of pure horror Feathertail recognised Star, the kit-mother who had spoken to them when they first arrived. Her mouth was open in a desperate wordless yowl, and her claws scored the earth floor as she fought vainly to free herself. Then all was dark again; Feathertail saw the faint outline of the lion-cat against the sheet of water as it whipped round and vanished through the entrance.

For a heartbeat a shocked silence filled the cave. Then a shrill wail of loss rose all around. Feathertail felt a cat nudge her roughly and spun around to see Brambleclaw.

"Out—now!" he rasped.

He bounded towards the entrance with Squirrelpaw and Tawnypelt hard on his paws. Crowpaw thrust Feathertail after him, though she did not move until she was sure Stormfur was following too. No cat tried to stop them; all the Tribe were still gripped by terror, crouched low on the cave floor or gazing after Sharptooth with bristling fur and their eyes glazed with fear.

At the entrance Brambleclaw paused, sniffed the air, and then led the way along the path. Feathertail detected Sharptooth's scent, mingled with Star's fear-scent and the reek of blood, but they were fading. The predator had gone, carrying his prey with him and leaving many more cats dead or wounded.

Sheets of rain were falling steadily, gusted by the wind, and thunder rumbled out again overhead. Feathertail was soaked within a couple of heartbeats, her fur plastered to her body, but she scarcely noticed. She followed Brambleclaw up the rocks as he led the Clan cats back the way they had come. Behind them, the Tribe's heartbroken wailing died away, drowned in the pattering rain and the endless, unchanging roar of the waterfall.

CHAPTER 16

A cold raindrop splashed on to Leafpaw's fur, and she shook it away irritably. Above her, a restless wind stirred the trees, sending brittle scarlet and gold leaves drifting into the clearing. Leaf-bare was barely a moon away, but it seemed like the least of the Clan's troubles.

"The rabbit smelled bad," Cinderpelt reported to Firestar. "Barkface said that cats who ate them died. I believe him. This rabbit we saw wasn't infected with any sort of sickness I've encountered. It must be something the Twolegs have done."

Crouched beside the fresh-kill pile in the ThunderClan camp, Leafpaw listened anxiously as her mentor told Firestar what they had discovered on their way to Highstones. Leafpaw's heart twisted with pity to see the shock in her father's green eyes as he listened.

"This means we can't eat rabbits either," he meowed. "Great StarClan, what next? We'll all starve."

"No cat has died in our territory yet," Sandstorm pointed out from where she sat a tail-length away, her tail wrapped neatly round her paws. She twitched as a falling leaf brushed against her ear. "Maybe the trouble's just in WindClan."

"But rabbits run across the border all the time," replied Cinderpelt. "It might be safe to eat rabbits from the other end of our territory, near the Treecut place, but I don't think we should take the risk even there."

"You're right." Firestar heaved a deep sigh. "I'll announce it to the rest of the Clan. No more rabbits."

"Well, we have to eat something." Sandstorm got briskly to her paws. "I'll get my hunting patrol together and see what we can find." She padded away and disappeared between the branches of the warriors' den.

"Meanwhile," mewed Cinderpelt, "we'd better get rid of any rabbits in the fresh-kill pile."

Leafpaw studied the pathetically small pile of prey. There was only one rabbit; it looked plump and inviting, and her mouth watered at the sight of it. She hadn't had such a good meal for days. Then her belly cramped at the thought of what the Twolegs might have done to it. She thought she could catch a whiff of the harsh scent that had clung to the WindClan rabbit, but this rabbit's scent was so mixed up with that of the other prey in the pile that she could not be sure.

"Take it outside the camp and bury it," Firestar directed.

"Wait—don't pick it up in your mouth," Cinderpelt added. "Push it out with your paws, and then clean them with moss."

Leafpaw had just separated the rabbit from the pile when Dappletail, the oldest cat in the Clan, came past and gave the prey an appreciative look.

"I hope that's for the elders," she rasped. "My belly's flapping like a leaf in the wind."

"No." Cinderpelt explained what she and Leafpaw had seen in WindClan territory.

"What? I've never heard such nonsense!" Dappletail snorted. "WindClan has a bit of trouble, so ThunderClan can't eat rabbits? Barkface might have been lying, just to weaken ThunderClan. They've always been a proud, deceitful Clan. Have you thought of that?"

Leafpaw exchanged a glance with her mentor. She could see there would be no point in trying to convince Dappletail. The old cat wanted the rabbit.

"The decision's been made." Firestar spoke with the authority of Clan leader. "No more rabbits. Leafpaw will take that one out and bury it."

"She'll do no such thing!" Outraged, Dappletail darted for the rabbit and began tearing into it hungrily and gulping down huge mouthfuls.

"No!" Cinderpelt exclaimed. "Stop!"

Firestar sprang forwards, pushing himself between the elder and her prey, and thrusting her gently away. "Dappletail, I'm ordering you not to eat that. It's for your own good."

The old cat's eyes burned into his, her gaze full of hostility. Seeing her skinny body, her tortoiseshell pelt dull and patchy, Leafpaw could understand her desperation. The old cat was usually one of the gentlest queens; only starvation would have driven her to this.

"Do you call yourself a leader?" she spat at Firestar. "The

whole Clan will starve, and it will be your fault."

"Firestar's doing the right thing," Cinderpelt insisted. "There's no point feeding the Clan with food that could kill us quicker than any hunger."

Dappletail turned on her, with lips drawn back in the beginnings of a snarl. Then she whipped round and stalked across the clearing towards the elders' den.

Leafpaw watched her go. "Please, StarClan, let that rabbit be safe," she murmured as she began to push the half-eaten remains towards the camp entrance.

A withered brown leaf spiralled down in front of Leafpaw as she padded up the ravine beside Cinderpelt. It was the day following their return from Highstones and the argument with Dappletail over the rabbit. Cinderpelt was stocking up on the herbs the Clan would need to see them through leaf-bare—weakened by hunger, the Clan would be in danger of greencough and deadly blackcough even more than usual.

"There's no point in going anywhere near the Twoleg monsters," Cinderpelt meowed. "Nothing grows where they've been. We'll head for Sunningrocks and see what we can find there."

Dead leaves lay thickly on the ground, stirred up by a stiff breeze. When she was a kit, Leafpaw would have loved to toss them in the air and chase them. Now she hardly had the energy to go on putting one paw in front of another.

Soon Sunningrocks appeared ahead of them, smooth grey mounds rising out of the grass like the backs of sleeping animals. Almost at once Cinderpelt found a thick clump of chickweed and began carefully biting off the stems. Leafpaw cast around to see what else she could find, looking longingly down to the bank of the river where plants grew thickly, their roots fed by the water. But that was RiverClan territory, and after being punished for the fishing lesson with Mothwing, Leafpaw knew better than to trespass.

She heard a scrabbling close beside her and turned to see a vole scuttling along the base of the nearest rock. In the same heartbeat the vole sensed her and darted for a crevice, but before it could gain safety Leafpaw had sprung on it and bit down hard on its neck.

Her belly was crying out to gulp down the prey, but instead she forced herself to pick it up and go looking for Cinderpelt. Her mentor was where she had left her, arranging the stems of chickweed, ready to carry them back to camp.

"Here," Leafpaw mewed, dropping the vole in front of Cinderpelt.

Her mentor looked up at her, blinking in gratitude. "No, Leafpaw. You caught it, so you eat it."

Leafpaw shrugged, trying to sound unconcerned. "I can catch another." She knew that Cinderpelt, with her crippled leg, would have more trouble hunting than any other Clan cat. "Go on," she added, when Cinderpelt still didn't start eating. "What will happen to ThunderClan if our medicine cat falls ill?"

Cinderpelt let out a purr, and touched her nose to Leafpaw's muzzle. "All right. And thanks, Leafpaw."

She crouched in front of the vole and disposed of it in rapid, neat bites. Leafpaw was just about to go look for more herbs, when she heard a voice yowling, "Cinderpelt! Cinderpelt!"

The medicine cat sprang up, ears pricked. "Over here!" she called.

Mousefur's apprentice, Spiderpaw, burst out of the trees, his long grey-black legs a blur as he raced across the grass and skidded up to Cinderpelt. "You've got to come," he panted. "It's Dappletail!"

"What's wrong?" Cinderpelt asked, while Leafpaw's heart began to pound.

"She's complaining of feeling sick," Spiderpaw replied. "She says her belly hurts."

"That rabbit!" Cinderpelt exclaimed. "I knew it. OK," she added to Spiderpaw. "I'm on my way. You run ahead and tell them I'm coming."

Spiderpaw dashed off again while Cinderpelt turned to Leafpaw. "You stay here; there's no need for both of us to go back," she meowed. "Collect more herbs. And bring that chickweed back with you."

She started limping as fast as she could towards the trees. Leafpaw waited until her mentor had vanished into the bracken before turning back to her search. What was it Barkface had said about treating cats who had eaten deadly rabbits? He had dosed the sick cats with yarrow, but almost all of them had died. Only the strongest pulled through—but Dappletail was old, and already weakened by hunger.

Oh, StarClan help us! Leafpaw prayed. *Show us what to do, before the Twolegs destroy us all.*

She had just begun to search for herbs again when she heard the shrill wailing of a cat coming from the river. For a moment she wondered if she ought to cross the RiverClan border. She made up her mind when the wail came again; some cat was in trouble. Without any more hesitation Leafpaw bounded down the slope.

The river surged along between its banks, swollen by leaf-fall rain. Branches and other debris were swept along in the current, bobbing and swirling on the white-tipped ripples. Leafpaw gazed out over the water, wondering where the cry had come from. Then she spotted a branch surging along close to the RiverClan side; half hidden by its few remaining leaves was the small black head of a cat. As Leafpaw watched, it opened its jaws wide to let out another terrified wail as it clung to a branch for its life.

Leafpaw tensed, ready to leap into the river even though her common sense told her that it would do no good. The current was too strong and swift, and the drowning cat was too far away.

Just before she leaped she saw another cat thrust its way through the reeds on the far bank and jump into the river, striking out with strong paws towards the floating branch. Leafpaw recognised the blue-grey fur at once: It was Mistyfoot, the RiverClan deputy.

She watched, claws flexing in and out in anguish, as Mistyfoot reached the branch and began to push it across the current towards the RiverClan bank. But before they reached it the waves rolled the branch right over, dragging Mistyfoot with it so that she disappeared into the black water. Leafpaw let out a gasp of horror. Then there was a splash and she resurfaced closer to the bank, where her paws found a foothold on the pebbles. Leafpaw shivered with relief as she watched Mistyfoot drag the other cat out by the scruff of its neck and crouch beside it. The tiny, bedraggled shape lay utterly still, water streaming from its pelt.

"Can I help?" Leafpaw called, wondering if Mistyfoot would remember that she was a medicine cat apprentice.

Mistyfoot glanced up. "Yes! Come over!"

Leafpaw raced down the bank until she reached the stepping-stones. Floodwater was lapping over them, but she launched herself on to the first without hesitating. Moments could mean the difference between life and death for the black cat.

She was leaping for the third stone when her paws slipped and she scrabbled frantically against the slick wet surface. The river bubbled around her and for a heartbeat she thought she would be swept away, drowning and tumbling in bottomless black water. In the midst of surging terror she felt a warm touch on her side, pushing her back on to the stone. A sweet scent drifted around her, strangely familiar.

"Spottedleaf?" Leafpaw whispered.

She could see nothing, but she sensed the reassuring presence close to her, the same as in her dream beside the Moonstone. As if she had grown wings, she leaped quickly over the other stones and dashed along the far bank towards Mistyfoot and the cat she had rescued.

Before Leafpaw could reach them, Hawkfrost and Mothwing pushed their way out of the reeds and stood over the black cat.

"What happened?" Hawkfrost demanded.

"Reedpaw fell in the river. We need Mudfur," Mistyfoot meowed. "Can you fetch him? Quickly!"

"He went out to collect herbs," Mothwing told her. "I'll go and look for him."

She sprang along the path that led upstream, but her brother called her back. "It'll take too long," he rasped. He flicked his ears towards the still black cat. "You see to him, you know what to do."

Just then he became aware of Leafpaw approaching. He looked up and glared at her with his eerie ice-blue eyes. Leafpaw felt a shiver run through her. "What's *she* doing here?"

"I called her over," Mistyfoot explained. "Reedpaw needs all the help he can get."

Hawkfrost let out a disgusted snort. Leafpaw ignored him as she crouched beside the black cat. He was very small— newly apprenticed, she guessed—and he lay quite still, with a trickle of water coming out of his parted jaws. There was a gash on his shoulder; blood was oozing into his sodden fur.

"He must have fallen," Mistyfoot meowed worriedly. "The apprentices are always playing too close to the river. It looks as if the branch hit him."

Leafpaw bent closer to Reedpaw. A huge sigh of relief escaped her as she detected the faint rise and fall of his chest. He was still breathing—but his breaths were fast and shallow, and seemed to grow weaker as Leafpaw watched. She glanced at Mothwing, waiting for her to start treating the injured cat.

Mothwing's huge amber eyes were fixed on the limp body of the apprentice.

"Well?" Hawkfrost meowed impatiently. "Get on with it."

Mothwing looked up, and Leafpaw saw the glare of panic in her eyes. "I—I'm not sure. I haven't brought the right herbs. I'll have to go back to camp. . ."

"Reedpaw hasn't time for that!" Mistyfoot rasped.

Leafpaw understood her friend's panic. They were only apprentices; they weren't ready yet to hold the lives of cats within their paws. Where was Mudfur?

Then a gentle voice spoke inside her mind. *Leafpaw, you can do this. Remember what Cinderpelt has taught you. Cobwebs for the bleeding . . .*

"Yes—yes, I remember now," Leafpaw mewed out loud.

Hawkfrost stared at her with narrowed eyes. "Do you know what to do?"

Leafpaw nodded.

"Right. Do it. You—out of the way." Hawkfrost shouldered his sister to one side so that Leafpaw could get closer to Reedpaw.

Mothwing let out a faint meow of protest; Leafpaw glanced up at her to see her amber eyes still wide and shocked and her ears flat to her head.

"Go and find me some cobwebs," Leafpaw instructed her. "Quickly!"

The RiverClan apprentice shot her a frightened look, then whirled round and dashed up the riverbank to the bushes at the top of the slope.

Now get the water out of him, Spottedleaf whispered. Leafpaw bent down and worked her shoulder under Reedpaw's, propping him up until water gushed out of his mouth.

Good. Now he'll breathe properly, so you can deal with his wet fur.

The apprentice started to cough feebly and let out a faint cry of pain.

"Lie still," Mistyfoot told him, giving his muzzle a reassuring lick. "You're going to be OK."

"That's right," Leafpaw meowed urgently to the RiverClan deputy. "Keep licking him—lick his fur the wrong way to help it dry and get him warm."

At once Mistyfoot bent down beside the young apprentice and began licking vigorously; after a moment's hesitation Hawkfrost began to do the same on his other side. Leafpaw licked at the gash on Reedpaw's shoulder, cleaning it of scraps of bark and leaf. She knew she had to get it clean to avoid infection setting in.

"Here," Mothwing gasped, reappearing beside Leafpaw with a wad of cobwebs. "Is this enough?"

"That's fine, Mothwing. Put them on just there."

She almost felt like Mothwing's mentor as she checked how the RiverClan cat put the cobwebs in place, making sure they covered all the gash, and patted them down carefully.

"That's fine," she repeated. "Reedpaw, do you hurt anywhere else?"

The apprentice coughed again; under Mistyfoot's and Hawkfrost's energetic licking he was beginning to revive. "No," he rasped. "Just my shoulder."

Leafpaw examined him for other injuries anyway, but she couldn't find any. "I think you're lucky," she meowed.

"He's lucky you were here," Hawkfrost growled, with a hostile look at his sister. "Mothwing, what was the matter with you? You're supposed to be a medicine cat!"

Mothwing shrank away, and would not meet her brother's gaze.

"Reedpaw, can you stand up?" Leafpaw asked, diplomatically not reacting to her friend's embarrassment.

For an answer the apprentice staggered to his paws. Mistyfoot supported him on his other side, letting him lean against her with his uninjured shoulder.

"Think you can make it back to camp?" Hawkfrost demanded.

Reedpaw nodded. "Thanks . . ." His voice trailed off as he looked at Leafpaw and his eyes widened. "You have ThunderClan scent!"

"That's right. My name's Leafpaw. I'm Cinderpelt's apprentice. Take him straight back," she added to Mistyfoot. "If Mudfur's there, he'd better check him. If not, you can give him some thyme leaves to chew for the shock."

"And poppy seeds for the pain," Mothwing added, trying to sound confident.

"Er . . . no, I wouldn't." Leafpaw hated contradicting her friend. "It's best if he sleeps naturally for now. He'll be worn out anyway from the shock."

Mothwing's gaze dropped to her paws again as Hawkfrost shot her a contemptuous glance. He turned away to pad upstream, towards the RiverClan camp. Mistyfoot followed, supporting Reedpaw. The black apprentice was still shaky, but he kept going until a clump of reeds hid all three cats from Leafpaw's sight.

As they left, Leafpaw couldn't help feeling envious of their sleek pelts and strong muscles. Even Reedpaw, with his fur drying rapidly in the cold wind, looked healthy and well fed. RiverClan was the only Clan that still had plenty of prey, the only Clan not to be affected by the Twolegs tearing up the forest.

Shaking off her resentment, Leafpaw glanced at Mothwing, who hadn't moved. "Don't feel bad," she meowed. "It's all over, and no harm done. Reedpaw will be fine now."

"It's *not* all over!" Mothwing whirled to face her, her voice rising. "I lost it. . . My first chance to show that I'm fit to be a medicine cat, and I totally messed up."

"Everybody makes mistakes." Leafpaw tried to soothe her. "*You* didn't."

But I had help, Leafpaw thought, wishing she could tell her friend about Spottedleaf, but knowing that she could never share such a momentous secret with a cat from a different Clan. She sent a silent prayer of thanks to her father's friend.

"*I* could have helped Reedpaw," Mothwing went on bitterly.

"I *know* all that stuff you did. I gave you and your friend thyme leaves, that time WindClan chased you. But now . . . somehow I couldn't think straight. I just panicked, and I couldn't remember."

"You will next time."

"If there is a next time." Mothwing tore fiercely at the ground with sharp, curved claws. "Hawkfrost will tell every cat how useless I was, and Mudfur will wish he'd never chosen me. And the Clan will never respect me now!"

"Of course they will." Leafpaw padded up to her friend and pushed her nose into Mothwing's beautiful golden tabby fur. "It'll all be forgotten soon, you'll see." She was shocked that Mothwing was so sure her brother would spread the news of her failure around the camp. She would have expected Hawkfrost to be more loyal to his sister.

"I know what you're thinking," Mothwing mewed bitterly, making Leafpaw jump. "Hawkfrost is loyal to the *Clan*, not to me or to any cat. He cares more for being a great warrior than anything else."

Like Tigerstar, Leafpaw thought with an inward shiver.

"You're so lucky, Leafpaw." Mothwing's voice was despairing. "You're Clanborn, and your father is a Clan leader. My mother was a rogue, and no cat will ever forget that."

She turned away, her head bowed and her tail trailing on the ground, and began plodding upstream as if every pawstep were an effort.

"I'll see you soon!" Leafpaw called, but her friend did not respond.

There was nothing more Leafpaw could do. Sadly she went back to the stepping-stones and crossed more carefully than she had done in her desperate race to save Reedpaw.

By the time she reached the ThunderClan border, she was beginning to feel better. With leaf-bare coming, Mothwing would have plenty of chances to try out her medicine-cat skills, and her Clan would forget that she had failed once. Besides, Leafpaw couldn't help feeling pleased with her own success. She had saved a cat's life—the first time, but not the last, she hoped.

"Thank you, Spottedleaf," she murmured aloud, and thought she caught just a trace of the medicine cat's sweet scent.

Feeling more optimistic than she had felt in moons, she collected Cinderpelt's chickweed and hurried back to camp. When she reached the top of the ravine she paused; her optimism vanished and an icy claw closed around her heart at the sound of the shrill wails and yowling coming from the clearing below. As she looked down, Mousefur and Rainwhisker burst out of the gorse tunnel and raced up the ravine, hurtling past Leafpaw without even noticing her.

Leafpaw bounded down to the camp and brushed through the tunnel, terrified of what she would find. Had the Twolegs reached this far already? Firestar was standing at the foot of the Highrock with Greystripe, Sandstorm, and Brackenfur clustered around him. Outside the apprentices' den Whitepaw crouched, wailing like a kit. Shrewpaw and Spiderpaw were trying to comfort her.

Leafpaw skidded to a halt, bewildered. Why was everyone so upset? There were no alien scents in the camp, and no signs of Twoleg devastation. She spotted Cinderpelt, limping wearily into the fern tunnel that led to the medicine cats' clearing.

Leafpaw raced after her. "What's the matter?" she demanded, dropping the chickweed. "What's happened?"

Cinderpelt turned and gazed at her, her blue eyes full of sorrow. "Dappletail is dead," she explained, and the lack of emotion in her voice scared Leafpaw as much as anything else. "And Cloudtail and Brightheart have disappeared."

CHAPTER 17

Stormfur's legs ached and the weight of his rain-sodden fur made his paws stumble painfully over the stones. He felt as if he had been fleeing through the stormy darkness for moons. The whole world seemed to have shrunk to nothing more than rock, wind, and rain.

As he scrabbled up a broken rock face he realised that the rain was easing off. Soon it was no more than a spatter driven by the wind. The sky began to clear, the moon struggling to show its light between the clouds.

Brambleclaw halted, and the rest of the cats gathered around him. They were standing on a wide ledge; above them was a slope covered with scree, while below the rock fell away into darkness.

"I have no idea where we are," Brambleclaw admitted. "I'm sorry, I meant to bring you back the same way we came with the cave-guards, but I've never seen this place before."

"It's not your fault," Squirrelpaw meowed, with a glare at Crowpaw as if she expected the WindClan apprentice to say something rude. "The rain has washed all the scent away, and it's too dark to see anything."

"That's all very well," Tawnypelt pointed out, "but what are we going to do now? If we're not careful, the Tribe cats will catch us."

"Or Sharptooth," Feathertail added with a shudder.

Stormfur cleared his throat. He was feeling guilty and betrayed that he had ever thought of the Tribe cats as his friends, and he wanted to forget them and everything to do with them as soon as he possibly could. But they had taught him skills that could be useful now, and it would be mouse-brained not to use them.

"I think I can find the way," he meowed. "I hunted with the Tribe, remember, more than the rest of you."

"You lead, then," Brambleclaw responded immediately. "Just get us out of these mountains."

Stormfur warmed a little at the ThunderClan warrior's trust in him. He wouldn't have been surprised if he had lost all Brambleclaw's respect, after the way he had settled in among the Tribe cats. He knew now how much Brambleclaw's friendship meant to him.

"It'll take a few days to cross the mountains," he warned the tabby warrior, remembering the day Brook had taken him to the top of a high peak and shown him the towering folds of rock stretching endlessly ahead. At least they would have the rising sun to guide them when daylight came. "But I think I can get you out of the Tribe's territory."

"The sooner the better," muttered Crowpaw. He was standing so close to Feathertail that their fur touched. There seemed to be an unspoken connection between them, and

Stormfur wondered what had happened while he'd been held prisoner in the cave.

Stormfur took the lead along the ledge and then diagonally up the scree, his paws slipping on the loose stones. Reaching the ridge, he paused to figure out the direction from the way the moss grew on the rocks and the trunk of a gnarled tree. Guilt swept over him again as he realised how easy it seemed to use Tribe ways, as if he had allowed himself to become a Tribe cat instead of a warrior loyal to RiverClan.

"What's the matter?" Feathertail asked quietly, coming up to him and brushing her side against his. He should have known she would be able to sense how bad he felt.

"I trusted them." Stormfur choked over the words. "Brook and Crag and the rest. I never thought . . . And then they took me prisoner, and the rest of you risked your lives to get me out of there."

"We couldn't leave you." Feathertail let out a comforting purr.

"They never told me anything about the prophecy, you know, not all the time we were hunting together. It was just as much of a shock to me when Stoneteller told us about it in the Cave of Pointed Stones."

"Yes, we know," his sister murmured.

"But do we have to stand here talking about it?" Crowpaw demanded disagreeably as he joined them on the ridge. "Let's just get *moving*."

"They *must* have been wrong." Stormfur ignored the WindClan apprentice, holding Feathertail's gaze and trying to convince himself as much as her. "I *can't* be the promised cat, right? It doesn't make sense."

"No, of course not," Feathertail mewed. "Don't blame yourself, Stormfur. None of us realised what was going on. And the Tribe, they aren't bad cats—just desperate."

Stormfur hoped his sister couldn't see the guilt that clawed deep inside his belly. What if the prophecy were true, and the Tribe of Endless Hunting really had chosen him to help the Tribe cats? StarClan had chosen four cats to save the forest, but he was not one of them. He had come on the journey because he couldn't bear to see Feathertail leave without him. Now he wondered whether somehow the Tribe of Endless Hunting had influenced his decision so that he would be in the right place to destroy Sharptooth.

But then he had turned his back on the Tribe at the time when they needed help the most. He remembered watching Sharptooth leave the cave, his fierce jaws gripping Star as she yowled vainly for help. What if the next cat to die was Crag? What if it was *Brook*? A picture came into Stormfur's mind of the beautiful she-cat trapped in those savage teeth, and he desperately tried to push it away.

He shivered, hardly aware that the rest of his friends were waiting for him.

"Is there something wrong?" Brambleclaw asked.

Stormfur shook himself. "No," he meowed. "It's this way."

On the other side of the ridge, the ground fell away into a slope broken up by shallow precipices, low enough for a cat to leap down from one level to the next. As he crouched on the edge of one of these, he saw a roosting mountain bird just below him.

Squirrelpaw, at his shoulder, prodded him and pointed with her ears. To be on the safe side, Stormfur flicked his tail lightly across her jaws and signalled to the rest of the cats for silence.

"I'll get it," he whispered. "You stay here."

He was appalled by the way his new skills seemed natural to him, as if he had known them all his life. The bird was on a narrow ledge, so he could not leap down on it without risking a bad fall. In the forest, cats wouldn't hesitate to jump out of trees, but that was onto soft earth, not jagged stone that sliced open paws and jarred bones.

Instead he cautiously crept down a few tail-lengths further on and worked his way stealthily back to the bird, using broken rocks for cover. When he was close enough he pounced, pinning the bird against the rock face, where it fluttered helplessly for a few heartbeats until he took its life.

"That was great!" Squirrelpaw exclaimed, curling her tail up in admiration. "You're just like a real mountain cat, Stormfur."

"I hope not," Stormfur mewed.

All six cats gathered around to eat their share of the bird. By the time they had finished, a thin rain had begun to fall and clouds were massing once more to cover the moon.

"This is hopeless," mewed Brambleclaw, swiping his tongue around his jaws. "I think we should shelter for the rest of the night."

"As long as the Tribe cats don't track us down," Tawnypelt warned. Stormfur noticed that her shoulder wasn't giving her trouble anymore; Stoneteller's herbs had worked well. At least that was something they could thank the Tribe cats for.

"I think we're far enough away by now," he meowed. "Brambleclaw's right. We can't keep going in this rain. Let's see if we can find a cave."

He took the lead again, this time looking for somewhere that would give them shelter. He found it soon enough, a dark hole leading into the mountainside from the base of a rock, overhung by a couple of scrubby bushes.

Cautiously he approached it and sniffed. "Stale rabbit," he reported. "It was probably a burrow a long time ago."

"Too bad," Squirrelpaw meowed. "I could do with a rabbit."

"Tribe cat scent, too," Crowpaw added, coming up beside Stormfur to sniff. "And that's fairly fresh. I'm not going in there."

"Stay outside and get wet, then," Squirrelpaw retorted, stepping forward.

"Hang on." Tawnypelt used her tail to bar Squirrelpaw's way into the cave. "Let me check it out."

She slipped down the hole while Squirrelpaw stared indignantly after her. For the first time that night Stormfur felt himself growing more cheerful, warmed by the ThunderClan apprentice's courage. She still couldn't bear to leave the dangerous tasks to full warriors.

A moment later Tawnypelt's voice came out of the hole, echoing as if she were speaking from a larger space below.

"Come on. Everything's fine."

Stormfur led the way down the cramped passage, his fur brushing the walls on either side. The opening narrowed until he had to breathe in, afraid of getting stuck, then suddenly grew wider. Though the darkness was unbroken, the echo of his pawsteps on the floor told him that he was standing in a fairly large cavern.

"This is great!" Squirrelpaw's voice came from just behind him. He felt her shake the raindrops from her pelt as she added, "All we need now is a good pile of fresh-kill."

Stormfur checked by scent that all six cats, even Crowpaw, had entered the cave. He was just beginning to relax when another scent washed over him and he froze with horror: It was a Tribe cat, yet somehow different from the Tribe cats he knew.

At the same moment a voice meowed from the shadows, "And who might you be?"

CHAPTER 18

All *night the Clan had kept* vigil for Dappletail, and now, in the pale dawn light, the elders were bearing her body out of the camp to be buried. The clearing was wreathed in mist and the leafless branches of the trees dripped rain from a sharp shower during the night. Leafpaw watched in silence. The old cat had been part of her life, and with her passing it seemed as if everything else she had known would slip away too.

As the elders departed through the gorse tunnel, the other cats gathered together in little groups, mewing urgently and casting anxious glances at one another. Leafpaw could not hear what they were saying, but she didn't need to. She knew they would be discussing the disappearance of Cloudtail and Brightheart. That made four cats that were missing from ThunderClan, but Leafpaw could not believe that StarClan had summoned Cloudtail and Brightheart away too—unless the others had already failed on their quest, and would never return. *If you can't help us, StarClan,* she thought desperately, *why are you taking our cats away?*

Cinderpelt broke into her thoughts, pushing her nose into Leafpaw's fur in wordless comfort, then limped forwards a pace or two to meet Firestar and Greystripe. Leafpaw spotted Mousefur loping across the clearing after them with Thornclaw and Ashfur just behind her.

"I'm taking out the dawn patrol," Mousefur announced as she came up. "Do you still want us to look for Cloudtail and Brightheart?"

"Not that there's much point, if they left on purpose," Ashfur added darkly.

Leafpaw's heart sank even further as she remembered the Clan's efforts the day before to find the two cats. Patrols had covered the entire territory, picking up a scent-trail leading towards the place where the Twolegs had destroyed the forest. It had broken off abruptly near one of the huge tree-cutting monsters, and after that there was nothing.

"Keep your eyes open," Firestar replied. "That's all you can do."

"I wouldn't put it past Cloudtail to have gone back to the Twolegs," Mousefur growled. "With so little prey in the forest, even Twoleg food must look tempting."

"And he ate it often enough when he was an apprentice," Ashfur put in.

"Yes, don't forget the time he left us," Mousefur mewed. "Cats were put at risk, rescuing him from the Twolegs."

"That's enough!" Greystripe hissed.

"No, she's right." Leafpaw couldn't believe how tired her father sounded. "Cloudtail has always had a paw in the Twoleg world. But I thought he was loyal to his Clan now."

"Of course he is. You're not being fair to him." Cinderpelt's voice was sharp. "It's been a long time since Cloudtail ate kitty-pet food. He was young and stupid then."

"Besides, Brightheart would never do that." Greystripe supported his missing Clanmates with a flash of his amber eyes. "And Cloudtail wouldn't go off without her. We have to figure out why they're *both* missing."

"And why they left Whitepaw behind," Thornclaw meowed. "She's their only kit."

Mousefur grunted. "True. I wonder if they went over to RiverClan?" she suggested. "Stealing fish?"

"Now I wouldn't put *that* past Cloudtail," Cinderpelt agreed, but there was no hostility in her voice.

Greystripe thought for a moment, then shook his head. "No. If RiverClan caught them they'd just chase them off. There'd be trouble at the next Gathering, but our cats wouldn't just disappear."

Unless they fell in the river, Leafpaw thought, not daring to put words to the idea. She couldn't forget the surge of flood-water when she nearly fell off the stepping-stones, on her way to help Reedpaw.

"Their scent trail didn't lead towards RiverClan," Firestar pointed out. "I can't help thinking it's strange that it ended so close to the Twoleg monsters. Suppose . . ."

He let his voice die away, but Leafpaw saw the anxiety in his eyes, and she could guess what his thoughts were. She had seen how the first Twoleg monster turned from the Thunderpath and began to tear up the forest. If a cat got in its way it could be crunched in those powerful jaws without the monster even realising it. She shivered, and her gaze met her father's. They were both fond of their wayward kin Cloudtail, and Leafpaw loved Brightheart fiercely for her courage in coping with the terrible injuries from the dog pack. The two cats would be a great loss to their Clan.

"Just carry on as usual, Mousefur," Firestar decided. "And report if you see anything odd."

"I always do." Mousefur hurried off with the two younger warriors behind her.

Firestar shook himself as if he was pushing useless thoughts away. "Cinderpelt, has StarClan shown you anything at all about Cloudtail and Brightheart?"

"No," Cinderpelt replied. "Nothing at all."

"Or any signs about more warriors going missing in the forest? It's . . . it's not all that long since Brambleclaw and Squirrelpaw disappeared." He choked the words out like half-eaten bones.

Again Cinderpelt shook her head. "StarClan is silent. I'm sorry."

Yet again, Leafpaw struggled with the urge to tell her father and mentor what she knew, that Brambleclaw and Squirrelpaw had been summoned away by StarClan to discover something that would help the forest. But she hardly knew what to say any more. Whenever she tried to reach Squirrelpaw she had nothing but confused, terrifying impressions of rushing water, darkness, and raking claws—blood, rock, and water churned together. She couldn't reassure Firestar that Squirrelpaw was all right, nor give Greystripe hopeful news of his missing children from RiverClan.

"Perhaps I ought to make a trip to Highstones," Firestar meowed. "StarClan might speak to me, if—"

He broke off as Brackenfur came up, his apprentice, Whitepaw, just behind him. Leafpaw's heart went out to her. The young cat's head was bowed, and her tail trailed in the dust. She was obviously grieving for the loss of her parents.

"Firestar, I think you ought to have a word with Whitepaw," Brackenfur mewed worriedly.

Firestar's ears flicked up. "Why, what's the matter?"

Whitepaw looked up at him. "I want to be excused from training," she begged, her eyes burning with the intensity of her plea. "I want to look for Cloudtail and Brightheart."

"I've told her she can't go off on her own," Brackenfur continued. "But she—"

"*Please*," Whitepaw interrupted. "I'm only an apprentice. The Clan can do without me. I've *got* to find them."

Firestar shook his head. "I'm sorry, Whitepaw," he meowed gently. "Apprentices are important to the Clan, just as much as any other cat. Besides, Brackenfur is quite right. You can't go wandering off by yourself, especially now, when we don't know what the danger is. In fact, no cat should leave camp alone."

"We've searched already," Greystripe added. "We did everything we could."

"But it wasn't enough!" Whitepaw wailed. Leafpaw knew that Whitepaw would never have spoken to the Clan deputy like that if she hadn't been driven out of her mind with worry.

"StarClan will be with them wherever they are," Cinderpelt murmured comfortingly, pressing her nose into Whitepaw's fur.

"Brackenfur, take out a hunting patrol," Firestar meowed. "StarClan knows, we can use the fresh-kill. Whitepaw, go with him; you can keep your eyes open for Cloudtail and Brightheart as well. But you're *not* to leave your mentor, is that clear?"

Whitepaw nodded; she was looking a little more hopeful.

"I'll go with you," Greystripe offered, "and I'll get Sand-storm to come as well. If any cat can find them, she can." He hurried off into the warriors' den.

"Thank you, Firestar," mewed Whitepaw, dipping her head respectfully before following her mentor towards the camp entrance.

Leafpaw watched until Greystripe and Sandstorm came to join them, and all four cats disappeared into the gorse tunnel.

"We aren't safe in our own territory anymore," Firestar murmured. "But surely *four* cats can't go missing without—"

He broke off as a low, feeble wail rose up from the nursery. Leafpaw whipped around to see Dustpelt emerge. He stag-gered forwards for a couple of tail-lengths and sank to the ground as if his legs would not hold him up.

With a glance at her father, Leafpaw dashed across to him, visions of disaster rushing through her head. Firestar and Cinderpelt followed, and came to a stop in front of Dustpelt.

"Are you hurt?" Firestar demanded.

The brown tabby warrior gazed up at his leader with eyes

as dull as pebbles. "It wasn't her fault," he whispered. "Ferncloud did her best. But she hasn't been eating enough to keep herself alive, let alone three kits."

As he finished speaking, Leafpaw heard the wail break out again, echoing with enough grief for the death of a whole Clan.

"What is it?" she cried.

Dustpelt gave her a long, hopeless stare. "Larchkit is dead."

Instantly, Cinderpelt whisked past Dustpelt, on her way to Ferncloud in the nursery. Firestar rested his tail-tip on the brown warrior's shoulder, in a vain attempt to comfort him. Dustpelt briefly pushed his nose into his leader's flame-coloured fur. Leafpaw felt her throat tighten to see the two cats, who had never been friends, brought close together by their shared grief.

"What next?" Firestar meowed, lifting his head to the grey morning sky. "StarClan, what trouble will you send to ThunderClan now?"

CHAPTER 19

What was that? Every hair on Stormfur's pelt shot up in fear. He and his friends were trapped in this dark hole; whoever had just spoken was blocking the entrance, and there was nowhere else to go. Desperately he tasted the air and picked out the scents of several cats, all of them smelling of Tribe, and yet not Tribe.

"Who are you?" he demanded.

For an answer he felt a powerful shoulder thrusting him aside as the strange cat entered the cave. There was the soft sound of pawsteps as the others followed.

Then he heard Brambleclaw's voice, tense but still calm. "We are travelling to our home far from here and we took shelter only for the night. We have no quarrel with you."

The strange cat spoke again. "This is our place."

"Then we'll leave," Tawnypelt mewed. She padded towards the entrance, and the other cats shuffled round to follow her.

Stormfur felt his fur begin to lie flat again. With any luck they could get out of here without a fight. These cats couldn't have come from the Tribe of Rushing Water, or they would have known who he and his companions were. Yet they carried the Tribe's scent; Stormfur was puzzled, but he was content to leave the mystery behind him if they could just get away safely.

"Not so fast," the newcomer growled. "How do we know you're telling the truth? I don't know you, and I don't know your scent."

"Talon, we should take them prisoner." A soft hiss came from one of the other cats. "We might be able to use them as bait for Sharptooth."

"You know about Sharptooth?" Stormfur exclaimed.

"Of course we know about Sharptooth," rumbled the first voice, the one called Talon. "Every cat in these mountains knows about Sharptooth."

As he spoke, Stormfur realised that the darkness was no longer unbroken. Gradually the shapes of the strange cats were outlined in faint grey light as dawn filtered down the tunnel. Every hair on Stormfur's pelt prickled with fear as he looked at them.

The first of them, Talon, was one of the biggest cats he had ever seen, a dark brown tabby with massive shoulders and huge paws. His ragged pelt was bristling with hostility, and a deep scar stretched across one side of his face, curling his lip in a frozen snarl. His amber eyes were narrowed, his gaze flicking suspiciously over the forest cats.

Behind him were two other cats, a scrawny black tom whose tail was little more than a jagged stump, and a grey-brown she-cat. Both of them flexed their claws as if they could hardly wait to sink them into the Clan cats' fur.

Although the Clan cats outnumbered the strangers two to

one, Stormfur didn't like their chances in a fight. They certainly wouldn't get away without serious injuries. He could see his friends were thinking the same; even the aggressive Crowpaw was silent, his gaze fixed warily on the strangers.

"We have seen Sharptooth and we know how savage he is." Brambleclaw was still trying to keep the exchange peaceful. "But we're on an urgent mission and we have to leave."

"You'll go when I say you can," Talon growled.

"You can't keep us here!" Stormfur winced as Squirrelpaw spoke up, her green eyes blazing. There was nothing wrong with her courage, but sometimes she hadn't the sense of a mayfly. "We've already escaped from the Tribe of Rushing Water."

Crowpaw let out a furious hiss, and for once Stormfur sympathised with him. Squirrelpaw needed to be a lot more careful about what she told these terrifying cats.

But to Stormfur's surprise, the suspicion in Talon's gaze seemed to fade. "You have been with the Tribe?"

"That's right," meowed Brambleclaw. "You know of them, then?"

"We know much, and too much," Talon replied, and the tabby she-cat added, "We were once Tribe cats too."

Stormfur stared at her in astonishment; he had assumed that these cats were homeless rogues. It would explain the puzzling scent, if they had once belonged to the Tribe, but he remembered how the Tribe had refused to turn the Clan cats out at night in case they met Sharptooth. If they had been that concerned about strangers, it seemed odd that they would let their own Tribemates live outside the cave. Unless they had committed a crime that outweighed the threat of Sharptooth. . .

"Did the Tribe make you leave?" he asked.

"As good as," Talon grunted. Slowly his bristling fur began to lie flat. He flicked his tail at his two companions, which they seemed to take as an order to guard the entrance, for they settled down one on either side of it. "Sit," Talon said to the forest cats. "Sit and we will talk. But don't try to leave, unless you want to lose your ears."

Stormfur believed that he meant the threat. Cautiously he sat down; his friends did the same, making themselves as comfortable as they could on the bare sandy floor. As the light strengthened Stormfur made out his surroundings more clearly: The roof of the cave was thickly interlaced with roots, stretching above earth walls, with more roots and stones jutting out here and there. He could not see any bedding, any fresh-kill pile, or any other sign that these three cats lived here permanently. Yet Talon had said it was where they regularly came to shelter. It must be a harsh life that they led here.

"My name is Talon of Swooping Eagle," the huge tabby began, raising one paw to the scar on his face. "An eagle's talon did this when I was a kit, and gave me my name as well as a mark to remind me how close I came to losing my life. This is Rock Where Snow Gathers and Bird Who Rides the Wind." He pointed his tail at the black tom and the she-cat in turn.

Stormfur's fear began to ebb. Somehow knowing the strangers' names made them seem less like enemies.

"Many seasons ago," Talon went on, "the Tribe of Endless Hunting sent a sign to Stoneteller. They chose six cats to leave the shelter of the caves and go out into the mountains to face Sharptooth and kill him. We are three of that six."

"What happened to the others?" Crowpaw put in.

"Sharptooth happened," Rock snarled from his place by the entrance. "He nearly had me, too. How do you think I lost my tail?"

"So, wait," Tawnypelt mewed. "The Tribe sent you out to kill Sharptooth?"

Talon bowed his head. "Stoneteller ordered us not to come back without his pelt."

"But that's mouse-brained!" Squirrelpaw burst out. "How could six of you kill Sharptooth when the whole of the Tribe couldn't do it?"

The tabby looked up again, and Stormfur winced at the depths of bitterness in his eyes. "I don't know," he replied. "Do you think we haven't asked ourselves that question? I'd give the fur off my back to save my Tribe, but what can any of us do?"

Feathertail let out a comforting murmur. "Could you not go to Stoneteller and tell him you've done your best? He might let you back in."

"No!" Talon's eyes blazed at her. "I won't crawl to him and beg. Besides, what use would it be? We all obey the will of the Tribe of Endless Hunting."

Stormfur blinked. There were times when the words of his own warrior ancestors seemed harsh and difficult to understand, but he could not remember StarClan ever banishing cats to a lonely existence that could only end in their death. *Would I have the courage to obey if they did?* he wondered.

"I'm surprised we didn't hear about you before," Brambleclaw meowed. "They told us about Sharptooth, but no cat mentioned you."

Talon snorted. "They've probably forgotten all about us."

"Or they're ashamed," Bird added grimly.

"You've just left the Tribe recently?" Talon asked. When Brambleclaw nodded, he went on with longing in his voice. "There's a cat . . . her name is Brook Where Small Fish Swim. Did you see her there?"

Stormfur's ears pricked up. For a heartbeat, jealous fury swept through him at the obvious affection with which this ragged loner spoke of the prey-hunter.

"Yes, we met Brook," Feathertail replied.

"Is she all right? Happy?"

"She's fine," Tawnypelt told him. "And as happy as any of them are with Sharptooth breathing down their necks."

"Because we failed . . ." All Talon's bitterness was in the three words. "Brook's my sister," he went on, letting out an awkward *mrrow*, half amused and half embarrassed. "You'd not think a pretty cat like that was related to me, would you? She's from a younger litter, and when Sharptooth took our mother I wanted to be there to look out for Brook."

Stormfur relaxed. What was the matter with him? Why should he care that Brook was Talon's sister, and not his mate?

"She would have come with me," Talon went on. "But it

wasn't the will of the Tribe of Endless Hunting. I was glad. This is no sort of life."

Stormfur knew he was right. He flinched as he thought about the destruction that Sharptooth had brought to the Tribe: not only the cats he had killed for prey, but the lives he had destroyed in their desperate attempts to kill him. Cats driven into exile, separated from their kin . . .

And what if he really was the chosen cat, destined to save the Tribe from Sharptooth? Had he any right to refuse his destiny? The thought crossed his mind that he ought to go back, but the idea terrified him so much that he pushed it away. He and his friends had their own mission, to tell their Clans what they had learned from Midnight, and nothing must be allowed to interfere with that. They had to tell the Clans to leave the forest before it was destroyed by the Twolegs' new Thunderpath.

The light in the cave had grown brighter and turned golden, as if the rain had stopped and the sun had risen above the mountaintops. Feeling as if he could not bear to be trapped belowground for another heartbeat, Stormfur rose to his paws.

"Will you let us out to hunt? We need fresh-kill."

Talon glanced at his companions.

"We're not going anywhere," Brambleclaw assured him. "We're all exhausted, and we need to rest."

After another pause, the tabby shrugged. "Go, stay, do what you want. It's nothing to do with us. We wouldn't feed you to Sharptooth, whatever Rock might say."

Stormfur pushed his way through the narrow tunnel and out on to the mountainside. The sun hovered over the top-most peak; that was the way they should be going, following the sunrise until they came home to the forest.

Squirrelpaw followed him out, and stood looking around alertly, as if she had not spent all night scrambling about on the mountain in the pouring rain. "Right," she meowed. "Where's the fresh-kill?"

In the rain and the darkness, Stormfur had seen very little of their surroundings before they found the cave. Now he saw that just below the entrance the rocks were broken up; thin soil had lodged in the cracks, enough for grass to grow and a few bushes. A trickle of water wound among them. "Down there," he suggested.

Squirrelpaw swept her tail back towards the hole. "The rest want to sleep, just as if they were hedgehogs in leaf-bare," she meowed. "Let's hunt, and surprise them when they wake up!"

"OK." Stormfur was pleased to be hunting with the deter-minedly cheerful apprentice, away from the ThunderClan warrior who took up so much of her attention. But since the beginning of their journey home he had been aware of how close she and Brambleclaw had become. It would always be easier for them to be together than for her to have any con-nection with Stormfur. Besides, he was starting to realise that he felt about Brook in a completely different way from how he felt about Squirrelpaw.

He had kept a check on his feelings for Squirrelpaw because they were in different Clans, but he was drawn to

Brook in a way that he couldn't ignore so easily. The sheen on her tabby fur, the glow in her eyes, her speed and skill, stayed with him even though he had escaped from the cave. Was that how Crowpaw and Feathertail felt about each other? he wondered suddenly, with a pang of sympathy he had never felt before. Would he cross boundaries like that to be with Brook?

Stormfur pushed the thought away. He would never see Brook again, so what was the point? He tried to focus instead on the sunny morning, and the pleasure of hunting with a skilful partner. It was good to have Squirrelpaw beside him as a friend, without the jealousy that might have threatened his friendship with Brambleclaw.

"Come on!" Squirrelpaw had already bounded down among the bushes. "I want you to teach me some of those new mountain moves."

As the sun rose higher they stalked through the sparse mountain vegetation, beginning to build a pile of fresh-kill on the ledge outside the cave. Squirrelpaw learned the new ways of hunting quickly, and couldn't stop herself bouncing like a kit with the delight of bringing down her first falcon.

"We need to teach this stuff at home," she meowed, flicking a feather off her nose with one paw. "We always hunt in the undergrowth, but like this we could hunt out in the open as well."

Bleak thoughts about the future of the forest rushed through Stormfur's mind. Squirrelpaw clearly guessed what he was thinking, for her triumph faded and she added somberly, "We might need to."

When they returned to the cave with more prey to add to the pile they had started, Stormfur saw Talon crouched on the ledge, his eyes half closed as he let the sun soak into his ragged fur.

He opened his eyes as the two Clan cats approached. "You've hunted well," he meowed.

"Help yourself," Stormfur invited him.

"Thanks." He padded over to the pile and dragged out a rabbit.

Squirrelpaw trotted back inside the hole. "I'm going to get our lazy friends," she announced.

Stormfur noticed that Talon had stopped eating after just one bite, and was looking at him expectantly. Almost without realising what he was doing, Stormfur pulled a falcon from the pile of fresh-kill, took a hasty bite, and shoved it towards Talon. The Tribe cat nodded and pushed his own piece of fresh-kill towards Stormfur.

"I see your Tribe shares as well," was all he said, and Stormfur looked down at his paws, suddenly feeling uncomfortable.

For a few moments, they ate their prey in silence. Stormfur was not sure how the exiled cats had changed from being enemies to something like friends, but he was certain that the Clan cats had nothing to fear from them now. He just wished that there were some way of helping them.

"I can tell you're worried about the Tribe," he began awkwardly, swallowing a mouthful of rabbit.

"Of course I'm worried." Talon fixed him with a piercing

amber gaze. "And so are you, even though you're not one of us."

Stormfur nodded slowly. He had been trying not to admit that, even to himself. Were his feelings so obvious, even to a stranger?

"Every day they live in fear," Talon went on. "Every pawstep out of the cave is filled with terror, when every rock might be hiding Sharptooth."

Stormfur nodded, thinking of the cave-guards who went out with the hunting parties. He tried to imagine what it would be like never to run freely through your own territory, always to feel the threat of claws and fangs. Cold shivers ran through his pelt as he remembered hunting with Brook in the first days of their stay with the Tribe. She had told him that Crag and the others were there to guard the prey-hunters from eagles, but now he understood that they were watching for Sharptooth as well. He and the Tribe cats had been in as much danger as any of the prey they hunted.

"I wish I knew what to do," he meowed. "We made this journey because of a prophecy from StarClan—"

"StarClan?" Talon echoed.

"The spirits of our warrior ancestors," Stormfur explained. "Like your Tribe of Endless Hunting."

He went on to explain how StarClan had prophesied great trouble for the forest and chosen four cats, one from each of the Clans, to make the journey and learn what Midnight had to tell them.

"I wasn't one of the four," he finished, "but I came to be

with my sister."

"And now you're going home," Talon meowed.

"Yes, but we don't know whether we'll be in time to help."
Even while he was speaking, Stormfur reflected that at least
they *could* go home; Talon and his Tribemates never could.

"Your Tribemate said that you'd escaped from the Tribe of
Rushing Water." Talon looked puzzled. "Does that mean they
kept you prisoner? That is not the Tribe I knew."

"It wasn't quite like that." Stormfur swallowed. If he
wanted to earn the trust of this cat, he had to tell his story,
but he didn't know how Talon would react. There was
every chance that the huge tabby would try to drag him
back to the Tribe to fulfil the prophecy and win the right to
return to his home. "There was another prophecy," he
admitted. "Stoneteller had a sign from the Tribe of Endless
Hunting. . ."

Talon listened to the story with his unblinking amber gaze
fixed on Stormfur. "A silver cat?" he rumbled, when the story
was finished. "Do you believe you are the one?"

Stormfur started to deny it, and found he could not. "I don't
know," he answered honestly. "At first I didn't see how I *could*
be, but now . . . The first prophecy, the one from StarClan,
matters more than anything to me. But I'm not one of the
chosen. I can't help wondering whether I'm meant to do
this instead." He sighed. "But I can't follow *both* prophecies.
Which one of them is right?"

Talon was silent for a few moments. Then he meowed
heavily, "Neither of them is right. And neither is wrong." He

let out a soft growl from deep in his throat. "Prophecies are strange things. Their words are never clear."

Stormfur nodded, remembering how he and his friends had thought that "midnight" meant just that, until they discovered that it was the name of the wise badger who had told them what they should do.

"Everything depends on how cats interpret the prophecy," Talon went on. "And whether the prophecy is fulfilled depends on what they decide to do about it. It is up to us to choose the code we live by. Isn't that true for your cats as well?"

Stormfur stared in surprise at the older cat. He was right. StarClan and the Tribe of Endless Hunting made exactly the same demands on the cats they watched over, with the same promises of protection and guidance if only they knew how to read the signs.

"What do you *think* you should do?" Talon challenged him.

Stormfur shook his head. "I don't know."

"But you will." The big tabby rose to his paws. "Your faith and your courage will tell you." Amusement glinted faintly in his amber eyes. "Just don't take too long about it," he added as he squeezed back into the tunnel that led to the cave.

When he had gone, Stormfur let out an exhausted sigh. These mysteries were too much for him; he was a warrior, and all he wanted was to follow the warrior code. But what should he do, when the code did not speak clearly to him?

The sun was warm on his fur, and it was a long time since he had slept. His belly was comfortably full of prey. He yawned, and his eyes closed.

Hardly any time seemed to have passed before he realised that he was lying in a forest clearing, though he could not have said exactly where it was. The scent of green, growing things was all around him, and he could hear the soft murmur of a stream. He opened his eyes to see moonlight filtering through the leaves above his head.

He stirred, puzzled. This was a forest at the height of green-leaf, though by now leaf-bare should be well on its way. Then another scent tickled his nose, something sweet and reassuring and somehow achingly familiar, though he had no memory of smelling it before. A voice behind him mewed, "Stormfur."

He turned his head and for a heartbeat thought he was looking at Feathertail. No, this cat had a silvery grey pelt very like his sister's, but he didn't recognise her.

"Who are you?" he demanded, rising to his paws.

The cat did not reply, but padded over to him and touched noses with him. Stormfur saw the glitter of starshine around her paws. With a shiver, he knew that he was dreaming, and that a warrior of StarClan had come to visit him.

"Dearest Stormfur, I am so proud of you and Feathertail," the strange warrior began. "You have come through great trials and proved your courage and faith, time and again. You have obeyed StarClan in everything, and we are well pleased with you."

"Er . . . thank you," Stormfur mewed uncertainly.

"Yet the cats of the Tribe have courage and faith too, even though they follow different warrior ancestors. You should honour them and the Tribe of Endless Hunting."

"I know," Stormfur agreed with feeling. Whoever this StarClan warrior was, she understood exactly how he felt. "Please tell me what I should do—and tell me who you are."

The cat bent close to him so that her sweet scent flooded his senses. "Don't you know?" she murmured. "I am your mother, Silverstream. And as for what you must do—Stormfur, remember that a question can have many answers. . ."

The light around her began to fade. Stormfur was left alone in the clearing.

"Don't go!" he pleaded.

He spun around, trying to see where she had gone. His eyes flew open, and he found himself lying on the ground outside the hole, with his friends dividing up the pile of fresh-kill a little way off.

He staggered to his paws. He had been sent a dream from StarClan! He had seen his own mother, who had died giving birth to him and Feathertail. But there was no time to mourn the fact that he had never known her alive. At last he knew what he had to do, although he had no idea how he was going to do it.

Feathertail looked up, her blue eyes startled. "What's the matter?"

"I . . . I have to go back," Stormfur rasped. "I have to fulfil the Tribe's prophecy."

"What?" That was Tawnypelt, leaving the mouse she was eating to come and stand over him. "Have bees swarmed in your brain?"

Stormfur shook his head. "I spoke to Silverstream. To

our mother," he went on to Feathertail. "She came to me in a dream."

Feathertail's eyes stretched wide. "And she told you to go back?"

"Well, not exactly. But she told me that a question can have many answers. I think one of those answers is for me to go back and accept the fate that the Tribe of Endless Hunting have laid down."

"But Stormfur . . ." Brambleclaw looked puzzled. "What about your duty to StarClan? What about *our* prophecy?"

"I was never one of the four chosen cats," Stormfur meowed. "And Silverstream said that the Tribe of Endless Hunting should be honoured too. They are warrior ancestors, after all, even if they are not ours."

He could see that Brambleclaw was unhappy about his decision, and he hoped that the ThunderClan warrior would not try to order him to continue the journey. He respected Brambleclaw, and had been content to follow his lead, but now that he knew that he had found the right path, nothing would turn him aside, not even the friendship that had grown between them.

"What do the rest of you think?" Brambleclaw meowed.

The Clan cats looked uncertainly at one another. While he was waiting for one of them to speak, Stormfur noticed Talon sitting a little way apart with Rock and Bird. For the first time Stormfur thought he could see a gleam of hope in his amber eyes, but when Talon caught his gaze he looked away, as if he would not allow himself a voice in this debate.

"Well, I think it's a mouse-brained idea." Tawnypelt's tail twitched back and forth. "I'm staying with Brambleclaw and going back to the forest. Or have you forgotten about what's happening there?"

"I'm not asking any cat to come with me," Stormfur meowed hastily. "This is something that I have to do, but the rest of you can go on with the journey."

Feathertail got up and padded towards him, pressing her nose against his shoulder. "Stupid furball," she mewed. "You don't think I'm going to let you do this alone, do you?"

"Then I'll come too." Stormfur was not surprised that Crowpaw wanted to go with Feathertail, but he was startled as the WindClan apprentice went on, "Actually, Stormfur, I think you're right. Ever since we rescued you, you've been mooning around like a rabbit without its tail. It makes my fur ache, just looking at you. You're obviously going to be no use at all until you've tried to help these cats."

Stormfur gave him a nod of gratitude. Crowpaw's bad-tempered words couldn't disguise that he had just made a courageous offer. None of the Clan cats could be sure that the Tribe would welcome them, not to mention the danger from Sharptooth.

"I want to come too!" Squirrelpaw sprang to her paws, her green eyes blazing and her tail curled up with excitement. Turning to Brambleclaw, she pleaded, "Can't we all go? We can't let Stormfur face Sharptooth by himself."

"He isn't by himself," Brambleclaw mewed dryly. With a rueful glance at Tawnypelt, he added, "It looks as if we're out-

voted. If one goes, we all go. I haven't forgotten about the forest—but we have to remember the warrior code, too."

Squirrelpaw let out a wordless yowl of triumph.

Tawnypelt's tail lashed once. "I think you're all as crazy as
hares in newleaf," she growled. "But I said I'd stay with you,
Brambleclaw, and I will."

Stormfur looked around at them, warmed to the roots of
his fur by their loyalty. Except for his sister, none of them had
any reason to support him apart from the bonds that had
been forged between them on their journey. Midnight
had spoken the truth when she said that four clans had
become one. Stormfur could see nothing but good in the way
that the old Clan boundaries were melting away, and he wondered if in the forest the Clans were learning to be friends as
well while facing the Twoleg threat. Perhaps at last the ache of
his half-Clan heritage could be soothed, and he would find a
place where he could truly belong. "Thank you," he mewed
solemnly.

"The Tribe of Endless Hunting will honour your courage,"
Talon meowed. "But what exactly do you mean to do?"

"I have an idea!" Squirrelpaw looked almost ready to leap
out of her fur.

Every cat looked at her. Talon let out a hiss of disbelief.

"Go on," urged Brambleclaw.

"What Silverstream said," Squirrelpaw began, "about
every question having many answers. Well, lots of cats have
tried to kill Sharptooth and failed, over and over again. Even
fighters like Talon. So we have to find another answer, and I

think I know what it is."

"What?" Crowpaw's voice was dry. "Are you going to go up to him and ask him nicely to go away?"

"Mouse-brain!" meowed Squirrelpaw. "No, if we can't kill Sharptooth by ourselves, we have to find something else to do it for us."

CHAPTER 20

❧

The mouse's tail slipped between Leafpaw's outstretched claws, leaving her to glare in frustration at the crevice where the tiny creature had vanished. She had left the camp to collect more herbs for Cinderpelt, and following Firestar's order that no cats were to go out alone, Sorreltail was with her.

"Bad luck," the tortoiseshell warrior meowed sympathetically. "But it was pretty scrawny to start with."

"It was prey," Leafpaw retorted. "I'd have caught it if I weren't so hungry that I can't see straight."

She began backing out from underneath the bush. Suddenly she noticed its familiar dark green leaves for the first time, and the red berries that clung to its branches and lay scattered around the trunk.

"Mouse dung!" she hissed. "And I've got the filthy stuff on my paws."

"What's the matter?"

Leafpaw backed out the rest of the way and pointed at the berries with her tail. "Deathberries," she meowed. "I was so keen to catch the mouse that I never saw them."

Sorreltail shivered. "Let's find some water and wash it off, quick."

Leafpaw was puzzled to see the look of horror in her friend's eyes. Deathberries were pretty bad, but only if you ate them. Sorreltail was one of the bravest cats she knew, yet she looked thoroughly spooked by the sight of the berries, her ears lying flat and her fur bristling.

"Are you OK?" Leafpaw asked as they padded on into the forest, keeping a lookout for a puddle where she could wash off any poison that might have gotten on to her pads.

"I'm fine." Sorreltail blinked. "Did you know that I once nearly died from deathberries?"

"No!" Leafpaw stopped, her eyes wide with shock. "What happened?"

"It was when I was a kit, before you were born. I'd followed Darkstripe into the forest—you won't remember Darkstripe; he was Tigerstar's biggest ally in ThunderClan. When I spotted him talking to Blackstar—he was Blackfoot then, Tigerstar's deputy—on *our* territory, he gave me the death-berries so I couldn't tell any cat what I'd seen."

"That's terrible!" Leafpaw pressed her muzzle against Sorreltail's side.

"It's thanks to Cinderpelt I survived," Sorreltail meowed. "Still, it's all over now. Whatever the Twolegs are doing to us, at least we don't have Tigerstar to worry about any more." She spun around, her tail held high in the air. "Come on; let's get your paws clean. A deathberry poisoning is the last thing the Clan needs right now."

Dark thoughts flew into Leafpaw's mind as she followed her friend deeper into the undergrowth. If Tigerstar really was the father of Hawkfrost and Mothwing, then perhaps that trouble *wasn't* all over.

The roar of the Twoleg monsters grew louder as they approached the Thunderpath. At last they found a small pool in a hollow where Leafpaw dipped her paws several times and rubbed them on the grass until she was sure all traces of the deathberries were gone. All the same, she knew she would feel uneasy about licking her paws for many days to come.

"There," she mewed. She had to raise her voice to make herself heard above the growling of the monster. "That should be OK. And look, there's a huge clump of chervil over there. Cinderpelt will—"

She broke off with a terrified gasp as the roar of the monster grew suddenly louder, as if the whole sky were splitting apart with thunder. A vast, glittering shape broke through the undergrowth, crushing the chervil she had just spotted. Sorreltail let out a startled yowl and fled for the nearest tree, clawing her way up the bark and coming to rest in the first fork, her fur fluffed up until she looked twice her size.

Leafpaw flattened herself in a hollow in the ground. She watched in frozen horror as the monster seized a half-grown ash tree and ripped it out of the ground with no more effort than she would have taken to dig up a burdock root. It lifted the tree high in the air, turning it in a huge, twisting limb as it stripped off the branches. Debris began to rain down around Leafpaw, pattering on the ground like hail.

"Leafpaw!" Sorreltail's yowl cut through her fear. Her friend had leaped down from the tree, perhaps realising there was no safety there any more. She pelted across the open ground and nudged Leafpaw to her paws. "Run!"

Leafpaw gave the monster one more terrified glance, to see it beginning to slice the tree into pieces. Then she was dashing through the forest behind Sorreltail, blundering into brambles and through deep troughs of mud in their mad rush to escape.

When the roar had died to a faint rumble behind them, the two cats halted, panting.

"They're taking more and more of our forest," Sorreltail gasped. "Soon there'll be nowhere left for us."

Leafpaw stood trembling, looking back and half expecting the monster to burst through the trees in pursuit. "I hate them!" she spat. "They've no right to come here. What did we ever do to harm them?"

"That's Twolegs for you," Sorreltail mewed. She was growing calmer, the fur on her shoulders beginning to lie flat again. After a moment, she touched Leafpaw's ear with her tail-tip. "Come on, let's go and look for herbs near the RiverClan border. We'll get as far from those horrible monsters as we can."

Leafpaw nodded, suddenly too scared to speak. She followed the tortoiseshell warrior through the forest, grief surging through her at the thought of the peaceful places that would never be peaceful again, the trees that would never again grow green in newleaf and cast their shade on the forest. StarClan must be grieving too, she realised, especially if they could do nothing to stop the destruction.

"What are we going to do?" Sorreltail asked after a few

moments. "I can't remember the last time I was full-fed . . . or any other cat in the Clan. Look at Ferncloud. She blames herself because Larchkit died, but it's not her fault at all."

Leafpaw thought of gentle Ferncloud, grieving over her dead kit, and Dustpelt's misery as he tried in vain to comfort her. She thought of Dappletail, dead because hunger had forced her to eat the tainted rabbit. Frostfur had become too feeble to leave the elders' den, and she had started to cough. Cinderpelt was waiting every day for an outbreak of greencough, which could so easily turn into fatal blackcough.

"Sometimes I think the Twolegs won't stop until we're all dead," Leafpaw mewed softly.

Sorreltail let out a murmur of agreement. "It's as if StarClan has abandoned us. Leafpaw, haven't they spoken to you, or to Cinderpelt? Why didn't they warn us? Don't our warrior ancestors care about us anymore?"

Leafpaw shut her eyes. She desperately wanted to tell her friend that StarClan had prophesied all this, though not to the medicine cats or their apprentices. But she had promised to keep the secret of the chosen cats, and if she was to break her word it must be to tell Firestar or Cinderpelt before any other cat.

And more than this, she was starting to think that wherever the cats had been sent by StarClan, they weren't coming back. It was days now since she had been able to reach Squirrelpaw in her mind. Leafpaw's heart ached at the thought that she might never see her sister or Brambleclaw again. There was no point in dangling hope in front of

Sorreltail and then snatching it away.

As they approached the RiverClan border, where the ground sloped down to the river and the Twoleg bridge, Leafpaw began to feel calmer. The sound of the Twoleg monsters did not reach this part of the territory yet; everything was so peaceful that she could almost imagine the forest was just as it used to be.

Tasting the air, she caught the scent of rabbit, and spotted the creature hopping between one clump of bracken and the next. Her paws itched to pursue it, but she remembered Firestar's order and Dappletail's dreadful death.

"Infuriating, isn't it?" Sorreltail muttered, with an angry flick of her tail. "I'd swear the stupid creatures are laughing at us."

Leafpaw nodded, water flooding her mouth at the prey-scent. She couldn't help wondering how long it would be before they were all so desperate that, like Dappletail, they would take the risk of eating the rabbits.

Just ahead of her, Sorreltail dropped into the hunter's crouch. Cautiously, so she didn't disturb her friend's concentration, Leafpaw edged her way forward until she could see what Sorreltail had spotted: a squirrel, moving slowly across an open space. *Yes!* Leafpaw thought. Prey that was fit to eat, to take back to the camp for Ferncloud and Frostfur . . .

Sorreltail leaped. Though she made no sound, the squirrel fled a heartbeat before the warrior's front paws hit the spot where it had been. Sorreltail let out a yowl of frustration and hurled herself after it as it made for the nearest tree.

"Sorreltail, no!" Leafpaw called out as she realised that the tree was on the other side of the border.

But Sorreltail was deafened by the hunger in her belly, fixed on chasing the squirrel. As it ran up the tree she launched herself up and managed to snag a claw in its tail, but the squirrel twitched itself free. Sorreltail fell to the ground, spitting fury.

"Come back!" Leafpaw cried. "You're on RiverClan territory!"

Sorreltail scrambled to her paws, bits of grass clinging to her fur. "Fox dung!" she snarled. "I nearly had it."

Before Leafpaw could call to her again, a familiar scent swept over her. A tabby shape appeared from behind the tree, and as Sorreltail spun round a huge paw slapped her to the ground and pinned her there.

"What's this?" Hawkfrost growled. "ThunderClan cats trespassing on our territory?"

CHAPTER 21

Sorreltail glared up at Hawkfrost. Twisting under his paw, she raked her claws over his leg, but days of hunger had taken the edge off her fighting skills. The warrior didn't flinch as he cuffed her over the ear with his other forepaw.

"You're coming with me to Leopardstar," he snarled. "Let her decide what to do. ThunderClan have no right to ignore our borders."

"Let her go!" Leafpaw meowed. "She's only a couple of tail-lengths inside your border."

Hawkfrost gave her an unfriendly stare. "Oh, it's you again."

"Yes, me again." Leafpaw drew herself up and met Hawkfrost's icy blue eyes, summoning all her courage. "You were glad enough that I was there when Reedpaw had his accident." Persuasively, she added, "You owe ThunderClan a favour. Let Sorreltail go."

Hawkfrost's lip curled in a sneer. "Clans do not owe each other favours. The warrior code says we should respect boundaries, which she"—he gave Sorreltail a contemptuous flick with his tail—"clearly does not."

Leafpaw felt her fur bristle and her muscles tense, as if her body were telling her to fight with Hawkfrost. Together she and Sorreltail had a chance of beating him. . . But she forced herself to stay calm and not move from where she stood on the border. She could just imagine what Firestar would say if he found out she had attacked a cat from another Clan on his own territory.

It was hard to beg such an obnoxious cat, but she had to make one more effort. "Please—it's not as if she was doing any harm."

Hawkfrost's blue eyes were chips of ice. "She was stealing prey."

"She was not!" Leafpaw's eyes flew wide. "That was a ThunderClan squirrel."

Sorreltail, who had been lying limp under Hawkfrost's paw, suddenly heaved herself upwards. Hawkfrost let out a screech as her teeth met in his leg. For a moment they writhed together on the ground, but for all her bravery Sorreltail was no match for Hawkfrost's size and strength. Soon she lay panting under his paws again.

"OK, take me to Leopardstar," she spat. "But I'll fight you every step of the way."

Hawkfrost looked bored. "Fine. You do that."

Desperately Leafpaw looked around; why wasn't Firestar or Cinderpelt here? They might be able to persuade Hawkfrost. There were no cats at all on her own side of the border, but she caught sight of a flash of gold in the reeds on the other side of the river, and a heartbeat later saw Mothwing running across the Twoleg bridge. The RiverClan apprentice bounded up the slope and halted beside her brother.

"What's going on?"

"You can see for yourself." Hawkfrost tapped Sorreltail with his tail. "I've caught a trespasser. I'm going to take her to Leopardstar."

"She didn't mean it," Leafpaw pleaded, feeling more hopeful now that Mothwing had turned up. "She was chasing a squirrel—one of ours—and she didn't realise that she'd crossed the border."

Mothwing looked from her brother to Leafpaw and back again. "Let her go," she meowed. "It's not important. She didn't catch anything. If you take her to Leopardstar you could start a war between our Clans."

Hawkfrost fixed his cold blue stare on his sister. "And why is that such a bad thing? Every cat knows that ThunderClan is in trouble. This could be our chance to move in and take their territory."

Leafpaw gasped. Was that what Hawkfrost really wanted?

Mothwing returned her brother's stare. "Don't be mouse-brained," she mewed frostily. "Remember what Leopardstar owes Firestar. He gave the Clan back to her when Tigerstar tried to take over. She'll never go to war against him."

"She will for a good enough reason," Hawkfrost argued. "This isn't about old favours; it's about the warrior code. The borders between the Clans have to count for something!" His voice was becoming high-pitched with desperation, and he took a deep breath before growling, "And you watch your tongue, Mothwing. Remember you could be talking to the next Clan deputy."

"*What?*" Leafpaw blurted out. "What about Mistyfoot?"

"Mistyfoot is a coward," Hawkfrost snarled. "She couldn't face what's happening in the forest, so she ran away."

"No cat has seen her for a whole day," Mothwing explained to Leafpaw, her eyes wide and anxious. "Not since she went to patrol the border near Fourtrees. We don't know what has happened to her."

"Even if she comes back, she won't be deputy anymore," Hawkfrost growled. "Clan deputies can't just go wandering off when they feel like it."

Leafpaw's head spun. She couldn't believe it. Mistyfoot was no coward; besides, she had assumed that RiverClan wasn't affected by what was happening to the other three Clans, because their territory was the only one the Twolegs hadn't touched. But now Mistyfoot had disappeared.

How many more had gone? Had *all* the Clans lost cats? A chill crept bone-deep into Leafpaw; these disappearances couldn't be related to the prophecy from StarClan. Even if the first cats had failed, StarClan wouldn't send out more and more to a nameless fate. Somehow the Twolegs and their monsters must be responsible.

She said nothing of this to Mothwing and Hawkfrost, and to her relief Sorreltail did not tell them about the disappearance of Cloudtail and Brightheart. The less RiverClan knew about ThunderClan's affairs the better, especially if Hawkfrost was spoiling for a fight because he thought ThunderClan was weak.

Instead, it was Mothwing who broke the silence. "You know, you're a fool, Hawkfrost," she mewed.

Her brother bristled. "What do you mean?"

"If you want to bring down ThunderClan, you're going about it the wrong way."

"And you know the right way, do you?" Hawkfrost sneered.

"Yes, I do." Mothwing's tone was cold. Leafpaw could hardly believe what she was hearing; she suddenly felt as if she didn't know this cat at all.

"Go on, then, enlighten me."

Mothwing turned her head to give her shoulder a couple of quick licks. "Be kind to them. Make them grateful to us. That should keep them quiet while they get weaker and weaker. Why fight and risk injuries to our Clan? Let the Twolegs do the job for us. *Then* we move in and take their territory."

Hawkfrost's eyes narrowed thoughtfully. "You could have a point," he grunted. "OK." He stepped back and let Sorreltail get up. "Leave, and don't come back."

Sorreltail shook herself and glared at him before taking the few steps that carried her back into her own territory. Leafpaw studied her closely as she crossed the border, but apart from a couple of superficial scratches, Hawkfrost hadn't hurt her.

"I'll tell Firestar what you said," she meowed to Mothwing, striving hard to keep her voice level. "He'll take it up with Leopardstar at the next Gathering."

Two pairs of eyes, ice blue and amber, turned their gaze on her.

"Sure, tell him," Hawkfrost invited. "Even if he believes you, what can he do about it? Don't you think Leopardstar will back me against a ThunderClan cat?"

Sorreltail nudged Leafpaw's shoulder. "Come on. Let's go back to camp."

Leafpaw turned away, her tail drooping. She had liked Mothwing and trusted her, and now it seemed that her friend had betrayed her. Even if Mothwing's first loyalty was to her Clan, Leafpaw hadn't thought that she would be so coldly calculating.

She had not gone more than a few fox-lengths when she heard Mothwing calling her name in a low voice. She stopped and looked back. Mothwing was standing on the border; Hawkfrost was nowhere to be seen.

"Leafpaw!" Mothwing beckoned with her tail.

"Ignore her," Sorreltail muttered. "Who needs friends like that?"

"Leafpaw, please . . ." Mothwing's voice was pleading now. "Let me explain."

Leafpaw hesitated, then took a few reluctant steps back towards the border. Sorreltail padded close beside her; Leafpaw sensed her tension and winced at the look of disgust she shot towards the RiverClan she-cat.

"I had to say that in front of Hawkfrost," Mothwing explained urgently. "Don't you see? He'd never have let your friend go otherwise."

Leafpaw felt relief flood over her. She hadn't wanted to think badly of Mothwing, not when they shared the bond of all medicine cats.

She could see her own relief reflected in the RiverClan cat's eyes as Mothwing added, "You do believe me, don't you? We are still friends?"

"Of course we are." Leafpaw stepped forwards to touch noses with Mothwing. She ignored a sceptical snort from Sorreltail just behind her. "Thank you."

Behind Mothwing, at the foot of the slope, she saw Hawkfrost emerge from the shelter of a bush and lope easily across the Twoleg bridge. She shivered when she remembered the cruel ambition in his eyes. Surely no other cat but Tigerstar had been so greedy for power?

"Mothwing," she murmured, unable to bear the uncertainty any longer, "who was your father? Was it Tigerstar?"

Shock flared in Mothwing's amber eyes. For a moment she hesitated, and then replied, "Yes."

CHAPTER 22

❧

This was madness, sheer madness. The words echoed to the thud of Stormfur's paws as he allowed Crag and another cave-guard to escort him back into the cave behind the waterfall. The other forest cats were ushered in close behind him, with more guards on either side, while Talon and his fellow outlaws brought up the rear. A patrol had spotted them as soon as they reached the river; Stormfur was pretty sure they were prisoners now rather than guests, and he did not know what the Tribe cats would do to them. They had fought their way out two nights before, so it was reasonable to expect hostility. Talon and his friends were taking an even bigger risk, because they had been ordered not to come back until Sharptooth was dead.

The first rays of glimmering moonlight were creeping through the sheet of water at the cave entrance, and soon Sharptooth would be on the prowl. Stormfur was not even sure that he could make the Tribe listen to Squirrelpaw's plan. As he sought inside himself for courage, Silverstream's scent drifted faintly around him. Stormfur glanced back, wondering if Feathertail could sense it, too. His sister was just behind him, her blue eyes troubled. But none of them had flinched when the cave-guards swarmed out from behind the rocks, as well hidden as ever by their mud-streaked fur. Stormfur felt humbled by his friends' bravery, by their loyalty to him and to the warrior code even this far away from the forest. He knew they would do whatever it took to help the Tribe, or die trying.

Stoneteller had clearly been warned of their arrival, and was waiting for them in the middle of the main cave. Under his coating of mud, Stormfur could see that a slice of his fur had been torn away in the fight against Sharptooth, and he had a raw wound across one ear.

Stormfur strode over to him and laid at his feet the piece of prey he had carried all the way through the mountains: a mountain hare, its pelt just beginning to turn white for leaf-bare.

"What's this?" Stoneteller's voice was cold, and his eyes were hostile. "Why have you come back?"

"To help you defeat Sharptooth," Stormfur replied.

His heart began to pound even faster when he saw neither welcome nor relief in the Healer's expression. "And just what do you think you can do?"

His gaze swept around the cavern; following it, Stormfur saw the Tribe creeping out of the shadows. They looked curious but wary. The friendship they had begun to show towards the cats had been scorched by the shock of Sharptooth's attack, and Stormfur's failure to save them in spite of their warrior ancestors' promise. Like Stoneteller, many of them bore raw scars or limped heavily from fresh wounds. Stormfur searched for Brook, but could not see her.

"Sharptooth took Star yesterday," Stoneteller growled. "Many cats were injured as we tried to drive him out. One has already died, and two others lie on the border of the Tribe of Endless Hunting. You didn't help us then. You ran away."

His contempt struck Stormfur like a claw. Even worse was the murmur of agreement from the gathering Tribe, as if they had felt betrayed by his flight, just as he had felt betrayed when they made him a prisoner. He heard a hostile hiss from one of the Clan cats—he guessed it was Crowpaw—and hoped that the apprentice would keep quiet.

"I didn't believe I was the promised cat," he meowed honestly. "And I didn't like being trapped in the Cave of Pointed Stones. But since I escaped, I've been thinking . . . and I've come back freely. Even if I'm not the cat who was named in the prophecy, I'll do all I can to help."

"We all will," Brambleclaw added, coming to stand at Stormfur's shoulder.

The Tribe's Healer began to relax. There were more murmurs from the cats around him, and some at least sounded approving.

Then he heard Brook's voice behind him. "Stormfur! I knew you would come back."

Stormfur turned to see her slipping through the crowd. A shiver ran through his pelt as he looked at her shining eyes and heard the welcome in her voice.

"We should listen to him," she urged Stoneteller. "The

Tribe of Endless Hunting has sent him to help us. Why else would he come back, after seeing what Sharptooth can do?"

Stoneteller looked as if he lacked energy to believe anything anymore, but he bowed his head. "Very well," he said. "But what are you going to do that we haven't tried before? Sharptooth has killed the best fighters in my Tribe as if they were puny kits."

Stormfur flicked his ears to beckon Squirrelpaw forwards. She carried a wad of leaves in her jaws. "Show Stoneteller what you have," he mewed, and added into her ear, "I hope you haven't swallowed any."

Squirrelpaw dropped the leaves. "I'm not mouse-brained!" she muttered indignantly.

Turning back to Stoneteller, Stormfur prodded the hare with one paw. "This prey is for Sharptooth," he meowed. "And inside it, we'll put these." Delicately he unwrapped the leaves to reveal a small heap of glossy red berries.

A kit who was crouched with its mother at the front of the tribe took a step forward to sniff them curiously; Squirrelpaw thrust her tail in its way and guided it back to its mother.

"Don't touch," she mewed. "Even one of those would give you the worst bellyache you've ever had—if you survived."

The kit stared at her with huge eyes and said nothing.

Gazing at the berries, the Tribe's healer let out a faint hiss and took a step back. "Night-seeds?"

"You know them?" Stormfur asked. "In our Clans, we call them deathberries."

"I know all the herbs and berries that grow in these

mountains," Stoneteller responded. For a moment a gleam of interest showed in his eyes; then he bent his head again and when he spoke his voice was defeated. "And none of that knowledge is any use to protect my Tribe. Sharptooth is too strong. Not even your deathberries will defeat him."

"Three will kill the strongest warrior." Squirrelpaw spoke up boldly. "I think what we have here would be enough even for Sharptooth."

Stoneteller looked surprised. "Are you sure?"

"Even if they don't," Stormfur added, "they'll weaken him so we can finish him off."

Stoneteller still looked undecided. His shoulders were bowed as if the whole weight of the mountains rested on them.

Then Stormfur heard a stir among the Tribe cats, hostile muttering that swelled to furious yowling. Talon was thrusting his way forwards to stand before the Healer; thanks to the shadows that darkened the cave most of the Tribe had only just noticed that the outlaws had returned.

Talon stood stone-still, while his former Tribemates hurled accusations at him.

"You were supposed to kill Sharptooth!"

"You failed us!"

"Stoneteller, he's disobeying you by coming here. Kill him!"

Instinctively, the Clan cats gathered round Talon, ready to defend him. Crowpaw's neck fur stood on end, and Tawnypelt had unsheathed her claws. Even the gentle Feathertail lashed her tail from side to side. Stormfur felt as proud of his warriors as any Clan leader.

Stoneteller lifted his tail for silence, but it was several heartbeats before the clamour died away. "Well?" the Healer growled. "I hope you have good reason for coming here."

"The best reason," Talon replied. "You can kill me if you like, but that won't make you any stronger against Sharptooth. Your enemy is outside this cave, not inside. The silver cat has come, and it is time to believe the prophecy of the Tribe of Endless Hunting. If we fail, then you can kill us."

The Tribe fell silent. Their hostility had changed to uncertainty; Stormfur let his neck fur lie flat again.

"We cannot kill the creature in its lair," Talon went on, "since we do not know where it lives. So we must bring it here to die."

"Here?" Brook exclaimed, one voice among many cries of outrage. "In our cave?"

Stormfur reached out with his tail and rested it on her shoulder. She had to trust him, however dangerous their plan seemed.

"Yes, here," Talon growled. "This is the place we know, where we have somewhere to hide, and where the whole Tribe can wait to ambush Sharptooth if we need to give him the death blow."

"And how do you propose to bring him here?" Stoneteller asked icily.

"With blood."

Talon lifted one huge paw and sliced it open with his teeth;

scarlet drops spattered to the ground like rain. Then he raised his head and let out a ferocious yowl that echoed around the cavern, louder than the waterfall outside. He spun round and dashed out of the entrance, Rock and Bird racing on his heels.

They left behind them a dizzy, echoing silence, apart from the sound of water. Stormfur let out a long breath. The plan had begun. The trail of blood was being laid.

Brambleclaw was the first to speak. "Squirrelpaw and Stormfur, you stuff the hare. Be sure you don't get any death-berry juice on your fur, and if you do, wash it off right away."

"Yes, O medicine cat." Squirrelpaw bowed her head with mock respect, her green eyes flashing. "We know what to do!"

Stormfur listened while Brambleclaw and Tawnypelt discussed the best place to leave the hare. Stoneteller was giving orders to his cave-guards, and sending the kits and kit-mothers to the nursery. Guards were placed at the entrance to that tunnel, while more of the cave-guards and the prey-hunters scrambled into places on the rocks around the cave walls where they could spring down on Sharptooth. Their mud-streaked fur blended into the walls so that Stormfur could hardly see where they were hiding.

All the while a sense of dread was growing inside him. Somehow he felt like something terrible was going to happen. But why, if this was what the Tribe of Endless Hunting wanted him to do? He drank in the air, but he could scent nothing of Silverstream now, nor sense her reassuring presence.

"It will be all right." Feathertail came up to him and pressed her muzzle against his. "I know you're scared, but StarClan sent you here as well, with your dream about our mother. We have to do this."

Crowpaw, a grey-black shadow hovering at Feathertail's shoulder, nodded but said nothing.

An icy paw gripped Stormfur. Something was wrong; he knew it. There was something they had not understood, something they had not planned for. He looked around for Brambleclaw, wanting to share his fears with him, and saw him dragging the hare across the floor to lay it in front of the entrance, a few tail-lengths inside the cave. Tawnypelt watched, measuring the distance between the bait and the entrance, while Squirrelpaw made helpful gestures with her tail.

Stormfur padded over to them, feeling the eyes of the hidden Tribe staring at him from every corner of the cave. But before he could say anything, a screech split the air outside. Talon, Rock, and Bird dashed into the cave and skidded to a halt.

"Sharptooth!" Bird gasped.

"He's here!" Rock yowled, his voice rising to a wail. "He's coming!"

CHAPTER 23

Stormfur froze. It was too soon!

The outlaws dived for the cave walls, and the Tribe cats who had not already taken up their positions pelted down the tunnel to the Cave of Pointed Stones. Stormfur and his friends were left in the center of the cavern, staring around in panic.

Their moment's hesitation was a moment too long. A ferocious snarling sliced through the noise of the waterfall. A shadow fell across from the entrance, etched in moonlight. Then Sharptooth burst upon them.

Just as the Tribe had said, he looked like a lion from the elders' tales, but without the fiery mane around his head. Lean muscles rippled beneath his short-haired pelt, and his massive gold head was lowered, following the trail of Talon's blood. When he entered the cave he looked up. He saw the hare, and swiped it aside with one vast paw.

"No!" Squirrelpaw yowled.

Her screech brought the huge head swinging around, the round, thick-furred ears twitching with interest.

"Get back!" snarled Brambleclaw. "All of you, hide!"

He leaped towards the lion-cat, lashing out with both front

paws and rolling aside before Sharptooth could turn on him. Stormfur saw Squirrelpaw dash in from the other side and spring on to Sharptooth's back, sinking her claws into the base of his tail.

"Squirrelpaw!" Brambleclaw yowled. "What in StarClan's name are you doing?"

As the lion-cat twisted, trying to dislodge her, Squirrelpaw leaped down and fled for the boulders that lined the cave wall. With a roar of fury, Sharptooth launched himself after her, but she was too fast for him, scrambling out of reach to stand hissing on a jutting piece of rock, her ginger fur fluffed up.

Stormfur fled to the opposite cave wall, following Feathertail up a series of cracks in the rock until they reached a tiny ledge tucked under the roof. Crouching in the narrow space beside his sister, he looked down at the cave floor.

The Tribe cats were all in their hiding places, too scared to move. Brambleclaw had gained safety too, on another ledge just below Squirrelpaw. He was snarling up at her, looking almost as furious as Sharptooth himself; Stormfur couldn't hear what he was saying, but he could guess.

For a moment Stormfur could not see Tawnypelt; then he spotted her head poking out of a cleft halfway up the cave wall near the entrance. That just left Crowpaw. Then Stormfur felt Feathertail tense against him and heard her murmur, "Oh, no!"

Sharptooth was scraping at the cave wall almost directly below them. Stormfur caught a terrifying glimpse of his eyes, glaring black in the moonlight, and his lips drawn back to reveal savage, dripping fangs. Crowpaw was trapped in a crevice at floor level that was too shallow to shelter him, desperately trying to press himself against the rock and escape the vicious claws. A cry of terror escaped him.

Stormfur felt his belly flip over. Everything was going wrong. Sharptooth had ignored the baited hare and pursued the cats instead. Within heartbeats he would have Crowpaw, and StarClan's mission would be ruined. How could four Clans become one if the WindClan cat were killed? Stormfur cursed himself under his breath; there was nothing that he could do, because he was not the cat the Tribe's warrior ancestors had promised. His stupid, thoughtless pride had gotten it wrong.

Beside him, he heard Feathertail whisper, "Crowpaw." She gave Stormfur a long look, filled with love and sorrow, her blue eyes glowing in the moonlight. "I can hear the voices clearly now," she murmured. "This is for me to do."

Then Stormfur felt her muscles bunch. Before he realised what she was doing, she leaped—not down, but up towards the cave roof, digging her claws into one of the narrow talons of stone with a grating noise that sent shudders along Stormfur's spine.

"No!" he yowled.

The rock split and broke away under Feathertail's weight. With a terrifying wail she plummeted down, straight at Sharptooth. The lion-cat looked up. His throaty growl changed to a scream as the spike of rock plunged into him; he fell writhing to the ground. Feathertail plummeted to the floor of the cave beside him.

Stormfur hurled himself down the wall, slipping on the rock and feeling his claws rip, until he reached his sister's side. Feathertail lay without moving, her eyes closed. Sharptooth was still twitching, but as Stormfur scrambled to a halt the lion-cat gave one massive shudder and died.

"Feathertail?" Stormfur whispered.

He was aware of Crowpaw creeping out of the rock to crouch beside him. "Feathertail?" The WindClan cat sounded desperate. "Feathertail, are you OK?"

Feathertail did not move. Stormfur lifted his head and saw the other Clan cats gathering around him, along with cats from the Tribe, creeping fearfully from their hiding places. He dropped his gaze back to his sister, and saw the faint rise and fall of her chest as she breathed.

"She'll be fine." His voice cracked. "She's got to be. She . . . she has a prophecy to fulfil."

Crowpaw crept forwards until his nose touched Feathertail's fur. He breathed in her scent, and then began to lick her gently. Blood from a slash on his shoulder smudged against her pelt. "Wake up, Feathertail," he whispered. "Please wake up."

There was no response. An achingly familiar scent wreathed around Stormfur, and he looked up. "Silverstream?"

Near the entrance to the cave, where moonlight rippled through the sheet of falling water, he thought that he could see a silver cat. She was nothing more than the faintest sliver of light, but her voice sounded clearly in his head, filled with grief. "Oh, Feathertail!"

There was a gasp from Crowpaw and Stormfur snatched his gaze back to see that his sister's eyes were open. Trembling, he spoke her name. She shifted her head and blinked.

"You'll have to go home without me, brother," she murmured. "Save the Clan!"

Her eyes focused on Crowpaw, and Stormfur saw in them a lifetime of love for the difficult young apprentice, enough to sweep their Clans' rivalry away forever. "Think you have nine lives, do you?" she whispered. "I saved you once... Don't make me save you again."

"Feathertail ... Feathertail, no!" Crowpaw could hardly get the words out. "Don't leave me."

"I won't." Now her whisper was scarcely audible. "I'll always be with you, I promise."

Then her eyes closed, and she did not speak again.

Crowpaw threw his head back and let out a wail. Stormfur crouched beside his sister with his head down, grief freezing his limbs. Around him he heard the voices of his friends rise in sorrow. Squirrelpaw huddled close to Brambleclaw, murmuring, "She can't be dead—she can't be!" Brambleclaw bent his head to lick her ear. Beside them Tawnypelt stared at Feathertail with misery in her amber eyes.

The Tribe cats started whispering to one another. Somewhere deeper in the cave a yowl of jubilation broke out. "Sharptooth is dead! We are free!"

Stormfur flinched. The price had been too high. He turned his head towards the mouth of the cave, where the faint outline of the silver cat still stood in the moonlight.

Silverstream's voice came to him through the roar of the water. "My dear son, try not to grieve too long. Feathertail will hunt with StarClan now. I will take care of her."

"We took care of her," Stormfur replied bitterly, and then he realised that he was lying. They had failed. If they hadn't, she would not be lying there, dead, her fur glowing silver in the moonlight.

"She came," whispered Brook. "The silver cat came."

"No," Stormfur growled. "I brought her."

Crowpaw turned his head, a terrible blank look in his eyes. "It's my fault." His voice was a hoarse whisper. "If I'd refused to come back to the cave, she would have stayed with me."

"No . . ." Stormfur murmured, reaching out one paw, but Crowpaw bowed his head.

A gentle voice said his name. Brook had drawn close to him, with Stoneteller behind her. Shyly she touched her nose to Stormfur's muzzle. "I'm sorry," she whispered. "I'm so sorry."

"The Tribe of Endless Hunting spoke truly," Stoneteller meowed. "A silver cat has saved us all."

But it wasn't me, thought Stormfur. *I wish it had been.*

He turned away from where Crowpaw lay beside Feathertail, his nose pushed into her fur, and looked at the sheet of falling water. Just for a heartbeat, he thought that he saw two silver cats there shimmering in the half-light, side by side, watching over the shattered remnants of the questing Clan cats.

He blinked, and they were gone.

CHAPTER 24

❧

"No! Help them!" A wail of sorrow and fear broke from Leafpaw. She opened her eyes with a jump and saw that she was in her nest outside Cinderpelt's den. The morning sunlight was pale and cold. The rumble of monsters from her nightmare had reached the camp in the waking world, too, and their stench hung in the air.

Shuddering, Leafpaw curled deeper into the moss, trying to find comfort in its warmth while the last wisps of her dream hung in her mind like mist. She had been standing near the Thunderpath, watching the Twoleg monsters as they roared through the forest, crushing cats under their huge black paws. Blood had run like a river across the forest floor. Spottedleaf had stood beside her, and Leafpaw had turned to her with a desperate plea. "Save them! Please! Why don't you save them?"

Spottedleaf's eyes had rested sadly on Leafpaw's dying friends. "There is nothing more StarClan can do to help," she murmured. "I'm so sorry."

Then she had faded away, and Leafpaw had woken up.

She rose to her paws, staggering, and padded across to

Cinderpelt's den. The medicine cat was not there; Leafpaw could see an empty heap of bedding at the back of the cleft and wondered if some emergency had called her away, and whether there was yet another disaster they would have to face. A whimper rose at the back of her throat, and she firmly closed her jaws on it. Whatever fate was coming, even if their warrior ancestors were helpless, she would go on helping her Clan while she had the strength.

A rustle behind her made her turn to see Cinderpelt brushing her way through the fern tunnel. The medicine cat's tail was drooping, though she tried to brighten up when she saw Leafpaw.

"What's happened?" Leafpaw asked, bracing herself.

"I've been to see Frostfur," the medicine cat replied. "Don't look like that; she isn't dead. In fact she's a little better. I'm pretty sure she hasn't got greencough."

"That's good." Leafpaw tried to sound pleased, but she couldn't help adding, "It's hunger, not greencough, that will be our real enemy this leaf-bare."

Cinderpelt nodded. "True. And if more cats disappear, there won't be enough warriors to provide food for the kits and elders, even if they could find prey." She let out a discouraged sigh.

"Shall I try to catch something for Frostfur?" Leafpaw offered. "I could join a hunting patrol, unless you want more herbs."

"No, we're pretty well stocked now. That's a good idea, Leafpaw—though I'm not sure you'll find much out there."

Leafpaw didn't argue. She padded through the ferns into the main clearing, and for a moment she felt as if she had stepped into the camp as it used to be. Sandstorm and Rainwhisker had just appeared at the mouth of the gorse tunnel, both with fresh-kill in their jaws. Spiderpaw and Shrewpaw were lying in a patch of sunlight outside the apprentices' den, while Dustpelt and Ferncloud shared tongues at the entrance to the nursery. Firestar and Brackenfur were talking together at the base of the Highrock.

Then Leafpaw realised what she was really seeing. Her father and Brackenfur both looked worried. The two apprentices lay still, instead of scuffling playfully as they used to. The fresh-kill pile where her mother and Rainwhisker dropped their prey was pitifully small. As Leafpaw padded past the nursery, she watched Dustpelt push a mouse towards Ferncloud. The she-cat's appearance horrified Leafpaw; she was little more than a skeleton, every bone visible under her dull fur.

"You must eat," Dustpelt meowed. "Hollykit and Birchkit still need you."

The reek of monsters hung over the clearing, and their roar sounded even louder to Leafpaw. Her eyes filled with a vision of them breaking through the wall of thorns that surrounded the camp, the sun glittering on their bright pelts as they crushed the terrified Clan. She blinked, forcing the images away. She could not stop the Twolegs from doing what they wanted, but she could do something small to help her starving Clan.

As she headed towards Firestar and Brackenfur, she remembered her encounter with Hawkfrost the day before. So far she had not told any cat about his plans to take over ThunderClan's territory, and she had asked Sorreltail not to say anything either. She hardly knew how to load more trouble onto Firestar's shoulders, when he had so much to bear already. How could she tell him that his greatest enemy, Tigerstar, lived on in Tigerstar's son Hawkfrost, in a Clan not weakened by hunger or ravaged by Twolegs? She knew she had to find the words, but she wanted more time to think.

Drawing closer to her father, she heard him meow to Brackenfur, "You could try a hunting patrol near Twolegplace. That's about as far as you can get from the monsters."

The anguished cry of a cat in pain interrupted him. Leafpaw spun around to see Greystripe and Mousefur stumbling out of the gorse tunnel. Greystripe looked anxious, and Mousefur was limping along on only three legs, one of her forelimbs hanging useless. Her brown fur was sticking up as if she had been in a fight, though Leafpaw could not see or scent any blood.

Firestar bounded across to her, and Leafpaw followed.

"What happened?" Firestar demanded. "Who did this?"

Mousefur was in too much pain to answer. Her teeth were gritted, and she let out a wordless moan of agony.

"Twolegs," Greystripe spat, terror stark in his eyes. "We went too close to the monsters, and a Twoleg grabbed her."

Firestar stared in astonishment.

"Come and see Cinderpelt," Leafpaw meowed before her

father could delay them by asking more questions.

She padded close to the injured she-cat on the way to Cinderpelt's den. Mousefur's eyes were glazed with pain; though she struggled along bravely, the effort of making it back to camp had obviously exhausted her. Leafpaw tried to help by letting her lean on her shoulder.

Behind them, Greystripe walked beside Firestar. "The Twolegs usually stay inside their monsters," he meowed. "But today they were swarming all over the place—StarClan knows why. One of them yowled at Mousefur and she ran, straight into the paws of another one."

"This is mouse-brained." Firestar sounded utterly confused. "The Twolegs have always ignored us."

"Not any more," Greystripe mewed grimly.

"At least I gave him a few scratches to remember me by," Mousefur gasped.

Leafpaw raced ahead to alert Cinderpelt, who was sitting at the mouth of her den with her eyes raised to the sky as if she were trying to read some message from StarClan in the movement of the clouds.

"It's Mousefur—she's hurt!" Leafpaw gasped.

Cinderpelt leaped to her paws. "Oh, great StarClan!" she exclaimed. "What next?" She squeezed her eyes shut as if she could barely brace herself to carry on, but her voice was as calm as ever when she meowed, "Come and lie down here, and I'll take a look."

Mousefur lay down in front of the den, and Cinderpelt ran her nose along the injured leg, sniffing carefully at the shoulder. "It's dislocated," she meowed at last. "Cheer up, Mousefur. I can put it right, but it's going to hurt. Leafpaw, fetch me some poppy seeds."

Leafpaw obeyed, and Mousefur licked them up. As they waited a few moments for the seeds to dull the she-cat's pain, Leafpaw listened to her father and Greystripe talking together near the mouth of the tunnel.

"I'll have to forbid cats to go anywhere near the Twolegs," Firestar mewed. "Soon there'll be nowhere safe outside the camp. Already some of the cats are too scared to go out on patrol."

"We're not finished yet," Greystripe retorted stubbornly. "StarClan won't let us be destroyed."

Firestar shook his head, and stalked back down the tunnel into the main clearing. After a moment Greystripe, with a worried glance at Mousefur, followed him.

"OK, Leafpaw," Cinderpelt meowed. By now the brown warrior was growing sleepy, her head lolling forwards on to her paws. "Let's do it. Put your paws there," she went on, pointing to Mousefur's other foreleg. "Hold her still while I put her leg back. I don't want to be clawed to death. And watch carefully what I do," she added. "You haven't seen this before."

Leafpaw carefully positioned herself as her mentor had shown her, while Cinderpelt took Mousefur's injured leg firmly in her teeth, bracing one paw against her shoulder. Then she pulled; Leafpaw heard a sharp click and Mousefur jerked, letting out a furious yowl.

"Excellent," Cinderpelt muttered.

She examined Mousefur's shoulder again while the she-cat lay limp and trembling. "That's fine," she mewed, nudging the brown she-cat to her paws. "See if you can put your weight on it."

Mousefur tried; she staggered, more from exhaustion and the effects of the poppy seeds than from her injury, Leafpaw thought, but stayed on her paws.

"You'd better get some sleep." Cinderpelt began guiding her to the ferns at the edge of the clearing. "I'll check you again when you wake, but I don't think you'll have any more trouble." Glancing back at Leafpaw, she added, "You did well there. I can manage now if you want to go and hunt."

Leafpaw paused while her mentor settled Mousefur among the ferns. "Are you sure you don't need me?"

Cinderpelt shook her head. "There's nothing more to do. There's nothing any of us can do," she added in a lower voice. "StarClan is silent."

Her despair appalled Leafpaw. Amid all the chaos caused by the Twolegs, she had always believed that Cinderpelt's faith would stand firm. And worst of all, there was nothing she could say to lift her mentor's spirits—not when Spottedleaf herself had admitted that StarClan was as powerless as the cats in the forest.

"I'm not going hunting," she meowed firmly. "I'm going to find out what happened to our missing cats."

Cinderpelt stared at her, puzzled. "What?"

"Don't you see? If Mousefur hadn't struggled free, the Twoleg would have taken her away. We might never have known what happened to her. That must be what happened to Cloudtail and Brightheart too."

The medicine cat's expression cleared. "Yes, I see that. But Leafpaw—what if *you* don't come back?"

Leafpaw gazed at her, half regretting that she had told Cinderpelt her plan. What if she refused to let her go?

"This is the first clue we've had about the disappearances," she meowed. "We *must* try to find out the truth."

To her relief, after a moment's hesitation, Cinderpelt nodded. "Very well. But be careful. And find another cat to go with you." As Leafpaw turned to go, she added, "You're a brave cat, Leafpaw. Remember that the Clan can't afford to lose you."

Leafpaw dipped her head, embarrassed by her mentor's praise, and slipped through the ferns. Back in the main clearing, she could sense that a change had fallen over the Clan. News of the attack on Mousefur had clearly spread; the air was full of the scent of fear and despair. Leafpaw wanted to spring up onto the Highrock and call out to her Clanmates, to make them realise that they mustn't give up. As long as they were alive, there was still hope. But who would listen to an apprentice? And what words could she find that would make a difference?

Taking a deep breath, she made up her mind. She would go to Firestar and tell him everything she knew about the cats who had been sent away by StarClan. Even though she had no idea where they were now, or if they would ever return, the news might at least give Firestar and the rest of ThunderClan reassurance that StarClan was not indifferent to what was going on in the forest. She would tell him about Hawkfrost too, and his plans to take over ThunderClan's territory. She was sick of secrets; it would be a relief to unburden herself after so long.

But first she would go and look for the missing cats, in case Firestar punished her for not telling him sooner by confining her to the camp. Quickly she made her way to the outside of the warriors' den and called, "Sorreltail!"

Her friend peered out through the branches. "Leafpaw? What is it?"

Leafpaw thought back to the morning not so long ago when she had called Sorreltail out to visit WindClan. Then there had been hope; Sorreltail had been bright and lively, eager for action. Now her tortoiseshell fur looked dull, and her eyes stared blankly at Leafpaw.

"I want you to come with me," Leafpaw began, and explained her plan to investigate the disappearances.

To her relief, Sorreltail's eyes brightened as she spoke. "OK," the tortoiseshell warrior meowed. "It's better than lying around the camp all day. Let's go."

She threaded her way out between the branches of the den, and both cats headed through the gorse tunnel.

Leafpaw followed Greystripe's and Mousefur's scents back towards the scarred section of the forest where the Twoleg monsters rampaged. She had been this way the day before, when she and Sorreltail had watched the monster uproot the tree, but she was astonished to see how much more destruction the Twolegs had created in such a short time. The ground had been churned into mud, with monsters crouched here and there, or roaring across the ground with a horrible slow movement as if they were creeping up on prey.

There were Twoleg nests there, too, roughly made of wood rather than the hard red stone in Twolegplace. The cats crouched in the shelter of one of them, peering out at the Twolegs walking around. Leafpaw could feel Sorreltail quivering, fear-scent coming off her in waves; she felt just as terrified, but there was no way she was going back now, not when she was so close to finding out what happened to Cloudtail and Brightheart.

"What's *that*?" she murmured to Sorreltail.

She pointed with her tail at what looked like a miniature Twoleg den, made of wood and open at one end, set underneath one of the few surviving trees. It was far too small for a Twoleg to get inside.

Sorreltail shrugged. "Dunno. Some Twoleg thing."

"I'm going to look."

Warily glancing from side to side in case a Twoleg tried to grab her, Leafpaw crept across the open ground. Behind her she heard Sorreltail meow, "Be careful!"

As Leafpaw drew closer, she picked up the scent of food coming from the den. Though it was unfamiliar, not the fresh-kill scent she was used to, water flooded her mouth. She needed all her self-control not to dash forwards and start eating. She knew that whatever it was, Twolegs must have put it there, and that meant danger.

Outside the small den, Leafpaw blinked as another scent reached her. Cat scent, familiar but very faint and stale, and at first she couldn't figure out which cat it was. Certainly not from ThunderClan. Then she remembered, and her paws tingled with excitement. Mistyfoot! The RiverClan deputy had been here, as well.

Cautiously Leafpaw peered into the den. It was empty except for a white, hollow thing that held the food. Mistyfoot was not there now, and there was nothing to tell Leafpaw where she had gone.

The food scent was even stronger inside. Slowly, one paw at a time, Leafpaw crept into the little den. The white thing held small brown pellets like rabbit droppings, smelling strangely of food and Twolegs at the same time. Leafpaw wondered if this could be the kittypet food Firestar had told her about. Kittypets ate it without being harmed, didn't they? She took a mouthful, shivering as it slid into her empty belly, and wondered if there were any way she could carry some back for Frostfur.

"Leafpaw! Get out!"

A deafening chorus of voices suddenly seemed to yowl in Leafpaw's ears. Sorreltail's was there, but there were many more that she did not recognise, and Spottedleaf's was loudest of them all.

She choked on her mouthful of pellets. Spinning round, she caught a glimpse of Sorreltail, staring at her in horror. Then the open end of the den slammed shut, and Leafpaw was left in darkness.

EPILOGUE

❧

Squirrelpaw was trapped in a small, dark space that rocked violently from side to side. Her head spun, and she swallowed the bile that rose in her stomach. Her paws scraped frantically on something smooth and solid. She let out a terrified yowl: *"Leafpaw!"* Then her eyes flew open and she found herself scrambling in a shallow dip in the ground.

"What's the matter? Yowling like that, you'll scare all the prey."

Tawnypelt was standing over her; she had dropped a plump, fresh-caught vole so that she could speak. The five Clan cats had left the mountains last night and were travelling across open moorland. The rising sun, relentlessly showing them the way they must go, had just cleared the horizon.

Squirrelpaw heaved herself out of her nest and shook scraps of grass from her pelt. "Nothing. It was just a dream." She gave her chest fur a few licks to try to hide how shaken she was. Her sister was in terrible danger; she knew that the dream had taken her to wherever Leafpaw was, and shown her the terror she was feeling, but Squirrelpaw guessed that the practical Tawnypelt wouldn't understand her fears.

Tawnypelt was looking faintly interested. "Was it a sign from StarClan?"

"No." Squirrelpaw knew she could share some of the details of her dream, without telling Tawnypelt it had connected her with Leafpaw. "I . . . I felt like I was trapped somewhere dark. I didn't know where I was, and I couldn't escape."

Awkwardly, Tawnypelt stepped forwards and pressed her muzzle against Squirrelpaw's side. "I think we've all had bad dreams," she meowed. "Ever since Feathertail . . ."

Squirrelpaw nodded. Like all of them, she found it hard to believe that they would never see Feathertail again. The Tribe cats had helped them to bury her, beside the pool where the waterfall fell endlessly, churning up spray that made the ground soft enough to dig.

"She has a place of honour here," Stoneteller had meowed. "We will keep her memory alive for as long as our Tribe survives."

That had been small comfort for the Clan cats. Crowpaw in particular was shattered by grief, spending all the next day crouched beside Feathertail's grave. Stormfur kept vigil with him, racked by guilt that he had done nothing to save Feathertail, and had not even imagined that she might be the chosen cat. Her silver fur had been slicked black with water when they first emerged from the waterfall, which was why the tribe cats hadn't paid any attention to her. At last Brambleclaw had ordered them both inside the cave to rest.

"We're leaving at dawn," the ThunderClan warrior had

told them. "You'll need all your strength. Our Clans need us."

The journey had begun again. The Tribe cats had escorted them part of the way through the mountains, and they soon came to easier country with flat green grass and hedgerows to provide prey. But they felt no sense of hope or relief that they would soon be home. Their hearts stayed with Feathertail, in the land of rocks and water.

Squirrelpaw soon recovered enough from her nightmare to help with the hunting so that they could get going and make the most of the rapidly shortening days. Though no cat wanted to eat, they forced themselves to gulp down the fresh-kill. Once or twice Stormfur caught himself looking around to ask Feathertail something, before he remembered that he would never speak to her again.

All that day and the next they travelled on, until their paws were cracked and bleeding. It was as if the horrors they had seen had numbed them to everyday pain. The sun was going down behind them again as they came to the top of a rise. Their shadows streamed out ahead of them, pointing towards a hill with a jagged crest. It seemed to smoulder in scarlet fire from the rays of the setting sun.

"Look!" Tawnypelt's voice was an exhausted croak.

For a few heartbeats no cat spoke. Then Squirrelpaw's green eyes flashed with a fire that had seemed dimmed forever by Feathertail's death.

"Highstones!" she exclaimed. "We're almost home."

KEEP WATCH FOR

THE NEW PROPHECY

WARRIORS

BOOK 3:

DAWN

The questing cats finally return to the forest, only to discover that their part in the prophecy is far from over. Now they must convince the warring, starving Clans to travel mysterious paths to find a new home . . . but how can they leave when so many cats, including Squirrelpaw's beloved sister, Leafpaw, are missing?